MW00677150

Auraria Dead

Melody Scott

Wolfmont

This novel is a work of fiction. Names, characters, places and incidents are either the product of the authors' imaginations or are used fictitiously, and any resemblance to actual persons, living or dead, business establishments, events or locales is entirely coincidental.

AURARIA DEAD

ISBN: 978-1-60364-038-1

Copyright © 2011 Melody Scott

All rights reserved

Printed in the United States of America

This book may not be reproduced in whole or in part, by mimeograph, photocopy, or any other means, electronic or physical, without express written permission of the copyright holders.

All trade names and trademarks contained herein are the property of their respective owners, and used by permission.

Published by Wolfmont Press
A division of Wolfmont LLC
238 Park Drive NE — Ranger, GA 30734
editor@wolfmont.com — www.wolfmont.com

Dedication

Dedicated to Donna Jean Small, 12/25/1939 to 2/16/2011, the best daughter, wife, mother and horse rider I ever met.

Acknowledgements

Once the machinery got rolling on this book, it turned into a village of lovely people.

I want to thank my preliminary readers, Joan McCall Keenan, Peggy McCall Ryder, Sally Steiner, Ron DeLaby, Afton Day, Ken Breeden, and Gerri Breeden. There's nothing like a reflecting pond. And then there's the cheerleader contingent consisting of Marcia Chelf, MaryJane Thompson, Kay Shumate and Ingrid Clark, all my fabulous book club members, my writer's group of two, Jan Dale and Pat Worley, who have sustained my belief in myself. The magic people who are responsible for my cover art, the electronic manipulations and the fruition of the whole kit and caboodle are:

Michaele Leah Tristram
www.sagebrushstudios.com
michaeleleah@att.net

Jennifer Herrara
Jennifer@azulitas.com

Arlene Ingram
www.lakelanier.net
arlenei@bellsouth.net

Tony Burton
Wolfmont Press
www.wolfmont.com

May the road rise up to meet you
May the wind be always at your back
May the sun shine warm upon your face;
The rains fall soft upon your fields and until we meet again,
May God hold you in the palm of his hand
Traditional Gaelic blessing

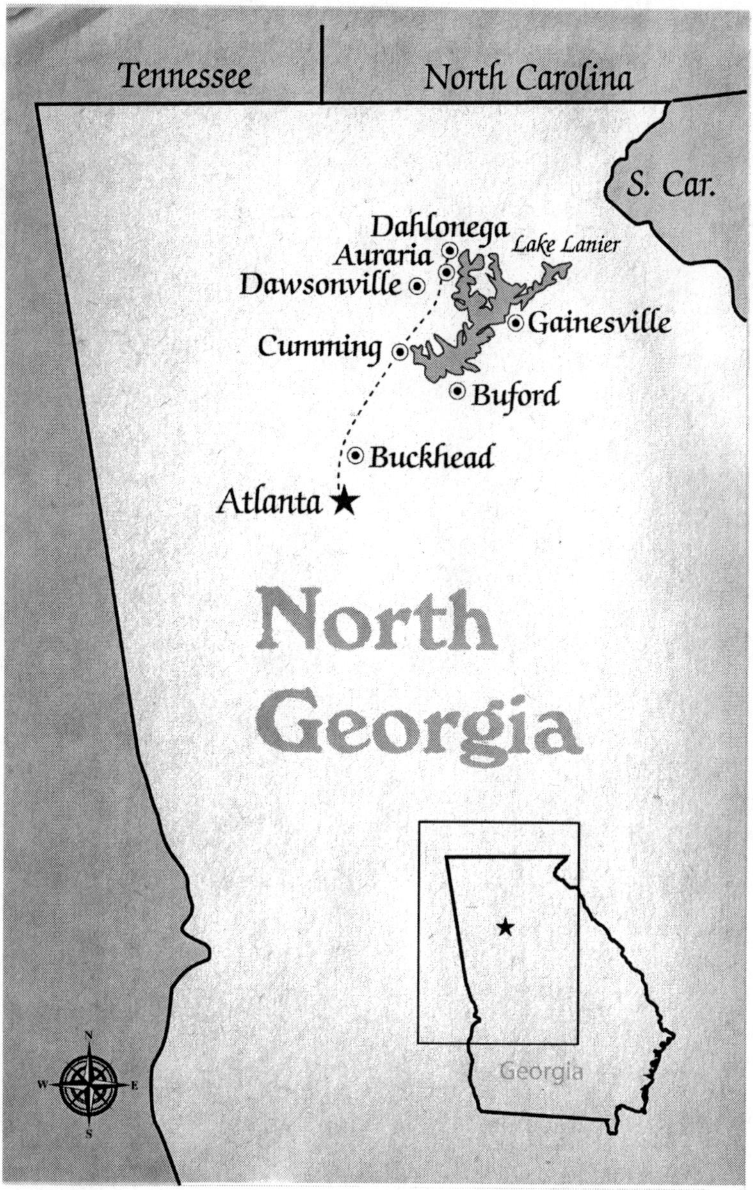
Tennessee
North Carolina
S. Car.
Dahlonega
Lake Lanier
Auraria
Dawsonville
Gainesville
Cumming
Buford
Buckhead
Atlanta
North
Georgia
Georgia
N
W
E
S

CHAPTER 1

Maria Sebastian figured her Jeep Cherokee could be the only motor-driven vehicle that had ever been on the trail in the center of this sea of trees with no beginning and no end. She bounced along the path with Bonnie Keen in Auraria, Georgia, perhaps on an old wagon trail, or even somebody's bridle trail running through the trees.

Mid-November in North Georgia meant the leaves were rain-washed and hung out to turn crisp, their color display as vibrant as any promised by laundry soap commercials. They made her lightheaded.

The other real estate agent seemed comfortably dressed in three layers of shirts. Even though the two women were here to estimate the value of the ninety-five acre tract a client wanted to sell, Maria couldn't decide if her dislike of Bonnie was because of a thirty-year generation gap between them, or if it was true that Bonnie could not be trusted. She'd heard the woman cheated other agents.

It wasn't fair to indict someone without evidence, but she knew the grapevine could be accurate. If she couldn't avoid working with the woman, at least she knew to expect the unexpected. Both she and Bonnie had turned out to be working with the same group of owners but different associates. They'd each invested up to six months with their respective sellers for that listing. By the time they found out they were walking on each other, the only way to avoid a conflict was to merge. Bonnie had made it clear she didn't like the situation either.

Maria stopped at the trail's end where a wall of trees blocked passage.

Prepared to walk the land, she'd felt obliged to know what she was marketing, even though Bonnie hadn't cared about potential home sites or whether water was available for livestock. Buyers could figure it out for themselves, she'd said. Maria had cajoled her into going anyway.

The women stepped out of the SUV to begin their trek. Steam wafted off Maria's fifteen extra pounds of clothing, trickling perspiration down her back, so she peeled off her down coat and tossed it in the backseat. She looked into the formidable woods for a path of least resistance.

They entered a woody gap, crossed through a thicket of junipers into a little valley loaded with dogwoods and hiked uphill to find the land's highest point. Under the kaleidoscopic canopy, branches seemed to wave to each other. Rolling land undulated around them like a swelling sea, offering wild rhododendron plants as a mainstay of the woodland floor. She'd had clients who would take on lifetime debt to purchase such serenity, and she would probably do it herself some day. She made a mental note to review her past clients who hadn't yet found what they were looking for. In a perfect world, she'd sell her own listing to a client and keep the entire commission. But that hadn't happened in a long time. Already having to split 50/50 with Bonnie wasn't what she had in mind either.

She started feeling exhilarated in the soggy cold air, yet a bit down. She'd probably never see this land in the spring. At least she hoped it would be sold by then. She'd never see the dogwoods in bloom. The mystic dogwood, by legend, was the wood used to make Christ's cross. It no longer grows large enough to be anyone's cross. Its wine-tipped pure white blossoms bob throughout the woods before the other trees leaf out, and look like fairy trees dancing under the giant hardwoods. "I bet this looks like Ferngully in the spring," she said.

2

"It even has Mountain Laurel and Creeping Cedar," Bonnie said, toeing a string of tiny cedar umbrellas nearby.

They crunched through calf-deep mulch to the top of the first hill. "We better pay attention to the lay of the land instead of the flora," Maria said as she opened her compass. No breeze ruffled leaves and only the anticipation of sound rang in her ears. "It's perfect land for one of those hermit types."

"Only till civilization catches up to it," Bonnie said as she stumbled over a rock. "Some day this will probably have hotels all over it."

Bonnie's sad look matched Maria's ambivalent feeling.

Between hills, starting to climb the second one, Maria reached for saplings to help her footing, holding back the switch branches so they wouldn't slap Bonnie in the face behind her. Three hundred feet into the woods she looked back, Bonnie was leaning against a huge white oak. To give the older woman a rest, she opened the aerial plat she'd picked up from the Clerk of the Court's Office at the Dawson County seat and calculated where she thought they were standing.

With the plat as a guide, she hoped to find corner markers designating which of the trees and hills might be on the property. Most properties had corner stakes. Since no lines were on the ground and the woods covered the whole state, only those markers could show where the listed property ended. She hated for people to find out the part of a piece of land they loved was really on adjoining property. She knew, when a consortium owned land, it was likely none of its principals had ever actually seen it in person. It was only about location and resale value to them, but a buyer could be different.

Maria heard a rustle in the leaves off to the left, and noticed Bonnie staring in the same direction.

"Surely it's too cold for snakes to be out," Bonnie said, her red-rimmed mocha-colored eyes basted with fear. A rabbit

3

twitched its nose at them from behind a spindly poplar trunk. Her voice quavered when she added, "I think if he wants to hide, he needs a bigger tree."

Maria relaxed enough to exhale. She kept her eyes at first glued to the leaves beneath her feet, scanning for burrowing reptiles, then let them flit over sticks lying about. *Don't be so silly*, she thought. *Snakes hate cold worse than I do.*

Bonnie squinted at the shuddering rabbit. "What's wrong with his leg? It's lying out to the side. He's dragging it."

If Bonnie's ownership of five spoiled dogs was any indication, Maria knew the woman would not rest until that rabbit was wearing splints and crutches.

"Aww the poor little thing!" Bonnie said, and took two steps toward the rabbit.

"What? You want to play catch the rabbit so we can take him to a vet now?" Maria asked as she looked hopefully for red or orange survey tape dangling from a tree. She kicked a stump lightly to awaken her cold toes, then searched through the branches overhead for the sun, but found only a sky that looked like steel ceiling above a crazy roadmap of tree branches.

"I can't stand to see him like that. Maybe we interrupted some animal trying to kill him." Bonnie hunched to sneaking position and tip toed toward the bunny.

Her round body suddenly surged through the scratchy underbrush, her fuzzy gray hair flopping with each step.

Maria looked up toward heaven and silently asked, *Why me?* "I am not going to track a rabbit around a hundred acres of trees, in case you're interested." She let out an exasperated sigh and followed Bonnie anyway.

Bonnie bobbed just ahead, darted left then right, disappeared, reappeared, whooped, and disappeared again.

"Bonnie! I don't see you." She heard only silence and felt foolish. She'd have to renew her gym membership if a seventy-

4

something-year-old woman could outrun her. She hurried toward the place she'd last seen her partner.

She scooped branches of mountain laurel away from her face, forgetting to look down. Freshly caved-in earth crumbled under her foot, sucking her right leg into the earth. She grabbed for a thick scuppernong vine tangled within the clump of surrounding brush and scrambled back from the caved-in hole, her heart racing. Feeling like a squirrel huddled in the thick underbrush, she looked around to get her bearings.

Heart racing, she gasped for oxygen lost with the onset of adrenalin, and looked around. The hole she'd almost fallen into gaped under her, partially camouflaged with sagging ragweed. Her phone vibrated and rang in her pocket.

With shaking hands, she answered the phone, feeling absolutely ridiculous. The phone had no bars and its light went out.

"Maria, it's me," Bonnie's voice said very faintly, but not from the useless phone.

"Where are you?" she nearly yelled, looking at her cell phone screen.

"I think I'm under you. A bunch of leaves fell on me, so you must be up there. Unless it was an animal! It's dark down here. Get me out of here!"

"Okay, okay, don't panic. Are you hurt?" Maria called into the hole.

"I don't know. I don't know. It's dark in here."

"Do you know how far down you are? Are you on the bottom? On a ledge? Is there water?"

"Uh… no. There's no water. Did you think it was a well or something? Not a ledge either. Yuck! There's something weird in here; I feel cloth! No, it's loose rock; it's so dark and scary! I'm scared! Get me out of here." Only static followed.

Maria felt like throwing the useless phone that was still clamped in her hand. She wanted to scream. Wait. Cloth? *In there?* Is that what Bonnie said?

The thick pithy vine that kept Maria from going down the hole seemed to have no end. Feeling slightly panicky, she noticed it spanned from her tangle of bushes up into an overhead tree. From there it made its way along a limb and down into some smaller trees and back into more undergrowth. *A vine like Tarzan used to swing through the trees*, she thought wryly. So, it should be tough enough to hold Bonnie's ample weight, since there was no alternative in sight.

"I don't know how far down you are," she shouted into the ground, "but I'm going to try to get you out. See if you can feel a vine coming down the hole. I'll be right back."

Bonnie didn't answer.

She ran her eyes to the other end of the vine as far as she could see into the blackberry bushes. She grabbed the Leatherman tool from its holster mounted on her belt and quickly opened the blade that was a knife-saw, then went to work on a section of the pithy wood.

At first it seemed hopeless that blade would ever gnaw through enough of that vine to drop down the hole, but she couldn't leave Bonnie alone while she found help. Finally ending up with a length of dried stalk that went to an apparent sky-hook overhead, she stuffed the other end of the vine into the hole in the ground. She wrestled with the vine like a water hose filled with cement. Stiff, rough, and sharply bent, it twisted left when she tried to turn it to the right.

She leaned as far into the hole as she dared and peered into the darkness beneath her feet. "Bonnie!" she shouted.

"What?" Bonnie answered, much too clearly.

Maria stood up from her hands and knees. Confused, she stared helplessly into the crumbling hole.

"My butt hurts. And I think I wrecked my ankle. What are you doing?" Bonnie appeared from behind Maria's right shoulder.

Maria swung around and saw the woman rubbing her backside. Bonnie's hair and plaid Pendleton shirt were dusted with leaves and dirt. "God! You scared me to death. I didn't hear you come up behind me. How'd you get out of there?" Her knees went weak and she sat down in the leaves with relief. What would she have done if Bonnie had been hurt? She'd have never found her, gotten her out. That thought made her woozy. She couldn't think about that now, grateful it wasn't worse.

"Are you OK? You scared a couple of lives out of me."

"I guess it's an old mineshaft." Bonnie's face contorted as she slumped down next to Maria. "I walked out of an opening in a cliff. I could just barely see light from inside the cave and was so scared I ran toward it. There's something creepy in there. Maybe a bear!" A spider walked down her jacket sleeve. Maria reached over and whisked it off before the woman saw what she was doing. *If it had been a yellow orbweaver spider*, she thought, *Bonnie would have been on her own.* She stood and lugged the other woman to her feet.

"Ow, ow, ow," Bonnie said as she turned and tried to walk back from the hole. Shock registered on her face as she looked down into a steady stream of blood oozing from the top of her foot.

"You're bleeding!" Maria said when she saw it at the same time. "Sit down—we've got to look at that!" For the first time that day, Maria noticed the crazy lady was wearing gold flats. "Where are your boots?"

"I can't wear them any more. I have this corn on my big toe that kills me when I wear them."

"There's no telling how many other holes may be out here, and we've got to get you to the car." One of the first things her dad had taught her was to wear boots when hiking. "We're going back." She rose and pulled Bonnie upright.

Maria knew she was strong enough at 5'8" to help Bonnie at 5'2" all the way back to the SUV, even if Bonnie did weigh about 170 pounds to her own 135. Maria needed something to stop the bleeding, so she took off one of her own boots, removed her sock and wrapped it around Bonnie's ankle. If she'd worn the thicker socks she'd considered that morning, her feet would have been warmer, but those socks were probably too thick to tie around an ankle. Then she slid the sturdy belt she always wore out of the loops of her jeans and made a new hole in the leather with her knife, to act as a tourniquet. She'd never tried to do this before, but had seen it done on a video once. When the blood was more under control, Maria slipped her arm around Bonnie's waist and lifted slightly. "Do you think your ankle is broken?"

"Ow! If it's not, it ought to be," Bonnie whined, then hopped three times on her other foot.

"Come on then, we'll go right to the hospital."

Maria half carried, half dragged the other agent up the first hill. On the way down the other side, Bonnie tried to steady herself, lost her balance and hopped onto a crumbing stump full of ants, which swarmed her uncovered foot. She tried to brush the beasts away from her foot but stepped down on the injured one. Balance lost, both women went down in a heap.

Bonnie screeched in pain while slapping at the ants. Maria snatched off Bonnie's gold flat shoe and brushed at Bonnie's foot with it.

"Oh, why did we come out here anyway?" Bonnie moaned after the ants were off. Pin sized red welts quickly turned white on her foot and ankle. "You made me come and now look

8

what's happened!" She rubbed the welts with the sleeve of her shirt.

Maria looked at the disaster sitting on the ground and wondered what she'd gotten into. She helped Bonnie stand again and they proceeded. At the crest of the next hill she knew the Jeep was still two hills away, but down was easier for the time being. When they stopped to rest at the top of the last hill, both of them panting, Maria seriously considered rolling Bonnie down the other side to the Jeep. She wanted to take off her sweater because she was dying of the heat, but had no way to carry it. The trek took more than an hour and exhausted both of them. Her white Jeep looked awfully good. Settled into the seats, her cell phone plugged in and charging, she drove as fast as the terrain would allow. Bonnie whimpered with every bounce of the Jeep, seemingly reluctant to put either foot on the floorboard. Another half hour and they reached the paved road.

Ten minutes later Bonnie whined, "Oh no! I've left my Daytimer in the cave. I can't live without my Daytimer. It has all my phone numbers, the addresses of all my clients, and even what properties they own. We have to go back."

"No way right now. That rabbit isn't going to eat your Daytimer before tomorrow. I'll come back for it this afternoon. We have to get you to the hospital. They've got to make sure you haven't lost too much blood and get my belt off your leg before you get gangrene. If your ankle's broken it's going to start hurting real soon. The Daytimer will be fine. I'll bring it to you later," Maria said. Then she added with a pang of guilt, "I'm sorry about the ants."

Bonnie glowered at her.

* * *

With Bonnie safely tucked into the ER, her relatives on their way to the hospital, Maria once more headed north on the

Georgia 400 freeway. Relieved the trauma was over, she considered driving home and getting under her covers, maybe starting the day over again tomorrow. She really wished now that she hadn't promised Bonnie she'd return to the mine to get the Daytimer. The place gave her the creeps.

Thoughts of what could have happened kept running through her head. What if they'd both been hurt? What if there were wild animals in the mineshaft? Bears had been seen only a few miles from there, according to the county newspaper.

Her good angel told her any bears would be sound asleep for the winter. Her bad angel said there were probably panthers in there with the bears.

Since she was close anyway, she drove toward the office to calm down while she ran some reports for another client she'd see tonight. She also needed to let Michaela, her office manager, know that Bonnie had been hurt.

Her freshly-charged cell phone rang.

"Hi, hi, *ma chère*. Where have you been? I've been trying to call you all morning."

Save me. "Oh, hi, Em."

"You remember my new name, now don't you?"

Maria knew her stupid cousin had changed her name from Emily Louise Tandy to All Knowing to boost her exotic dancing trade. Fat chance she'd ever call her that.

"Listen, Em, I've just taken my partner to the hospital. There's been an accident and I have to go back up to some property this afternoon, after I run some reports."

"But, I have to see you in your very person, *ma cousine*. Today perhaps? One o'clock? Please, please, please?"

"Em. Did you hear me? I'm very short of time and I've got to go forty miles away and into the woods because there's been an emergency. Go away!"

"Aww, Cuz. I can come to your office. It's only eleven fifteen now. You will have two whole hours. Pleaasssseee?" she whined.

Maria snapped back. "There's a little more to it than that. First of all, I promised to go back to the mine where she was hurt this afternoon to get Bonnie's Daytimer. Second, it's colder than a well digger's nose right now. We almost froze in the icy wind," she lied outright. "Third, we saw a snake up there earlier today, and I don't know how you feel about maybe meeting it again. And, before you mention it, no, we can't take the truck the whole way because the trees are too close together." That should solve the cousin problem.

"Ooooh, you have such an exciting life! What should I wear?" Emily cooed. "A real snake? Did he have an apple in his hand? Oops, I don't guess he had a hand at all, did he?"

Maria waited until her dopey cousin quit laughing at her own stupid joke. She supposed it would be better to have another person along in case of trouble. Even if it was Emily.

"Oh, all right. You can come. Wear lots. With boots. Twelve thirty, my office. Bye."

Sheesh.

* * *

After a detour to pick up a milkshake, Maria arrived at her office and dived into the computer research site.

Michaela poked her head in the door and said, "Whoa, you look like you've been rolling in leaves." She paced across the floor and flicked at Maria's sweater. Leaf crumbs danced to the floor. She did a double take when she looked at Maria's face. "Okay, what's been going on?"

Maria looked up at her friend. "It's been a dumb day already and it's only about noon." She reiterated the whole story, ending with the part about Bonnie being at the hospital with her son.

11

Two agents Maria didn't know came into the computer room and sat at terminals behind her.

She stood and motioned for Michaela to follow her around the corner to the kitchen area where they were alone. "Mikey, I'd like to keep the fact of the mineshaft under wraps until I get more information about it for the file. I don't want agents to get into the same mess Bonnie and I did today by showing the property blind, possibly getting hurt. I need a better plat and a warning about the mineshaft, but first I have to find out how the tunnel runs and mark it above ground with flags or something. Right now I'm going to note on the computer listing to not show the property until further notice."

"Good idea. I won't mention it to anybody but Phillip, since he's our broker, after all. And we can explain it to everybody else at the weekly meeting. Are you sure you're all right?" she asked.

"Sorry if I scared you, I haven't been home to clean up and I promised to return to the mineshaft to retrieve Bonnie's Daytimer." She paused to look down at her clothes and noticed blood on the lower leg of her jeans. Bonnie's blood. Her head swam. She leaned against the doorjamb.

Michaela grabbed her, stepped her toward a kitchen chair and sat her down. "You shouldn't go back up there alone today," she said.

"Sorry. I just didn't know I had blood on my jeans from Bonnie's cut. I'm okay, really. And my cousin is going with me back up to the property. Bonnie will be out of business without her Daytimer, since she doesn't have a PDA. And I promised her I'd get it. She blames me for her getting hurt." Guilt washed through her for the second time today.

"You know better than that," Michaela said. "Nobody twisted her arm to go with you today. It was all just an accident."

Maria, who'd done the arm-twisting, thought Michaela looked like an angel standing there with her cloud of red hair, wearing a long woolen skirt and boots, making her guilt go away. "You're a sweetheart. Really, I'm fine, especially after you put it back into perspective for me." She smiled to show she meant it and went back to her desk just as Emily came through the door.

She wore camo pants, shirt, boots and hat. There was a canteen belt strapped around her lean waist and her ebony hair was stuffed up into a green-mottled campaign hat, with crinkly curls spilling out from under it around her ears and forehead. GI Jane with a little Fruit Loop thrown in.

"Hi ya, Cuz. Bet ya didn't know it was me. I thought the rifle was *tres* overkill, so I left it home." She nudged Maria's shoulder with her own.

Maria tossed the papers she was carrying into the top desk drawer and bundled her purse, keys, cell phone and a change of shoes into a canvas bag. She really wasn't in the mood to spar with Emily. Ever since they'd been children, Emily had made a production out of every event and she wouldn't be likely to change now.

"Don't I look *tres chic*, now? You can be honest, don't I? Huh?" The cousin twirled in front of Maria's desk.

"Yeah, right," Maria mumbled as she stood up again to go.

"Okay, then, we're outta here!" Emily said and strode commandingly behind Maria toward the exit. The excited child going to day camp.

Maria sighed and pulled out of the office driveway again. It was one-fifteen.

"OK, now we've got time to talk, don't we?" Emily asked.

"I suppose."

"I need to know whether I should pay quarterly taxes. And what the advantages are of being incorporated, before I go that

13

direction, and I hope it doesn't tickle." Emily flashed a huge smile at Maria and waited for a response.

With no reaction, she continued. "Wellll. I'm not going to be able to stay at *le chateau* after January first, so I must seek more income."

"You mean the mansion where you house sit so you don't have to pay rent? Well, oops, what WILL you do? More exotic dancing?" Maria set her cruise control at seventy and stretched her left leg into the firewall.

"I called you because I'm going to start a new business and I need your acumen for incorporating, et-ce-ter-a."

"Hmmm. What type of business?" Maria was almost afraid of the answer.

"Clothing design, *ma chère*. Aren't you just excited for me?"

"You're going from no clothing to designing?"

"Come on. It's going to be fabulous and I have very key personnel to assist *moi*. You are going to be sooooo impressed!"

Maria took a deep breath and launched into explaining about how quarterly taxes were required by the government for self-employed people such as herself. Then she went through the S Corporation versus the C Corporation advantages and disadvantages, glad that her broker had arranged for CPAs to come to the weekly office meetings several times. Peering sideways, she stopped for a breath to see if Emily had glazed over yet. Nope, she was still in there.

Maria was beginning to feel like she was standing on a soapbox with a cartoon balloon pointing at her mouth that said "Blah, blah, blah".

Em took notes on a pad she pulled out of a pocket on her sleeve.

Maria swerved her Cherokee into the left turn lane, and turned onto a dirt road going down, in and under thick hardwood trees that were giant pickup sticks pointing at the sky. Leaves that had been stuck to the trees earlier seemed to be gone now.

Emily perched on the edge of her seat as they bounced along, seatbelt flopping next to her. "What is this place, anyway, Cuz?"

"Remember Frank Denning? He's the guy you referred to me?" Maria glanced at Em.

"Oh yeah, Frankie. He said he really likes you. This is his property? Wow!"

"Not exactly. It's a consortium of eight owners who bought it from a tax sale off the courthouse steps up in Dawson. I had to co-list it with another agent named Bonnie Keen because she'd been working on listing that land with one of the other owners for about six months. Since Bonnie and I work in the same office, it was the best thing to do. Not to mention there's a huge commission. I think it'll work out okay."

Emily started in again on how wonderful her new business was going to be while Maria's mind wandered. As soon as summertime was over people started thinking about year-end holidays. This year had been slow anyway and Maria was spending far too much time on each of her properties. She was going to have to learn to live on oatmeal or dog food if she didn't get the ball rolling soon. Listings were money in the bank. They paved the way for income in the future. Today's listing equaled tomorrow's rent payment.

After eight miles, the road ended and it was time to walk. The weather hadn't improved. The fib Maria told Emily about the wind blowing was now true. They arrived at the old mineshaft entrance twenty minutes later, Emily exclaiming over every tree and critter she saw along the way. "Oh Maria, it's so exhilarating! Out in the fresh air, breathing deeply, feeling

15

healthy!" She stretched out her arms and spun around with her chin in the air.

Her goofball cousin wasn't worried about starving to death. She'd compromised herself a long time ago when she'd found that men would support her in trade for what she euphemistically called "her company." What Maria couldn't figure out is why being a moral upright citizen of the world didn't pay well. Maybe she just needed a real job.

"Come on Twinkle Toes, the shaft opening is over here, I hope," Maria said. Not looking forward to creeping through a pitch-black cave, she'd remembered to bring her father's new invention with her. He'd hit the jackpot with his limelight and it would soon be patented. She carried the prototype in her purse. Without being pressured by the trauma of her last trip, her confidence returned. She'd been in deep woods, inside caves, up trees and over fences for fifteen years, and knew the possibility of a bear or wildcat being in that mineshaft was small. A wildlife agent once told her animals avoid the scent of man. They also prefer to make their dens in very small locations. A mineshaft is not small. Still, she hoped he was right.

Emily followed her cousin into the earthen hole.

Maria extracted the limelight from her purse and clicked the switch that turned it on. It fanned into a phosphorescent crystal ball. She set it on a musty beam extending out from the wall of the shaft.

"Ooooo. Isn't this cozy?" Emily said as she walked from side to side of the tunnel looking at dirt.

The shaft entrance, nine feet in diameter, continued back about ten yards before branching slightly to the left and out of the light.

Maria examined the structure around the entrance before she picked up the glowing globe of light and proceeded further into the tunnel.

16

Emily gave a double-take then examined the light Maria held. "Whoa, Cuz. I know, that's another of Uncle RJC's toys, isn't it? Even though your dad isn't really a blood relative to me, I think he's the only honest-to-God genius I've ever known."

Maria's chest swelled with pride as she watched her cousin admire the light. But her cousin's attention was short lived.

"I can't believe I'm in a real gold mine!" Emily said. "Look at this cute little train track. Just think, wouldn't it be fun to ride a tiny train all through this tunnel? Another Disney World. Frankie and his friends could make miniature pretend villages all in through here and over there, and real people could be charged to come through here. Wouldn't that be grand?"

Maria began to feel a lift—was it possible her cousin's craziness was infectious? "Grand? No, I don't think so. The liability insurance alone would prohibit that, I think." Noticing mud on her boot, she kicked a post, which caused a shower of dirt to sprinkle down on Emily.

"Ohoooh." Emily jumped and Maria grinned.

"That was not very nice, *ma chère*," Emily said, flicking dirt off her hat.

Maria felt a twinge of guilt. She hadn't known the post was that rickety when she'd kicked it.

"Sorry," she mumbled. With the limelight she couldn't tell if there was any daylight coming in from overhead, so she simply looked along the earthen floor for Bonnie's Daytimer.

Emily finally noticed just how creepy it was in the moist tunnel. "Ew, ick, cuz. Do you suppose there are bats and snakes in here? Maybe creepy crawlies?"

Actually, Maria still hoped for no bears. "Let's just get the book and get out of here. Watch where you're stepping," she told her cousin. Junk lay everywhere.

Old broken carts lay off the tracks. Forlorn wooden crates were stacked in tiers, and rusted sickle-shaped tools loomed in niches resembling weird shrines along the walls. Everywhere, spiderwebs netted sections of infrastructure. Overhead they dangled, and along the walls they cocooned rotted pieces of wood and clusters of rocks, as if they had knitted them in place.

Raising her eyes to a dim shaft of light, Maria noticed a dried vine dangling along the shaft wall from its dirt ceiling. Loose dirt piles cluttered the floor. This must be the spot where Bonnie fell through and more earth caved in after her.

The Daytimer lay against the rocky red Georgia clay floor several yards ahead of them. It seemed iridescent in the tunnel gloom just beyond the light's edge. Maria headed that direction, stooping to retrieve it. Emily huddled closely behind her, following the light. One of the indented alcoves just beyond the Daytimer had some red fabric trailing around the corner into the main corridor.

Emily shimmied past Maria, snatching the light globe as she passed toward a corner.

Spooked, Maria said, "Hey!" and went to get the light back.

Emily stood frozen. There sat a skeleton, exactly like Pirates of the Caribbean's bone piles in Disney World. Oddly, a leathery covering that had to be skin seemed to hold the face bones together. Other bones had piled up inside the clothing and it all resembled a misshapen gnome.

"Well, this guy doesn't look too healthy now, does he?" Emily said. "Pirates, do you think, Sweetpea?" she added softly.

Maria gasped out a scream. Though muffled by walls of dirt, her scream made her ears ring. Her hand, of its own accord, flew up to cover her mouth. How could her cousin be so calmly macabre?

18

The statement about "something weird" being in the cave that Bonnie made earlier was true! In their worry and haste, Maria and Bonnie had both forgotten about it.

"Whoa! I'm outta here!" Emily said. She backed away toward the direction they had come. Then she flinched and stepped back toward the creepy vision. "You know, I've seen that guy before."

"What are you talking about, here? You've seen him before?" Maria whispered. The tomblike feel that settled inside her matched the surroundings.

"Maybe it's the red coat."

"How do you know it's a coat? That pile of cloth could be a blanket, or something else entirely," Maria said.

"Because I remember seeing it on your ex-husband. Oh yeah, it's a coat. Poor Normy."

CHAPTER 2

"Do you mean you really think this... these bones are... were Norman?" Maria asked her cousin. It was preposterous. Still, moisture formed under her shirt and chills ran down her back. Nausea made her knees weak. She slumped against a six-by-six stud. Was there no bottom to her cousin's audacity?

She didn't remember the jacket. On the other hand, Emily, while morally challenged, never forgot a piece of clothing. Steeling herself, she rose, held her light closer to the coat. She stooped and made herself tweak back the collar of the jacket propped around the bones. The label read, "Eprifam."

"Yuck!" Emily said. "You touched a dead guy!"

"I didn't touch a dead guy! You dope! It's a coat, not a dead guy," Maria answered, her hand shaking.

Emily peered from Maria to the shriveled coat on the ground. "All I know is Norman had a coat like that. Don't you remember it? He was YOUR husband!" She ran her eyes over the ceiling, yanked a strand of loose hair out from under her jacket collar and folded her arms in front of her with a huffy sigh.

Maria tried to remember any red clothing that Norman may have had, but drew an absolute blank. She remembered the musty smell of outdoorsy fabric and leather that emanated from his side of the closet, where she'd hidden from him a few times. The mirror she'd hung on the inside of that closet door reflected her frightened image the morning she'd left him. She'd never noticed a red coat.

"Think we should call somebody? I mean, an archaeologist? A coroner? A policeman? Or should we just put him in a box and carry him home? He wouldn't complain much. Hee, hee, hee," Emily said.

"Em. Shut up!" Maria stamped her cold feet and tried to think clearly.

"Right, right, right. We going to just leave him here?"

"NO! WE'RE NOT GOING TO JUST LEAVE HIM—IT—HERE!," Maria yelled. She unclipped her cell phone from her waistband, her hand shaking so badly she could barely keep her fingers on the small numbers. Nine-one-one got no reception. She walked out of the entrance and down a ways from the twelve-foot opening. When the angle was gradual enough to climb, she made her way up over the top of the shaft to the hole Bonnie fell through, Emily right on her heels. Her freshly charged cell phone showed three bars, so she tried the number again.

"Ah, yes, we're here in Auraria, and we've found... my cousin and I... yes... Maria Sebastian... Emily Tandy. What? No, it's a cell phone, not a land line." She told the woman her number. "No, we're fine...."

Emily grabbed the cell phone from her cousin and said into it, "Look lady, do you want to know about this body we found or not? We're not answering any more of your stupid questions. This guy is REAL dead and he's in a cave in the woods. You can have him or we'll just leave him here for another bloody ten years if you don't. 'Bye." She pressed the red button that ended the call.

Maria gasped, "I can't believe you just did that," snatched her phone back, and for what must have been the 500th time, felt like smacking Emily.

"They'll call back," Emily said, brushing strands of her hair away from her eyes. "I didn't think they should be hassling you in this, your hour of need."

Maria clenched her fists so tightly her nails bit into her palm. "That guy is not Norman," she nearly croaked.

"Well, it sure looks like him, if you ask me."

Maria's stomach clenched. She didn't want Emily to know how easily her cousin upset her, and always had. She'd long ago decided her painful reactions to her cousin's antics and words somehow entertained Emily.

When the phone rang, Maria stepped out of Emily's reach, gave all the particulars, and closed her cell phone.

"OK, the Sheriff's deputies will be here soon. I don't want you to mention your theory of that body belonging to Norman. And I think we need to go out to the road and meet them at the turnoff so they don't miss it.

"Why? Aren't you worried it might be him?" Emily asked as they hurried toward where the truck was parked.

"No, I'm not. And I don't want a whole bucket of worms getting dumped on top of whatever the real story is."

As Maria picked up her pace through the woods, she wondered what the chances were that the bones actually could be Norman.

The last time she'd seen him in Arizona, he was yelling over the phone at somebody in the VA office for screwing up his file.

Later that day, a Friday, he'd gone to a survivalist camp for the weekend. The opportunity she'd planned and waited for had finally arrived. Twenty minutes later she'd left in a taxicab, stopped at the bank and kept going. She never returned.

Maria barely heard her cousin say, "I'm glad we're not in that cave any more." She knew the corpse in the mine was *not* Norman Sebastian. Arizona was too far away from Georgia, and nobody from her home state had said anything about Norman being gone. It had been, after all, fifteen years.

* * *

23

They'd led the sheriff's caravan of four-wheel drives to the mineshaft. Maria pointed the way to the bones but didn't go inside the mineshaft again. Several men steadily chopped saplings with axes to allow the vehicles through to the mine entrance along an ancient roadbed. She and Emily sat in the warm front seat of her Cherokee with the motor and heater running. The Cherokee's outside thermometer registered 31 degrees. While ice formed on the side mirror, one black-coated, red-nosed Lumpkin County Detective took pictures and another directed the coroner's wagon to a small opening between trees. Soon Emily, Maria, a fireman, and an Emergency Medical Technician were all collected on the Cherokee's seats. Both of the men stared at Emily, who sat, blinking doe eyes and drinking coffee the EMT provided.

When her cell phone rang, Maria heard the static-filled voice of Mason Walker calling from Florida. She nearly wept with relief. Until she heard his voice, she hadn't realized how tense she was. But soon, frustrated by static gaps in their conversation, she jumped out of the Jeep and quickly walked to the nearest clearing, hoping she'd have better reception. "I'm in the woods at my new listing and there's a skeleton inside a mineshaft. Where are you?"

"Are you okay?" he said through static.

"Yes, I'm fine. I'll tell you about it when we have better reception." She repeated that louder and slower two more times. She visualized how he'd looked when she'd first met him at a Business After Hours networking meeting six months ago. Dressed easily in a blue chambray shirt and light linen jacket with the sleeves rolled up, black hair and ebony eyes. Beautiful.

"What's Tom saying about it?"

"He doesn't know yet." The static became violent and the connection was lost. She shouted that she'd call him back later. She really wanted to tell him everything while sitting on his lap.

Emily, in her element, smiled at her cousin. Her eyes said, "Are you having a bad day?" Since Emily's greatest joy in life was to bait men, it was her perfect environment—night shift. Surrounded by men. "How about we go to your house and hit the pillows, cousin? I think I'm tired," she said over the rim of a cardboard cup the EMT handed her. Then she stretched her arms and yawned to support her statement.

Dennis Livermore, the Lumpkin County Sheriff Deputy, according to a name tag on his jacket, appeared at the Cherokee's front passenger window. He opened the back door and crowded his bulky frame into the back seat with the other two. "Everybody can go," he said as he handed a business card to first Emily and then Maria. "If you think of anything else, call me at the number on that card." He looked expectantly at the fireman and the EMT, who made no effort to move.

"I can drive you home," the fireman jerked back awake from the warm somnolence of the SUV and volunteered to Emily.

"Nah, it's too far for you," the EMT said. "Ms. Sebastian's house is down in Cumming, and we have to head that way anyhow, so Jim and I'll take Ms. Tandy back on our way to the hospital."

"Jim?" Emily turned to ask him.

"My partner. He's in the ambulance with the remains." The EMT never took his eyes off Emily as he spoke from the backseat.

Maria squirmed. She'd always had a hard time believing men could be so easily manipulated. Once she'd wanted to be able to have that kind of power. But the few times she'd tried it, she felt ridiculous. Besides, she'd never gotten the response Emily did. She looked at Emily and said, "Somebody should write a book about you."

She saw a flash of white teeth.

25

The big deputy sucked in a breath of heated air, ran his wrist across his nose. He snuggled down into the fur-lined collar of his duty jacket and said, in a professional voice, "Thanks, but I'll," he paused, "escort the ladies home."

Maria wanted to choke Emily, who wasn't even flirting, just leading them all on. "This is a four wheel drive vehicle, which brought us in here, and it can take us back out. So, thanks, but no thanks. We can handle it just fine."

Emily gave each male his own private smile then said, "Thanks for thinking of us," and batted her eyelashes.

Three men dropped their eyes.

* * *

Maria dreamed that night she was in an underground hole, complete with the smells of dark pungent earth and musty roots.

Instead of panicking, like any sane person, she'd methodically prodded, first with her foot, then with her bare hands around the earthen pit, gauging how she could ladder herself up and out with an imaginary tool her father had invented. The foot and hand holes she prepared to carve out of damp clay wall seemed perfectly logical during the middle of the night. Absurd and claustrophobic in the morning. The red Georgia clay she'd felt seemed so real, she checked under her fingernails after she awakened. She eyed the limelight she'd left on her nightstand. Were her father's inventions starting to make her feel overly confident?

CHAPTER 3

In her kitchen the next morning, Maria related the whole adventure to her friend, Dena over coffee.

Dena's response was, "Call your ex." Her unruly hair belied the German ancestry that made her direct golden eyes snap with confidence. She'd shown up on Maria's porch to hear the whole story and share a Danish she'd brought with her.

"I don't want to call him," Maria said, "I don't want anything to do with him. That's why I'm in Georgia and not in Arizona."

"Well, it seems to me that you're going a little crazy. If you hear Norman's voice, at least you'll know he's not dead and you can continue hiding in peace." She dusted Cherry Jubilee Coffeecake crumbs off the counter onto her saucer then held her coffee cup toward Maria for a refill.

"No—he'll be able to find me by caller ID," Maria said as she grabbed the nearly empty pot and poured the few remaining drops.

"OK, I'll call him then. What's his number?" Dena slipped her cell phone out of the purse she'd set on the floor next to her seat.

"Wait a minute! I have to think about this. I don't even know if I still have the number because he's so paranoid. He used to change it all the time—you know... they're tapping his phone, following his car, watching his house."

"I'm calling him, I'll pretend I'm a lending institution or something." She grabbed Maria's tattered address book from the counter top and shuffled through its pages.

"Where's Mason, anyway?" Dena asked as she punched in some numbers.

"In Miami." Just like a cop, never around when you need him.

"Well, it's a hard life, isn't it?" Dena said. She peered toward the window and clowned a frigid shudder. "He goes from living on the lake to working in Miami. Hmmmm."

"He's rebuilding a houseboat on the lake, if you recall, Dena. He's investigating some dude who lives in Miami for an attorney in New York. He says he hasn't been lying on the beach." Her mind wandered to the image of Mason's tan body in swim trunks.

"Hoo haw, I believe that, don't you?" Dena held the phone to her ear. "I know *I* wouldn't be lying on the beach. Not me, not in Miami's warm cozy sun, water lapping at my sand-covered feet. Noooo. I'd much rather be wearing four layers and sitting by the fire, sweating." She pointed at the phone, shushing Maria.

"Hi. Is your mommy home?" Dena asked.

Maria scanned Dena's face wondering who in the world she was talking to.

"Oh. Well, is your daddy home then? No? Okay, I'll call your mommy back later. What's your name?" Dena winked at Maria as she listened. "Okay, thank you Donnie. Bye-bye.

"What a cute kid!" she said as she put her phone on the counter.

"Little kid? A wrong number."

"Donnie Salali Sebastian—at least that's what it sounded like. I think he's your ex's son."

"Norman's a father?" Maria felt stunned. "Ooo, that's scary. The poor baby. How could Norman ever raise a child to be sane if he's nuts himself? Why would anybody marry him?"

Dena grinned and rolled her eyes.

"Well, that was dumb. I married him, didn't I?" Maria turned to a wall mirror and shook her head at her image. She

28

looked both too old and too young to have a baby. Especially Norman's baby. "A baby makes Norman a sixty-year-old-daddy, since he's twenty something years older than I."

"Donnie didn't know where his daddy was or when he'd be back. His mommy is sleeping. So I guess we're back to square one," Dena said.

"How old do you guess he is?" Maria asked.

"I think three or four."

"Maybe we should call back and wake the mommy up?" Maria suggested. "I'm not sure I care enough to do that." She sure didn't want Norman back in her life, either.

"If your ex has another woman he won't be obsessing about you any more, right?" Dena said.

"It wasn't an obsession. It was ownership. He thought he owned me." Suddenly needing to talk to Mason, Maria picked up her landline phone. She pushed the six.

"Hi, beautiful!" Mason said.

The sound of his voice washed over her, warm and comforting. "We were just talking about you suffering down there in the heat!"

"Yep, that's me, suffering."

She pictured his smile.

Her blonde hair fell in a veil over her face, as she leaned into a private place with him. "I want to hear you tell me that when the world gets upside down, it always turns back over again. Goofy Emily thinks a skeleton we found in a mine shaft is Norman, my ex. She's calling it 'Normy' and making me crazy."

He hesitated. "You found a corpse in a mineshaft? Why were you in a mine shaft with Emily?"

"Yep. It's a long story, but basically that's what happened."

"Now that'd be the coincidence of the century. I thought he lived in Arizona."

"I know. It's ridiculous. I don't want it to be Norman. I want it to go away."

"Maria, it's not your ex."

"I know. Emily irked me when she said it was him. I can't tell if she wants to pull my chain or if she really believes it."

"Why would she say that if she didn't have some reason? And remember who we're dealing with here."

"I know she's off the wall. It just gave me the creeps I guess."

"You realize that the lab will set it all straight."

"I know, I know. She says the coat on the skeleton was Norman's coat. Why would she remember his coat, even if it was true?"

"Think about it, Maria. Why *would* she know that?"

Confusion took over her brain for a second. She stared at Dena and sat down. "Do you mean she and Norman were..." She felt zapped by a cattle prod. She grabbed the back of a chair for support.

"I'm just saying, would it be in character for her to have something going with your husband?" he asked.

Her head started nodding of its own volition. "Yes. Yes, of course it would. God! With a family like mine, I really don't need any enemies."

"Look, I can be there in four hours if I catch the early flight to Hartsfield."

Dena came around the counter and put her hand on her friend's shoulder, her eyes clouded.

"No," Maria said into the phone. "I'm being a baby." She shook her head and turned to smile at Dena. "Honest, I'm fine." She felt ridiculous causing him to feel like he needed to hurry home to be her security blanket. She knew better than to believe anything Emily said. What was she thinking?

"Yes, I'll see you soon," she said. "I know everything will be all right. Take care." She hung up the call.

"What'd he say?" Dena asked expectantly.

"Oh, that. He inferred Emily probably laid Norman, and that's how she knew that he had a red coat. Double damn that cursed cousin! She's never changed. I have to say that for her." Maria slammed her hand on the counter.

"That was a long time ago," Dena said. "And Norman's out of your life now. I don't suppose she caused you to leave him."

"No, no. He had more women than her anyway."

Concern washed over Dena's face. "The man was a real prize I guess."

"Probably the problem with our marriage was that I was co-dependent. I don't want that to happen with Mason."

"From what you've told me, I'd say Norman was the needy nut in your relationship. If you were so needy, you wouldn't still be single—you'd have to have somebody—anybody," Dena said.

"I don't want Mason to need me, I just want him to want me."

"But why would he want you if he didn't think he was necessary to the arrangement? Sammy wouldn't stay with me for five minutes if he didn't think I needed him. I think *want* and *need* are pretty much the same thing. Don't you think Mason needs you? I mean, I see such a sweet expression on his face when he looks at you."

Maria turned to look her friend full in the face. "He does that? I never noticed." Loneliness fought with pride in her chest. "I read once that women who marry alcoholics and finally get rid of them, will go right out and marry another alcoholic, because they're programmed to be life savers." She opened the can of coffee, refilled three scoops into the filter basket, then turned on the water to refill the coffee pot. "Do you think I'm uncomfortable about my relationship with Mason because he's not the loser that Norman was, uh, is?" A chill blew through her. "That I'm only wired to be with a loser?" She stepped over to the coffee maker, poured water and set the filter full of coffee in its place.

"No, I definitely don't think that," Dena answered. "I think you're waiting for the other shoe to fall. The thing is, Mason isn't Norman and you'll have to get used to it."

Feeling a warmth of understanding, Maria suddenly stood, leaned over and hugged Dena. "Thank you for that. I think you're right. Faith has been just a word to me for too long."

Her own words echoed in her head while she heard Dena say, "With a man like your ex, I shouldn't think you'd care if he was alive or dead anyway."

"How did you know that's what I was thinking?"

CHAPTER 4

Maria sat at her desk and stared at the numbers in her checkbook. She poured more coffee then looked at the pile of bills.

If only her last three deals hadn't fallen apart. One client changed his mind about his purchase at the last minute. Another buyer found out her newly-wed husband's credit was not good when the check was run on their loan application—a detail he hadn't shared with her before their marriage. The third deal faded when the seller's house turned out to be located partly outside the property lines. It would take weeks to straighten any of them out, even if one or two could be salvaged. She had enough money for two more months if she was conservative. She closed and opened her eyes. The numbers didn't look any better.

A Carolina chickadee with a tiny mantilla cape of black feathers landed in the bird feeder outside her kitchen window. It gulped seeds then sprang to an oak branch ten feet away. Another chickadee took its place at the feeder. Maria smiled. *Maybe I could live on seeds.*

Selling the new Auraria listing could solve her problem, but that wasn't probable in November. Cold keeps people indoors. Dead bodies don't add charm either. The few listings she had were not moving and the season was at an end. She needed more listings to insure future income.

A couple of old clients should be ready to make a change soon, she reasoned.

She scrolled though her BlackBerry, looking for likely prospects.

* * *

When Detective Sergeant Tommy Larken answered his phone at the Sheriff's office, Maria asked without preamble, "Don't you think you need to buy Erica the new house you've been talking about?"

If she'd ever had a brother, she'd have chosen Tom Larken. Tom, his wife, Erica, and Maria had been through a lot together.

"You talk like I'm made of money!" Tom responded with a laugh.

She adored him for always knowing her voice.

Tom Larken, Maria's teddy bear neighbor had been her friend for as long as she'd been in Georgia.

"Please," she said, with drama. "Then I won't have to eat seeds, like a bird."

When his wife, Erica, became crippled from a spinal cord disease called arachnoiditis, Maria was there for them both. Erica had been washed by bad luck, withstood surgery for cysts on her spinal cord and left to fight constant pain.

"Speaking of lunch," he said, "why not meet me at Chili's? I'm starving and it sounds like you need to talk anyway."

"Uh, OK, order me their Oriental salad and I'll meet you in twenty."

Maria hung up and looked in the bathroom mirror. *This is going to take a miracle.* She couldn't consider the cost of a beauty parlor, but her blonde hair looked ropy and sad. Lack of makeup accentuated blemishes she'd been trying to ignore for two days. She twisted her hair on top of her head, stuck a barrette in it, and went to work on her face. Ten minutes and a lot of eye makeup later, she was a new person, who would only be five minutes late!

Tom was seated four booths from the front door. He stood, said, "Welcome to the fern bar. You look wonderful," and ushered Maria into a seat across from him. Then he rubbed the top of his soft brown crew cut.

34

Maria briefly noted he wore black lace up shoes, his right sock was tan, and his left one was chocolate brown, the combination a product of his colorblindness. Once Maria accused him of buying a dozen of the same shirts, the same khaki pants. She wasn't really sure he had more than one set of clothes, actually. He wore the same jacket every day to cover the weapon at the small of his back. However, he always smelled good.

The server swept up to their table and laid down a dish mounded with Mandarin Orange slices, crispy Chinese Noodles, grilled chicken and lettuce so fresh it looked artificial. "I should send you on ahead every day. I hate waiting for food when I haven't eaten for twelve hours." She picked up her fork and speared an olive. "What have you been doing since I saw you last?"

"Absolutely nothing. No dead bodies, no burglars, no riots or family beefs. Everybody's gone straight and it's boring as hell," Tom said as he hunched over the table, an ice tea dangling from his left hand.

Maria knew he would go home after ten hours work to relieve Erica's caretaker then help his wife to a kitchen chair where he would pull out the makings and fix them both a small exotic drink—a pina colada, margarita, or tequila sunrise.

After he fixed dinner, he'd sing the latest Clint Black song, using a can of peas for his karaoke microphone, while he did the dishes and cleaned up the kitchen.

Maria was in awe of their love.

"Have you heard about the, ah, body I found in the mineshaft?" she asked. Her throat went dry and she grabbed the nearest water glass for a sip.

"No shit?" He dropped his fork. "A body? Where?"

"Auraria. My co-listing agent literally fell right onto it."

35

"In Aurora, huh? Oh yeah, one of the deputies mentioned that at roll call—but I had no idea it was you who found the guy. What's the consensus?"

"A-rar-i-a, is how it's pronounced. It means 'golden,' or 'city of gold'." She ran through the whole story for him. "Maybe you can find out something further. Mason said they can get DNA from a body, even if it's been there for awhile. This guy was basically just bones."

"Will a pile of bones scare off potential buyers?" Tom asked.

"Maybe I'll advertise it as a pirate's retreat," she said as she chased a sprig of lettuce around her bowl.

"Yeah. You could tag it The Den of Thieves Land, or, how about Legend Land? We'll make treasure maps to distribute with the listing pages. I have a brother who works at an art supply store. He'll make it look old and legitimate."

"Fine," Maria said. "We can all go to jail for fraud."

"Maybe we'll just call it Adventure Land, so all of the stories can be believed."

"They'll be true stories at the rate I'm going," Maria answered. "So far they're a bit difficult to absorb."

"What do you call that, tainted property?"

"Stigmatized. But I don't know if that applies to a mine. If it were a house, it's enough to squelch a sale. With land, I don't really think it makes much difference. Not so personal."

"What was the guy doing in the mine? Can they tell?" he asked.

"Nobody's speculated—at least not out loud."

"It's a gold mine?" he asked between bites of his French dip sandwich.

"It's some kind of mine, and gold is the logical choice." With this, Maria's mind started turning over.

"Well, maybe the killer wanted some gold?" Tom said.

36

She grinned at him. "You'd be the one to come up with that. The gold rush up there was in 1829. I'm quite sure if there was still gold, people would be digging away, as we speak."

She chewed on crunchy noodles, then said, "Dena called Norman's house for me since my nutty cousin Emily said the dead guy looked like Norman...like she could tell anything from a pile of bones. Dena knew I'd worry about it, so she made the call. A little boy answered, who said the mother was sleeping. He said his last name was Sebastian. Norman doesn't know where I am and I mean to keep it that way, but maybe he's got something else to think about now that doesn't include hassling me. Dena's going to call back later and see if she can talk to the mother."

"Wait a minute! When did your cousin see the remains?" Tom asked as he dusted crumbs off his shirt.

"I took her along with me to pick up the lost Daytimer that Bonnie dropped when we were out there the first time..."

"When she fell on the body."

"When she fell through the air vent. Yes. I'm glad I had somebody with me, but I could have made a better choice. Do your cousins make you crazy?"

"No. My only cousin, Richard, tried a few times, but I kept punching him and he quit."

"Maybe I should try that," Maria said.

Tom's eyes glazed slightly as he stared at a fern. "If there was a corpse in there then somebody besides you found that mine too. I gotta wonder why."

"Are you on speaking terms with Lumpkin deputies?"

"Yes, I am." He smiled at her. "Maybe I'll just speak with a few of them."

CHAPTER 5

Emily Louise Tandy opened up an alligator attaché case and pulled out a stack of papers, which she tossed onto Maria's kitchen table. "See, *ma cousine*! I told you there is a lot being done on this—just look at these fabulous drawings that Monique designed for *moi*."

Maria stood with her hands on her hips, looking down at the clothing designs. "Em, is there a reason you don't have many business clothing designs? All of the suits are form-fitting, pantsuit styles and I have to admit, they're pretty tasteful. But maybe more sexy than they need to be."

"*Oui*, Cuz. See, the designers tell me they all have to be very severely tailored. Just look at the sleeves on this one." She tapped a long pink fingernail on a design with three-quarter sleeves that had a flounce at the elbow. "Isn't it just divine?"

Maria couldn't get excited about them. They looked pretty much the same, though with different necklines. "I just hope you know what you're doing."

Em's eyes sparkled with excitement as she gathered up the drawings. "Oh yes, I've never been more sure of anything in my tiny life. I am so jazzed." She replaced the papers into their case, then whirled once in place. She ran long tan fingers through her ebony mane, scrambling it all on top of her head, into what should have been a big mess. It reincarnated itself into a dewy coltish look as easily as sliding silk.

Maria doubted lips could stay so puffed and smooth and never lose their luster…but there they were, right on her cousin in front of her. *Go figure.* Emily, probably a botox-collagen queen. "Are you into botox and collagen? I mean we've been

39

out all day. Here I look like warmed over death and you're an ingénue for an Estee Lauder ad."

"Grumpy Cuz, are you a teensy jealous about my permanent makeup?"

"Jealous? I don't think so. What's *permanent* makeup?" Maria peered at her cousin's eyebrows and lips as Emily's smile lit up like facial neon with perfect teeth.

"Look! No lipstick!" Emily lifted a tissue and scrubbed at her perfect pink lips. She was right—no lipstick.

She repeated the movement at her eyebrows, then raised them and made a face at Maria. "No eyebrow pencil either! Ha!"

Maria recalled hearing something about permanent makeup. *I've been out in the woods too long.* "OK, how's it work?"

"Ms. All Knowing has been tattooed!" Emily batted her eyelashes, her face so close to Maria's she felt a small breeze they created. "I have rose on butt also," Emily added.

"Pink? Pink tattooed lips?"

"Oh, yes, yes." Emily's head bobbed like a 1950's dashboard toy.

"Black tattooed eyebrows?"

"Uh huh." Em rolled her eyes.

What a good idea! Maria thought. "What a dumb idea!" she said.

"So," Emily said, "Where's Normy's box?" She craned her neck to see behind the sofa, then inverted her head to look between her feet under the stuffed chair where she sat in Maria's living room. "Is he under your bed?" she asked. "Now, that would be unique, keeping your ex under your bed!"

Maria gritted her teeth. "Emily! Stop it! You're driving me crazy. That pile of bones is NOT Norman, and whoever it is— was, is NOT here. Now, go home."

* * *

40

"Ms. Sebastian, I have to tell you, it's very upsetting to think about a death on our land." Frank Denning, contact man for the consortium practically whispered over the phone. "I can tell you I never would have become involved in the purchase if I'd known. I've no idea how we'll sell it."

"Who knows, maybe notoriety will attract a buyer," Maria offered.

"I don't suppose we can just keep this under wraps?" Frank almost begged.

"It will be tough to keep the media from exposing it, since it's a matter of public record. I can't really think somebody interested in that land would be put off by some bones in the mineshaft." Maria tried to sound reassuring. There were people who would definitely be put off by it, she knew. But there were also those who would think it added mystery to their property, that it was kind of cool to have something notorious about it. Shoot, Emily would be just the one to charge admission to show people where the bones were found!

"What if there's something else out there we don't know about?" Frank continued.

"The Lumpkin deputies and the Georgia Bureau of Investigations have been all over that mineshaft. They'd have found it by now," she said without knowing for sure.

She still had to go back out to the property she'd never had the chance to see. She leaned sideways to see out of the window next to her office desk. If the predicted rain held off, she could go today.

New property on the market always caused a prideful stir among real estate agents, especially notorious property. She knew it would get a lot of talk.

She called six of her friends, told them about the new listing, countering their questions as best she could. When she contacted Eileen Douglas and said she planned again to walk the land, Eileen volunteered to go with her. The more she thought about it the better the idea became. Eileen was cool, calm and resourceful. She also carried a gun.

Eileen stood five feet ten and showed up wearing western boots and a sheepskin lined denim jacket. She wore no makeup, little jewelry and didn't bother with niceties like ceramic nails. She'd built more than one house practically with her own hands.

They drove out to the land, parked and walked from the opposite end of the property toward the mine. It was cold but sunny for a change. Trees stood like sentries waiting for spring.

After a crunchy ten-minute hike, the women crested a knoll. A sudden loud blast careened through the empty sticks overhead, followed by a light metallic ping. Eileen dropped to the ground, grabbed Maria's waist as she went down, the two women tangled together under scratchy shrubs.

"Shit!" Maria said in a whisper. Numb except for the place where her hip hit the ground, she lay there breathing for what seemed an eternity.

"Yeah," Eileen said back, grimacing. "I think we've got us some hunters out here."

With a glow of panic beginning, Maria jabbered to herself, "I should just write 'target' across my forehead." *Why can't I just have a normal, quiet, boring listing?* She curled into a ball.

Eileen low-crawled back to the top of a ridge on their left. Maria flipped back on her stomach and did likewise until they could peer over the edge.

"Can you tell what's going on?" Maria asked. "Is somebody shooting at us?"

"Well, somebody is shooting, but the good news is, I don't think it's at us."

Maria squeezed her tearing eyes together and lay there feeling like a groundhog. "If somebody is hunting, we could just yell so they'd know we're here." She flipped out her cell phone—no bars.

She noticed lead pellets were not flying over their heads. But she'd worked the area for fifteen years and did not know of a shooting club.

Eileen said, "I think we should go away and come again another day." She lay on her back looking up.

"I am never going to see this land. Maybe God simply doesn't want me to see it. Maybe I don't belong here." She considered covering herself with leaves and staying there until spring.

"Well, *I'm* not going down there," Eileen said.

Shots ceased and a motor started. They heard a car motor rambling then revving along what must be a very rough road.

The sound grew more and more faint and no more shots were heard. Nothing could be heard at all.

Ten minutes passed before Maria stood, knocked the dirt and leaves from her jeans, picked stickers and little fuzzy seeds called hitchhikers off, then started down the hillside. Eileen said, "I still think we should go."

Maria checked her compass, pulled out a pen and wrote the heading on her hand. Soon she saw a three-sided concrete block structure with a man-made, Y-shaped "tree" in the center of the opening.

"That thing is for resting a rifle on. For better aim. This is some kind of rifle range," Eileen said.

A slab of hinged steel sat on a post, obviously a target. Fragments of colorful stickers dotted on the slab marked shots.

About fifty feet beyond the side of the hut was another just like it.

"I wonder if the sheriff's office should know about this range," Maria said.

"You dang sure right they should," Eileen said. "That guy in the mine might have been shot. This is some more spooky land you've got here, girl."

Maria sighed. "I know."

"Is this listing firm yet?"

"Bonnie's supposed to get the signatures this weekend."

"From the hospital?" Eileen asked, her eyebrows wrinkled with doubt.

"No, she'll be home tomorrow. She's got a walking cast thingy on her foot. She's got an appointment to have the papers signed on Saturday."

"You know, it's dangerous to show this property with people wandering in and shooting guns. What if another agent comes to show it and doesn't know this range is here? They'd do the same as us and think they're being shot at. And they might come in from another direction and actually get shot. You might want to rethink keeping this listing."

They began the trek back to the Jeep Cherokee. Maria thought, *So I'll just have to sell it without seeing it. Nobody else walks their listings. I don't have to walk my listings.* "I'll just have to make sure nobody shows it without Bonnie or me going with them."

Eileen went on, "Well, what about those agents who want to preview the property and don't call you first?"

"Right," Maria said. "I'll have to emphasize I MUST be called before showing or previewing or going on the land, because of the shooting range. That'll get their attention."

* * *

When Maria called her contact, Frank Denning about the shooting range, he said, "Oh, yeah, I forgot about that. My partner, Adam, has a bunch of friends who use it to pot shoot.

They're not going to hurt anybody, they just dress up in their cammies and play with their guns."

"When you sign the listing, I'm going to need to make it very plain about that range. Also we're going to have to make sure nobody will be on that range when the property's being shown. I'll need to call Adam and find out their schedule—do you have his last name and number?"

"Dan signed the listing already."

Maria's breath caught. "Oh yeah? I thought y'all wouldn't be available until tomorrow night." *Now what?* Obviously Bonnie had been busy instead of laid up.

"I thought it was kind of funny, your partner insisting that way. Dan said she showed up at his office and said she had to take care of it right then, even though she was hobbling along in a cast." He paused. "Uh, oh. You didn't know anything about this, did you?"

"I'll take care of it, don't worry about it. Bonnie probably was going stir crazy laid up with her ankle sprained and needed to get out." *Yeah, and my grandmother wears combat boots.*

"Well, let me know if you have any problems with it. I'll talk to the guys and we'll make it right."

Maria steamed. Her half of the income from a sale on that property would be lost if her name was not on that listing. She checked the new listings file drawer in her office and found the new paperwork all signed, sealed and delivered under Bonnie's name as agent, with Daniel Duke as representative of the consortium. Maria's name was nowhere in sight.

Bonnie is older and getting forgetful, Maria thought. She got caught up in the zeal of the moment. She planned to add Maria's name but forgot about it temporarily. Then Maria's evil angel popped up on her shoulder. *The bitch had taken over the listing.*

45

Her grandma used to say, "Every once in a while all the apples fall out of the basket and you just have to go get 'em back."

She took a new listing form on the ninety-seven acres to Frank Denning, who took it to Daniel Duke and explained a few things to him. They both signed the listing, and Maria signed it for herself and Bonnie. She destroyed the sheet Bonnie'd put in the file, and replaced it with the corrected one.

She couldn't wait till she got her hands on Bonnie.

CHAPTER 6

Staring into her morning coffee the following day, Maria couldn't get over the idea of Norman having a family.

Why had another woman done better than she? What was wrong with her? God knows she'd tried to keep her marriage together. Her parents had done it, but she couldn't. Norman hadn't exactly looked like the white knight she was sure would come carry her off to the Cinderella castle, but he had some good qualities and she was sure she could change the bad ones. She never considered mental illness though. And what if they'd had a child? She shuddered at what might have happened. Mental illness can be inherited.

A psychologist once told her she was in mourning for the death of her marriage. For the loss of a child she never had. Yeah, right. More like a death wish staying with him, she'd guffawed. And hell to pay being tied to Norman for the rest of her life through an innocent child. *But it was still there after all these years, wasn't it?*

Maybe she just hated to lose. She certainly didn't want to have Norman back, especially after all the silent prayers she'd wasted on him. She noticed she hadn't moved from her barstool since the coffee had finished dripping, yet the coffee in her cup was lukewarm. She rested her arm on a dishtowel, away from the cold granite countertop.

If she'd stayed with Norman then she would have never met Mason Walker, Maria reasoned. Maybe she wouldn't have lived to meet Mason if she hadn't left Norman when she did. That thought almost buckled her knees—he'd restored her faith that a man could believe in her. Even if it was too late for a child, he

47

looked a lot more like a white knight than Norman ever had. Besides, just having him in a room warmed it up for her.

The ringing phone drew her attention.

"Maria? This is your mother."

"Oh. Hi, Mom." Her mother never called to chat. Her heart skipped a beat. "Is everything all right?"

"I've been wondering. Are you coming home to Phoenix for Thanksgiving?"

Why would her mother waste money on a long distance phone call, much less just to invite her to Thanksgiving?

Since Maria had divorced she'd also more or less washed her hands of her nutty family when she moved to the Southeast, she hadn't been home and didn't plan to return. She'd started her life all over with a clean slate. "Uh. I've been thinking about it. Do you need me to be there? Is something wrong?"

"Well, it's your dad, you know."

Her sweet dad? The only one in a family full of mixed nuts that ever understood her? Maria thought she might hyperventilate. "He's been awful grumpy lately," her mother continued. "I don't think he feels well, but of course he won't talk to me. I thought maybe if you came out…."

She listened for the possibility of an ulterior motive in her mother's voice. Possibly her mom actually wanted to see her. Not much chance of that. Maria was oil, her mother was water, and they hadn't understood each other since Maria's birth. Her mother talked around a barn better than anyone else. Maria never knew where she was going or what she wanted. "I was just going to hang out with friends." Her breath caught in her chest. "Is Dad really sick?"

"I just don't know." Her mother's voice trailed off. "He got mad at the neighbor kids for messing up his rocks in the front yard last week. He's still mad. It just isn't like him."

"That's funny." The man was a saint to stay in that Tandy family, but maybe it was finally getting to him. "Did he say why?" She couldn't remember him ever going to a doctor. Maybe it was time he did.

"He doesn't talk to me. You know, I saw on TV that people can die from high blood pressure. He's never talked to me."

"Did you ask him why, Mom?"

"Well, no. He wouldn't answer me if I did."

Her mother was probably right. Thirty years ago her dad had stopped trying to talk to his wife, who found fault with absolutely everything,

"Okay, look, I'll call you back when I know about a flight. Do you mind if I bring a friend with me?" Maybe this wouldn't be so bad.

* * *

Maria shuffled through her airline file folder until she found the phone number for frequent flier tickets. She'd been saving them for an emergency. This situation qualified. While in Phoenix she could go by and see if Norman still lived in the old house. His old phone number hadn't been changed. Strange. Norman, Mr. Paranoia-R-Us still had the same number.

She knew she could go standby if she had to but began scanning computer sites for an airline ticket. She'd covered Dena's calls when she'd gone to Hawaii for her anniversary, so she could ask Dena to handle her business calls over Thanksgiving.

When she called Mason to ask if his current schedule could accommodate a trip to Arizona, Maria heard delight in his voice.

"Sure, I can get away. Nobody's open down here in Florida on holidays anyway," he said.

Three hours ago she felt so alone, so bad over her lost chance at marriage. Yet she had an incredible support group. A psychiatrist would have fun with that. *Yes, Ms. Sebastian, I see you feel undeserving to have success and to have friends who care about you. Why is that, do you suppose?*

Maria began packing sweaters, then remembered where she was going, and changed out the warmest clothing to a couple of light slacks and jackets she hadn't worn since summer. Though it could happen, she reasoned, snow wasn't likely in Phoenix in November. She'd obtained a non-transferable reservation, printed her boarding pass on her computer and prepared to do the battle of the holiday traffic at Atlanta's Jackson/ Hartsfield International Airport the next day.

After calling Dena, organizing her deals that night and eventually getting out the door the following morning, she became exhilarated on the hour drive to the airport. The traffic needed all her attention, but it was something else causing her light mood. Even the aspect of being scanned or searched didn't bother her. Usually she felt down—no, *challenged*—when she contemplated seeing her mother. So either she was finally getting over that after forty something years, or it was the excitement of seeing Mason that brought it on. Her cousins Yvette and Sharon could be reasons the trip should be fun too. They were always fun, even if they did have dysfunctional lives. Sharon was married to Evan, who she wouldn't let in her house, but they shared a child and a business together, worked every day together. Yvette, only 38, married an 80-year old man and spent her days taking care of him.

She'd left Atlanta in damp, forty degree weather and landed in seventy-five degrees of dry sunny skies. Even the jacket she'd needed to get to the airport was unnecessary. Mason's plane would arrive in only three hours, according to a text message in her BlackBerry.

She immediately felt comfortable in the southwestern ambiance of Phoenix's Sky Harbor International terminal.

Basking in the patchwork rays of sunshine on tile, she sauntered past gift shops that offered ceramic coyotes, Indian pottery and turquoise jewelry. She caught herself dealing with a big lump in her throat. She never thought she'd feel homesick. *Holy Cow.*

At a shop of western hats she mooned over a Stetson she would have killed for fifteen years earlier.

To hide her embarrassment, she leaned down and stuffed a sweater she'd shucked into her carry-on case. She remembered to call her mom before she searched out an airport hot dog.

Perched on her hand luggage, munching a hotdog, she began a favorite pastime she shared with her father, the ex cop. They had often come to this very location just to eat a hotdog and watch people. He pointed out idiosyncrasies that made individuals stand out in a policeman's mind. She never would have noticed such things if he hadn't spent the time teaching her what to look for. Only a hobby for her, people watching is why he'd been such a good officer.

The all-important thing was the eyes, he said. The expression found there created an identifying characteristic, something he never forgot. Maria had yet to master that one.

Her mother was attentive to physical problems ever since her own mother, Maria's grandmother, had saved the leg of a ranch worker a doctor had wanted to saw off. The leg had been caught in a wagon wheel and had an infection that was running out of control. Her mother helped her own mother nurse that infection back to a completely restored leg. She'd learned to take care of any wound immediately. Timeliness was all, in her mother's opinion. If she'd said something was wrong with Maria's father, then it was likely something was wrong.

Just as she began to think of confiscating an abandoned newspaper section lying on top of a trashcan, the carousel started, whereupon bags began sprouting from the conveyor opening.

Angled behind a carousel, she wanted to just look at Mason without being noticed before he stepped off the escalator.

As he waited to step off the moving stairs, Mason searched through the sea of faces, peering at one after another with continuously scanning eyes.

God, he was gorgeous!

His black hair fell capriciously over the perfect eyebrows that sheltered searching brown eyes.

The remnants of a grin slept in the tiny creases along his cheeks and at the corners of his eyes.

His blue chambray shirt lay easy across his shoulders, khaki slacks impossibly fresh after being wadded into a plane seat for several hours. His Florida tan glowed.

She waited until the last possible moment to show herself, then stepped into his vision the same millisecond his scanning eyes held her fast. The full-force grin materialized as he encircled her with his free arm.

If ever there was going to be a home for her, it was this place, this capsule of air that joined them, separated them from the world. The baggage section faded into a blur. His kiss made her forget failures in her life.

"Ummmmm," he said. "Remind me to not be gone so long next time."

"Yes," she said, wishing to not be turned loose.

"You're making a spectacle of yourself," he murmured through her hair where his nose was buried.

"Yes."

"I'm willing to stay until the janitor comes," he said.

"Okay, Okay." She backed up from him with a sigh.

When he lunged and grabbed his leather suitcase from the carousel, she jumped back. She remembered why she was there and her breath caught for a second. She'd have to figure some way to get her father to a doctor.

CHAPTER 7

By twilight Mason drove with Maria away from the Sky Harbor Airport in Phoenix, plain, dull, dead grayness everywhere on the hills, the lawns, the roadways. Obviously rain had become a memory and a pall of brown smog hovered over rush hour traffic.

"How far do your parents live from the airport?" Mason asked as they made their way east on McDowell Road.

"About twenty minutes. Scottsdale isn't far."

Four lanes of traffic in both directions were stopped dead on 44th Street by stoplights on every corner. Maria looked around while Mason drove past landmarks so familiar, yet so far removed from her present life they seemed like she'd seen them in a dream. Her eyes settled on the traffic jam surrounding them. All she wanted to do was get it over with.

"I think we should go have a cup of coffee until the traffic breaks," Mason said. He rubbed the back of his neck then inched the rental car toward the bumper of the car ahead of them.

"It's funny how sitting on a plane wears you out, isn't it? That's probably a good suggestion. We can relax for a while." As they came to the next intersection, she realized where she was in relation to her old neighborhood and said, "Just two more blocks up on the left is the turnoff for my ex's house. We could use the time to drive by and see if anybody's home. I don't want to go in, but maybe we could see if Norman's there?"

"Good idea," Mason said as he looked at her. "We can put that demon to rest."

She read something in his eyes. "Will it make you feel bad?" She asked. She brushed back a strand of hair escaped from the clasp behind her head.

"No. We're not going anywhere right now anyway."

"OK, then, when you get to the next signal, turn right."

The one-time middle class neighborhood had been reduced to blue collar. Sort of blah Spanglish architecture, the houses had been built in the sun-country style of single-story flat-roofed stucco.

The piles of scrap cars blocking driveways baffled Maria, along with the lack of anything green in the yards. Block fences full of graffiti and chunks of concrete missing from the curbs indicated the entire area devolved into nearly a ghetto in the fifteen years she'd been gone. The whole neighborhood showed graceless neglect, with each house overdue for paint or roofing, screens or lawncare.

Mason pulled the rental car against the opposite curb, two doors past Maria's old home. They turned around in their seats to see the house from where they were parked, well past its driveway. Maria appreciated the surveillance tactic he'd used. She certainly had no wish to see or be seen by Norman.

A broken window, haphazardly bandaged with duct tape leered from the porch, and the sagging chain link fence encompassing the front yard kept the tufts of dried grass safe. A dark-haired child played in the dirt with toy cars. Misshapen rings of apparent dirt splotches covered his face and abdomen. Was that Donnie? Maria thought, the child whose voice Dena heard on the phone?

They watched the child, clad only in cartoon-figure underwear, push toy trucks over well-worn tiny tire tracks. He was oblivious, caught up in his fantasy.

"He's filthy," Maria said, something tugging within her.

"He's playing," Mason answered.

56

"I know, but he looks like he hasn't had a bath in a couple of weeks."

"Boys get dirty."

She looked at Mason, who looked back at her in mock innocence. Then he rolled his eyes. "Some get dirtier than others?"

"Nice try." She searched his face for some real explanation. "The kid's neglected. I wonder why the neighbors haven't called social services or something."

He shrugged his shoulders. "Have you looked at some of the neighbors' yards?"

"He looks neglected to me." Maria looked around the street, feeling sadness for the desperation of the neighborhood. A neighborhood she'd called home, and where she'd had dreams. Yet another reason to be grateful she'd left when she did.

"You see any movement around the windows?" Mason asked.

Maria craned her neck to look again. "No. Nothing's stirring. There're no cars parked in front and there is no garage. Looks like Norm isn't home. He'd never be caught without a car, trust me. Maybe he doesn't live here any more."

"Shall we go have a talk with—what's the boy's name? Donnie?" Mason asked, looking back toward the child again.

Maria wanted to yell, *No!* Then she thought he must be joking. "The child must have a mother in there somewhere. Are you out of your mind?"

"And if there isn't one? How would you feel about that, Ms. Worry Wart?"

"Nobody'd leave a kid that young by himself."

Mason raised his eyebrows.

"Would they?" she asked, and then shuddered despite the heat.

"I think we'd better find out." Mason opened the car door and stepped onto the street. Maria followed him.

"Donnie?" Mason called to the child and approached a dip in the fence.

The boy looked up from his concentration and grinned.

Yep, Maria thought. *That's Norman's child, Norman's smile.* She waved to him. He looked curious, but waved back, then picked up a truck, held it close.

The adults waited at the fence.

"Is your mommy home?" Mason asked.

He nodded his head. "Mommy sleep."

Maria felt something wrong. Does an adult put a kid outside, even in a fenced yard and go back to bed?

"We want to talk to her," Mason said.

"Sure." The child looked at his truck.

"Is your daddy home?"

"Daddy work." He nodded in agreement with his answer.

"We're going to come in the yard and knock on the door to talk to your mommy. OK?"

"Okey Dokey," he said.

They made their way along the fence line up the drive to a covered stoop at the side kitchen door and Mason knocked loudly. No response.

Again they tried.

Still no response.

"Donnie? Will you go get your mommy for me, please?"

He scrunched up his face, then said, "Mommy sleep," and dropped his head.

"I know, but will you wake her up?"

The boy's chest heaved with a big sigh.

"It must be difficult to deal with such obtuse adults," Maria said softly to Mason.

"Ohh kay!" Donnie said and toddled over to the front door, holding the back of his underwear up so he wouldn't lose them. He was about three feet tall. He wrestled with the worn screen door. It clattered when he grabbed it and Maria feared it may fall on him. But he managed to reached up and turn the knob without the whole thing falling off and disappeared inside.

After five minutes, the boy slid back outside, walked over to his trucks and sat down in the dirt to play.

Mason said, "Donnie, did you wake up your mommy?"

He hunched his shoulders, pursed his baby lips and looked at Mason like he was demented, but politely said, "Mommy sleep."

"OK, that's it, I'm going in," Mason said to Maria.

Maria stuck close to Mason as they made their way through the kitchen door.

The refrigerator sounded like a threshing machine with its door standing wide open and its contents spread around the floor before it. Small containers spilled foodstuff in various smelly heaps onto the linoleum where sauces were spread like finger paintings.

A peanut butter jar lay abandoned on its side next to an empty jelly jar. Melted sticks of butter pooled half in their paper wrappers, blended with catsup, mustard and au jus from some forgotten meal. All of the cabinet doors stood ajar with bowls, pots, pans, cookie sheets flowing in progressive trails from their openings.

"It looks like Donnie's been busy in here," Maria said.

"Probably hungry. This doesn't look good. Maybe you should open up the peanut butter and make him a sandwich while I go on to the bedroom," Mason suggested.

"No way. We're in this together. Go." She nudged him forward, noticing a putrid odor.

"But..."

"Go."

The first room on the right, a type of den, varied from the rest of the house because it was extremely neat. Mason paused apparently for the same reason Maria did. It was too clean. Why?

A laptop computer sat closed on a small wooden desk, with an attached printer. A forgotten paper sat in the basket of the printer. Mason picked it up by the edges and turned it over.

"What is it?" Maria asked as she looked around the desk.

"A shopping list."

"Add eggs. Nobody's going to eat the ones on the kitchen floor."

He stared at the paper, memorizing it, then turned it back over and replaced it in the printer where he'd found it.

Down the hallway, in the last bedroom, they found Mommy. She was permanently sleeping, with a neat hole behind her left ear.

Maria felt the blood rush out of her face. Her head spun. She leaned briefly against the wall, understanding the bad vibes from earlier.

She saw Mason's built in cop scanner click to ON as his eyes searched the woman's body for signs of life.

No need to check for a pulse, her left arm was pasty white as it rested along the side of her body. Her right arm, a lurid blue-purple, lay partially buried between her abdomen and the bed surface. She appeared frozen into a semi-fetal position.

A pillow with a case bearing an orange, black and white cartoon bird was beside her face on the bed. As they stood there taking in the grotesque scene, Donnie darted past them, scrambled up on the bed, grabbed the bird pillow, snuggled down against the woman's body, stuck his thumb in his mouth and closed his eyes.

Tears welled in Maria's eyes as she said, "Donnie, come show me your room. We'll take care of your mommy." She choked the out the words in the putrid room.

Mason pulled out his cellphone and stepped into the hallway.

As Maria picked up the child and the pillow clutched in his arms, she noticed a label dangling from beneath the sunny pillowcase. It read *Eprifam*. Where had she seen that name before? Maybe on her own pillow at home?

CHAPTER 8

Only twenty minutes had elapsed from the time Maria and
Mason got into the rental car, to when the Phoenix Police
showed up. Maria had made a peanut butter sandwich for
Donnie. She wanted to go examine the bedroom for the hole
Norman had put through the drywall when he swung a punch at
her so many years ago. She'd circled the gaping evidence with a
magic marker and written YOU MISSED inside the balloon
before leaving for the airport. She remembered for that entire
flight to Atlanta she'd made up other things she should have
added to that balloon.

Well, her nerve didn't hold now. She felt like a trapped
animal and reached for the door, left it wide open while she
encouraged Donnie to eat his sandwich.

A Homicide Investigator named Dirk Singletongue caught
the call. He was slightly rounded where many people have
angles. He had silver hair, an incredible tan and nut brown eyes.
Turquoise beads glinted at his wrist as he shook hands with
Mason.

The detective wrote down all the information from the time
Mason and Maria arrived and found Donnie playing outside,
until he arrived from the Central City Precinct in his city-issued
car.

He said, "I'll get back to you in a while. Right now I've got
some business in the back. Will you keep an eye on the boy for
me? It looks like you've done a good job of making friends
already."

The detective stepped over the floor clutter and approached
the child, then stooped to talk with him. "Hi, Buddy. Is that a
pretty good peanut butter sandwich?"

Donnie sat on the only kitchen chair. He nodded in response, and chewed.

Maria found a dishcloth in a cabinet drawer and used it as a washcloth to clean the child's face and hands.

"You finish your sandwich, then I'll take you to get an ice cream. Is that a good idea?" the detective asked.

The boy nodded again.

The mob of homicide squad members showed up and immediately began marking, measuring, taking pictures, going through everything in the immediate bedroom where the woman apparently died, then merged into the other rooms of the house.

Meanwhile, two uniformed policemen walked around the outside of the house with flashlights, checking under shrubs and yard clutter, and took notes from the nearest neighbors. People stood outside the fenced front yard, talking to each other.

Some time later, Detective Singletongue finally approached Mason and Maria. "Isn't this a hell of a deal?"

Mason answered, "It may be the weirdest I've seen."

"Woman's been dead for maybe two days. Little kid's been surviving on his own."

"It makes me sick to think about it. What if we hadn't come by?" Maria said.

"Sooner or later she'd have been in such a state that the neighbors would have noticed or the boy would have hollered until somebody came along. At least I hope that would have happened. We shouldn't think about that."

"If the deceased is the wife of Norman Sebastian, maybe there is some way I can help you," Maria said. "I am Norman's ex-wife and I know most of his family and friends."

"So, you came all the way out here from Atlanta, Georgia with no knowledge of this situation?" Singletongue asked, settling himself on the edge of a stout coffee table.

Maria sat down on the arm of an old couch. "We actually came out for Thanksgiving, and happened to stop by to see if Norman Sebastian, my ex, might be home, since we were stuck in traffic anyway. My parents live in Scottsdale. Which reminds me, I've got to call them."

"You have a working relationship with your ex?"

"Not exactly. You see, it's been brought up that a skeleton that was found in a mineshaft in Georgia had clothing that was similar to something my ex-husband owned. Naturally I was upset by that comment. I only wanted to reassure myself that isn't possible. When I called this house, the little boy answered the phone, said no adults were present—it was two days ago I called—and it was too strange to not just drive by and settle my mind. It probably sounds foolish to you, but there's more to it than that.

"Uh, excuse me right there," the detective said. "Why do you think the skeleton may be the remains of your ex-husband?"

Maria felt her face flush. "Because the jacket found with the remains looked like one my husband used to own."

This is so dumb, she thought. It was really her cousin who'd said the jacket was Norman's. She'd opened her mouth, now she had to try to not look like a total idiot.

"You can see why this whole coincidence has me spooked. Don't you think it's weird? Of course, it's silly to assume the bones are really Norman's, but in process of trying to put my mind to rest by driving by to get a glimpse of him, we found a dead lady. I'm frankly chilled." Her shudder was certainly real. "Not to mention Donnie may be Norman's child. It's complicated, but I feel a certain responsibility to him."

"We're all upset, ma'am."

"Detective, do you know who the deceased is?" Mason asked.

Singletongue riffled through his notebook and stopped to read from a page.

"According to the neighbors, her name is Nita Sebastian. The child is Donnie Sebastian, as far as we know."

"She was shot, right?" Mason said. "I know shot when I see it."

Singletongue's eyes seemed to glaze over. "There's no weapon to indicate it was a suicide, but I don't like to discuss these things until the forensics guys have finished up. She was shot in the head, as you know," he answered.

"Execution style," Mason added.

The detective nodded in response.

"What are they going to do with the child—Donnie? Donald is Norman's father's name," she added.

"I don't know that yet. Child Services will be notified and we'll proceed as they say. I'll take the little guy back to the station if I can't reach somebody from their office because of the holiday weekend. The process takes a long time, and the kid obviously needs a bath and some decent food. Child Services will take care of him until a relative is found." He looked at Donnie across the room quietly playing with some alphabet blocks. The child's eyes closed from time to time, during which he slumped against the back of his chair.

The detective stopped to speak with a uniformed officer, who talked to Donnie for a few minutes, then picked him up and carried him out toward a patrol car.

Singletongue looked up from a notebook in his hand with a question in his eyes then said, "Apparently you're not a blood relative, right?"

"That's right," Maria answered with a sigh.

"How did the guy in the mine die?"

Maria started to answer, then shook her head instead.

"We don't know yet," Mason said. "And the reality is, it's probable these two things are not connected."

"Norman has an aunt, who will be pretty elderly by now, but I know where she used to live. If she's still there, maybe she'll know something about him. Maybe she knows about the child, too. Do you want me to see if I can find her? I can go by her house while we're in town, but I don't know the address," said Maria.

"Yeah, that's a good idea. I'll need all your contact information, as well as Mr. Walker's."

"I'll see if I can find her and I'll call you," Maria said. "What'll happen to the child if we can't find relatives?"

"Child Services will take care of him and he'll probably be adopted. He's young, so there will be people wanting him." The detective smiled sadly. "I'm sorry this happened and hope you can find the aunt. We'll let you know what turns up for Donnie. He's a sweet child."

Maria felt terrible for the child. She hoped he was young enough that one day he'd have no memory of the past few days. She stood in thought, staring at the cluttered floor.

A toy tucked under the corner of the couch in the living room caught her eye—a plastic wind-up toy, the image of which was on the pillowcase Donnie had clutched while next to his dead mother. It apparently held some significance for the boy. In hopes the toy might bring him comfort, Maria pocketed it to take to Donnie as soon as she could.

Their names, identifications, phone numbers and addresses were logged into the police report. Singletongue verified their driver licenses and exchanged business cards with both of them as well. Maria promised to contact him with the aunt's name and address right away.

Finally free to leave, Maria and Mason went back to the rental car. She was exhausted, and felt nauseous. "Do you feel as bad as I do?"

"Like I could sleep for a week. It's been a busy day." Mason looked at his watch. "With the time change, I've been up for twenty hours. How about you?" He started the car.

"I need food and a bed."

"Yes, ma'am. Coming right up. Do you want to stay at your parents' house? I can get a hotel room."

"You wouldn't really make me do that, would you? You have no idea what prison is like until you've been told when to go to bed, when to eat and what to wear. I'm staying with you." She paused. "Oh my gosh! I need to call them. It's so late, they're going to wonder what happened to us." She checked her phone to see if she'd missed a call from her parents, but found she'd left it turned off ever since she'd entered the airplane. She keyed in their home number, got their voice mail and left word they'd run into a problem after they landed and would call in the morning and explain. She added she was sorry and looked forward to seeing them bright and early.

Maria's favorite Mexican restaurant was still in business, so they stopped for dinner. It was just past midnight when they pulled into a Marriott Courtyard on the edge of the city of Phoenix. The next block began Scottsdale.

"My headache left with my second enchilada, but the rest of me feels swept under the rug," Maria said as they entered the elevator. Not to mention she'd seen a dead person with macabre circumstances involving a child.

Mason sighed. "I know what you mean. God, you smell good," he said as he leaned into her hair. "Hmmm. You taste good, too." He nuzzled her cheek.

Maria felt a misty surge of warmth enclose her with his embrace. It was like they weren't two people when they were

68

together like this, but only one. She'd seen movies where a person stepped into the body of another, and she imagined herself being neither herself nor him, but another entity, created from the two of them. *What was going on?* He kissed her face, both hands cupped along her jawline.

He flashed his beautiful white teeth and his special smile lines ran down his cheeks. Canyons, actually. "I loved watching you today." He kissed her eyes. "You seemed so at ease with all those people. I lose my ability to think when I've got you so near. All I can do is feel your life, your heartbeat, your gentleness. It's like there's a door open into you that I can walk through and everything I see is different because of it. What is this about?" Delicately he kissed her cheeks, her nose and her lips. "Soft," he said.

"Am I still here? Can you see me?" she asked, kissing him back gently. *Should I fear disappearing into him?"*

The elevator stopped and the door slid open, but they made no move toward exiting.

Her hands were shaking. All the grimness of death, the morbidity of murder, the worry over Norman, the abandonment of a child lessened, then blipped off the screen.

Here and now was all the reality she wanted, as unreal as it felt.

"There's no tomorrow, Maria. There's no yesterday. There is only now. Come be with me now."

Maria's knees weakened at his words. How did he know the perfect words to say exactly when she needed them?

The doors shut on the elevator. Mason jumped back and pushed the 'door open' button, and it slid open again. "Clever, these electronic gadgets," he said as he picked up the suitcases and ushered Maria out of the metal box.

Room 215 was a semi-suite with a living room and separate bedroom. He dropped their bags on the floor then reached for her again.

She wasn't sure exactly when it was she started dreaming, but she knew they were both too tired to be awake long. Reality mixed with fantasy which mixed with the fragrance of him, an embedded flavor that was his alone, hers alone. Time meant nothing. Harbored bad feelings, guilt, memories, all got lost in there somewhere and they entered a new land.

* * *

Maria woke early and took advantage of her chance to be a voyeur. Mason lay eighteen inches away from her in solid sleep with his left arm flung up over his head. His unanimated face looked almost like it belonged to another person, with eyelashes so long they were black satin against his skin. Even thrown back against his pillow, his hair looked like a dark pool with glints of blueness in the morning light. His lips looked chiseled from bronze marble and were surrounded by the shadow of a morning beard. The facial creases she loved so much could not be seen as more than a slight line along his cheeks on either side of his mouth. His nose was the best nose she'd ever seen. He'd won the coin toss for looks.

Though they'd been so tired they were nearly ill the night before, the healing togetherness had rebuilt them both. Their relationship was so comfortable, she could not imagine a life without Mason.

His eyes opened, blinked, focused. His face came to life and he was hers again with its smile.

"Come on, dude," she whispered to his ear as her lips touched his briary cheek. "The parents are going to wonder what happened to us." She planted a kiss on Mason's right eyebrow before she headed for the shower.

He rousted himself up and into the shower as she passed by him smelling warm and shampoo-sweet five minutes later.

Mason was dressed and out the door before Maria set gold earrings into her pierced ears. She looked around for missing items. "They're going to wonder what happened to us, we're so late," she said as he stepped back into the room. She picked up her luggage and started for the door.

He handed her a cup of coffee he'd obtained from downstairs, took her bag from her hand, and said, with a smile and a kiss on her nose, "Let's go see dad."

CHAPTER 9

The old neighborhood where her parents lived held only tiny glimpses of her past. Stubbled fields that had been behind their subdivision were covered in newer subdivisions. Walls now separated each area like tiny fiefdoms.

The miles rolled by with increasing unfamiliarity. Gone were the stubble fields where Maria had played high school softball. In their place were maze-like warrens of walls and rooftops, an unending crop of Scottsdale's hidden houses. Where *did the kids play*, Maria wondered as they turned onto her street.

Squaw Peak Mountain shaded her parent's yard in the early morning. In the softer light, their cream-colored stucco house and pristine lawn looked picture perfect. Maria fought the odd tide of emotion that coming home always brought.

Her Mom met them at the door, her natural reticence seemingly forgotten. She hugged Maria with tears in her eyes. Then Maria took Mason's hand and said, "I'd like you to know my mother, Elizabeth." She turned to her mother and followed with, "Please meet Mason Walker."

The father who met the couple in the backyard patio of the cream stucco house surrounded by a variety of cactus plants looked perfectly healthy to Maria. Questions crowded her mind.

The gray hair taking over the remnants of dark brown looked noble in contrast to the sun-browned skin that leathered his face and neck. His daughter was swooped off her feet in a tangle of arms and blonde hair.

"Daddy," Maria said, but it meant so much more. It meant, 'I love you, I've missed you, you're still my hero, I'm awed by you, I wish I could get in your lap again.' But "Daddy" was all she said.

When Maria was back on her own two feet, she backed away from her dad, pulled Mason forward by his arm and said, "Mason Walker, this is Robert John Charles Walton, my father."

Mason stepped forward. A flash of puzzlement crossed his face but immediately was masked with his familiar grin.

As they shook hands, Mason said, "I admire your inventions that Maria shared with me."

"I have to keep myself busy, you know. Retirement can get you down if you let it."

They'd swept past the pies lining the granite counter top in the kitchen behind them, where a fragrance of spices combined with baked sugar crusts filled the room and brought a familiar rumbling to Maria's stomach.

A barrage of unasked questions hid behind the politeness of the logistics of their arrival to Arizona, the thinly disguised excuse of a Thanksgiving holiday wafting about in the air between the four of them.

Yes, they'd both had good flights, the airline food was better than nothing and they compared safety procedures from other recent flights.

"We landed right at rush hour, so we avoided a bit of traffic when we stopped by the old house in Phoenix on our way out," Maria told her parents. She related the story of Donnie. "I didn't know Norman had a child, did you?"

Mason watched their response. Maria glanced at him, reading something there.

"Really? No dear, I hadn't heard about that," Elizabeth said, wiping her hands on her well-worn apron.

"You wouldn't know if Norman's aunt Ada is still in town, would you?" Maria continued.

"No," her mother answered thoughtfully, searching deeply into her past for an answer. "We haven't seen anyone from Norman's family since…." She glanced at Mason. "Well, you know."

Robert John Charles looked at his feet and said nothing.

"Mom, the pies smell fabulous."

Elizabeth beamed with the compliment. "Well, I've tried to make everybody's favorites. Howard was so glad to hear you were coming—he likes chocolate pie, you know."

"Howard is my mother's brother," Maria told Mason.

"Do you men want drinks? I've got to check my rolls," Elizabeth said. The women started toward the kitchen as they talked about the arrival of family members, the huge Thanksgiving reunion.

"We've got it covered," Robert John Charles answered and waved a half-consumed drink toward his wife. "I'll take care of the guys."

Maria opened drawers with no need to hunt for aluminum foil, potholders, or pie cutter. They were in the same places they'd been when she was five years old. She and Elizabeth organized food to travel while chatting about recipes and relatives. She snatched glances toward Mason and Robert John Charles, noticing the similarities between them, standing eye to eye, a low roll of conversation unbroken. They could have been a picture of a man in his youth vs. the same man in his elder years.

"I think we're about through in here," Elizabeth said as she pulled the strings of her apron, and ducked her head out of the neckpiece.

Maria finished tucking plastic wrap across the top of a pumpkin pie and dusted her hands.

Their respective histories caught up by their short conversation, when Maria returned to the patio, Mason was saying, "There's more to the story than what Maria mentioned. We were delayed yesterday because the boy's mother, Nita Sebastian, was dead when we got to the house. She'd been murdered."

Shock registered on the elder man's face. "Murdered? How?" His green eyes bored into Mason's brown ones.

"Assassination style, bullet behind the ear. Small caliber gun. No exit wound."

Robert sat back in his chair and put his drink down on a glass-topped table, missing the coaster assigned to it.

"Holy Christ! That blasted idiot finally got somebody killed."

Mason's ears appeared to perk up.

"I know you probably don't know Norm, but he's an accident waiting to happen," John Robert Charles continued. "He keeps an arsenal in his house—always has. What a fool." Maria winced at his words. Though somehow they didn't make her feel responsible for Norman.

Elizabeth had returned with a tray full of iced tea glasses and pitcher. She sat them down on a chair-side table. "Who's a fool?"

Maria stepped to take the tray from Elizabeth and wrapped an arm around her mother's shoulders. "When we were at Norman's house, we found his current wife in the bedroom, dead."

"Ohhhh. My. Was she sick? Why was she dead? Where was Norman?" Elizabeth asked. "Where's the child? How old is he?"

"The detective was going to take him to Child Services. I think he's about two," Mason said.

Maria sat down next to her mother and took her hands in her own. "We don't know. We were hoping maybe one of you had seen him recently. I'm going to try to find Norman's aunt

Ada, and see if she's heard from him. Have you seen Norman at all?" Maria looked at her father.

Robert cleared his throat, "Just a couple of times. You know —in passing."

"Where?" Maria asked him.

"Out at the range, once. Actually, a couple of times."

Mason said, "A shooting range?"

Robert nodded his head.

"Do you shoot?" Mason asked.

"Yes. I have a few weapons, and like to keep current on them. Old habits die hard. Look, I'm sorry to hear about the woman. Did you know her?"

Maria answered, "No, I didn't know Norman was seeing anybody, let alone that he was married. Maybe that's why he stopped trying to contact me. I hope he didn't kill the woman."

"You should have married someone closer to your own age," Elizabeth said to Maria.

"I know. We've already been through all this a dozen times. If you don't mind, I really don't want to talk about it." She wondered why her mother persisted in making her feel such a failure. Still.

"If you had, maybe we'd be grandparents by this time," her mother said.

"Mom, don't do this to me. I didn't come here for this." Maria stood and took up her purse and her jacket. She knew she shouldn't get so angry, but she knew her mother wanted to hurt her. What she didn't know was why. She'd never known why.

"Honey, come on. Calm down. Your mother didn't mean anything by it. She just wishes everything had gone well instead of bad for you," Robert said. He stood and took the things from Maria's hands and pulled her back to her chair seat.

"I do too. But the fact is, it's a dead issue and I'm not talking about it again." She couldn't keep the tears from forming in her eyes.

"Would you like some pie, Mr. Walker?" Elizabeth asked.

Mason blinked his eyes several times. The corner of his lips tightened and muscles clenched along his jawline. "Uh, yes, thank you, I would," he answered, then looked over at Maria. She was still marshalling her thoughts and wondered if he thought she was a loser, since her mother had pointed it out for him so well. With an almost imperceptible grin, he winked at her.

Elizabeth left for the kitchen.

Maria composed herself, dreading the next episode of domestic bliss.

"Tell me about this firing range you use," Mason asked Robert.

"It's a local one over in the hills halfway across the reservation." Robert nodded toward the East. "Been there for years."

"Daddy was a policeman a long time ago," Maria told Mason. Did you start using the range during that time?" she asked her father."

"Uh huh. It belonged to the sheriff's office at that time, and we all went out there to qualify every month—the city police as well as the county sheriff's deputies."

Elizabeth smiled at Mason as she set a piece of warm pumpkin pie down before him on the coffee table, then glided back toward the kitchen.

"Was Norman on the department?" Mason quizzed as he picked up his fork.

"No, he started using the range later—when it went public. You had to have a background check and buy a membership when it changed over. Most of the department guys continued to use it rather than be stuck with an inside range. It's the noise, you know. Bad enough outside. Worse inside."

"Do they allow AR-15s at that range? Maybe M16s?" Mason asked.

Maria wondered why he asked that. She felt guilty not running into the kitchen to help her mom, but she wanted to hear her favorite two men in the world talk together.

"Yeah, it's OK for the AR-15s. The M16s are illegal, you know, at the outside range. Neither of those can be used inside."

Maria was fidgeting around in her pockets looking for a pen when she came across the toy she'd found at Norman's house. She set it on the table while she looked through her purse. Her father picked it up.

"Where'd you get this?" Robert John Charles said, looking at her intently.

"Uh, it belongs to the little boy—Donnie. I was saving it for him."

"Are you sure about that?" her father asked.

"Sure about what, Dad? That it's Donnie's, that it's a toy or that it belongs to him?" Why was her father being so irritating? Wasn't her mother enough for one day?

"Any of those. All of those. You found this at Norman's house?"

"Yes, Dad, that's what I said." *Sheesh.*

Robert stood up just then and jammed his fists into his slacks' pockets, suddenly looking angry. "You shouldn't be messing into this, Missy."

"Dad? It's a toy! What's wrong with you?"

Just then Elizabeth announced everything was ready to pack in the car for the trip to the extended family's Thanksgiving Dinner.

It seemed they would have to talk later.

79

CHAPTER 10

The annual Tandy Thanksgiving Day Feast and Meeting was held at Maria's Cousin Irene's historically significant old house. Hedges and pathways through tiny gardens covered the two-acre grounds and had been maintained well, courtesy of a succession of husbands provided by cousin Irene.

It was gorgeous. A lovely painted lady with gingerbread balustrades irreverently perched in a desert setting.

Elizabeth brought two casseroles, three pies and fifty dinner rolls, which they carried to the function in two cars, each item perched on towels, wedged by trunk junk and covered with more towels. Ferried into the period home, cousins talking to them the entire way from the street to the kitchen counter tops, each cousin they encountered stopped what they were doing to size Mason up and down. The facial expression known as the "cousin smirk" was plastered on each face as they noted Maria's new beau, as Cousin Patsy referred to him.

"I tried to warn you," Maria said to Mason when they had a rare minute alone.

"Yes, you did. I think it's kinda sweet, actually."

Suddenly a blur whizzed past Maria and attached itself to Mason in the form of Emily Louise Tandy. "Aaaiiieee! You gorgeous devil!" she wailed before landing against Mason's chest with a thump that nearly knocked him over. She tipped up to his face and planted a big kiss on his lips. "Didja miss me?"

"Sorry," Maria said. "I forgot to warn you Emily would be here."

Emily wore skin-tight blue jeans with a glistening silver-threaded tee shirt. Her hair was piled loosely in sort of an ingénue waif free-form look. Maria began figuring out a way to get her off of Mason, before he got to liking her cellophane act.

Cousin Sandra stopped on her way by with a huge sweet potato soufflé, leaned into Maria and said, "All's got him already? That's fast, even for her! It may be some kind of record."

"No, Sandy, she already knows this one," Maria said.

Maria watched Mason's face recoup from the attack, swatted Emily on her butt, and said, "lay off, dopey."

"But *ma cousine*, you must learn to share your goodies."

Maria was thrown. Surely the other cousins thought it just as stupid. Mason hadn't caused the situation with Em and was too polite to tell her to buzz off.

She shouldn't have come, or brought Mason with her. She shouldn't have exposed Mason to her goofy family yet. Or maybe ever. She'd long ago ceased to let them embarrass her, but it was difficult to explain them to other people she cared about.

Mason stood back from Emily, slipped over to Maria's side and wrapped one arm around her waist. Then he looked back at Emily and said, "How good of you to come. Did you have a nice flight?"

Color rushed up Emily's neck to the top of her head, painted there by some sudden and unforeseen brush. Her teeth ground together. Her eyes narrowed to slits. She stared at Mason, then dropped her head forward. When she pulled it back up again, it was with a little girl pout, complete with pursed lips and big innocently rounded eyes.

"I know you're really glad to see me," she said, and batted her eyelashes at Mason.

He said, "Oh, boy! Let's go see what's on the dessert table," to Maria and took her arm.

Food piled high on plates, the family merged out to the lawn where awnings covered twelve picnic benches. Babies crawled on blankets spread near the tables, and older children ran between and among them, playing with their cousins.

Mason and Maria sat at a table with two sets of cousin couples and one of her aunts and uncles. Aunt Grace met Mason and asked how Maria liked Atlanta, compared to the desert. "Do you miss our dry weather?" Grace asked.

"Yes," Maria answered as she cut a piece of ham. "Especially during the rainy months. Atlanta gets about sixty-five inches of rain a year. Most of it comes over four months."

Grace laughed in an alto tone. "That's quite different than our four inches a year! Of course our weather is more humid now that people planted all those lawns and the aquifer is being tested! When people want to sell their homes they water like crazy in the middle of the night to make their yards look lush. You can always tell a home for sale—it has the only green lawn in the neighborhood. Personally, I like my rock yard. Never any trouble. Of course right now nobody's selling anything. Is your real estate as bad as ours? All those foreclosures!"

"It's bad everywhere right now, Grace. The only thing to do is wait it out."

"Yes, and be grateful if you can make the payments."

"Absolutely," Maria said.

"This potato casserole is wonderful! Did you try some of my aspic salad? Of course you did—I see it right there on your plate. Do you hear anything from Norman?" Grace slipped in.

"No. As a matter of fact, Mason and I went by his house on the way out here. I don't know if anyone has told you, but there was a death at his house."

Grace's eyes widened. "Norman died?"

"No, I think the woman was his new wife. He wasn't there. I've been worried about him since last week. "

"Norman? I saw him at the airport swap meet yesterday. He was shopping knives."

Maria and Mason looked at each other. She let out a big sigh. He slipped his arm around her briefly, and gave her a hug.

"Whew. I didn't realize I was that concerned until just now. Thanks, Grace." As she said the words she thought about the dead woman lying in Norman's bed.

Mason said, "Now all we have to do is wonder where our boy is."

Maria asked, "Grace, did Norm look upset or anything? I can't imagine someone shopping for knives with his wife barely cold and not even in her grave yet. Hmmm. Maybe they were divorced or something."

Grace stopped to chew on the bite of pecan pie she'd just inserted into her mouth. She swallowed and said, "Well, he seemed perfectly normal to me. At least normal for him. Which I guess isn't really so normal, is it?" She laughed and cut another piece from her pie wedge.

* * *

The day was pretty familiar to Maria. She'd spent every Thanksgiving she could remember until the age of twenty-two attending the event. It had been hit and miss after she'd married Norman and after she'd moved to Atlanta. She hadn't attended for seven years.

When she'd moved to Atlanta, she'd been glad to be rid of her cousins and all their strange problems. She'd only gone back once.

Mason asked if he could drive Elizabeth back over to Scottsdale. Elizabeth agreed, so that left Maria to ride with her father in the rental car.

"Did you have a good time, kid?" her father asked.

"I hate to admit it, but, yes, I did. I've always thought our relatives were a strange bunch of people."

"Yep. You don't get to choose your family," Robert answered. "There was a time when I wouldn't go either, because they were so irritating."

"I remember that. Mom dragged us anyway, and all the cousins asked about you and planned all the ways they could get you to come. Remember when they had your birthday party one year at Thanksgiving?"

"Yes. What a put-up job that one was. My birthday is in July."

They laughed.

"Dad. What did you mean about that toy I picked up of Donnie's at Norman's house? How could a toy upset you so much?"

Robert's jovial mood darkened.

"That thing is a symbol for survivalists. So they can recognize each other and their paraphernalia."

"What? A toy?"

"A logo. An innocent one. One the rest of the world won't notice. A secret code."

"Are you sure?"

"Absolutely."

"But the cartoon bird was all over Donnie's pillow case. Why would survivalists use it?"

"I looked that bird up once. It's a Striped Tanager. There have always been street insignias, logos. The underworld understands them as contact points. This is the same thing, for illegal weapons and contraband." Robert stared hard at Maria. "You need to be aware. You need to leave it be."

"Maybe in this case, it's just an innocent toy."

"That could be, of course, but who's fooling who? Those guys suck a lot of people into their paranoia, cause a lot of trouble. Illegal weapons are only one inch away from illegal drugs, prostitution, numbers running, anti-American activities."

"Sheesh. Now who's sounding paranoid?" Maria said.

"You've already got one dead woman. An orphaned child, a missing ex-husband. What do you want, a diagram? Open your eyes Maria."

CHAPTER 11

Mason's rental car made its way into an area of older homes
spaced and partially hidden by huge boulders and small
hillocks. Maria squinted at the homes they passed, searching her
memory for Norman's aunt's house. But, with the architecture
of the homes confined to adobe, they all looked alike. Flat
roofs, shades of walls that varied from beige to brown, cactus
and rock yards. Small acreage tracts for each home. *Boring?*
Picturesque? Who knows? Maria thought. "They've done a
good job of keeping the homes in the same architectural vein. I
can't tell one from the other. Let's drive past again. There must
be something I can remember about that house," she said.

"You say Norman is sixty?" Mason asked.

"Yep."

"Is his aunt still alive? She'd have to be in her eighties, or
so."

"Not exactly. She's only about twelve years older than
Norman. Norm's mother was the second of thirteen children.
Ada is the youngest."

Mason pulled the rental car onto the road's berm and turned
to Maria. "We're back where we started from now. Shall we
make another pass?" he asked.

"That mailbox looks familiar." Maria stared at the entrance
to one house. "But there are three others that look right too. I
remember only part of the house could be seen from the road.
The other ones with similar mailboxes are all totally hidden."

Mason turned into the driveway and followed it over the
landscape sand dune in front of the house and stopped. "Yes.
This looks right. I hope she's home."

"Well, she certainly isn't out watering her flowers."

"What flowers?"

"Exactly."

Bright brown eyes with flecks of gold and green looked expectantly through the wrought iron security screen door when the heavy front door opened to their ring. "Do I know you?" a frail woman asked.

"Ada? Yes. I'm Maria—Norman's ex-wife. Do you remember me?" The woman looked as frail as a bird.

"Yes I do remember you. And I think I'm mad at you."

Maria glanced at Mason, who winked at her. The wink made her lose the confusion the old woman's words had started. "It's been a long time for you to still be mad," she said.

Ada opened several locks on the security-screened door as she spoke, then stepped to the side when it swung open. "Come in, then. I can be just as mad inside as out."

Mason grinned at Maria as they went inside. She whispered, "What?" at him as she passed through the doorway.

Maria scanned the room of musty furniture as she recalled the plethora of china cups and saucers on every surface. "You have your curtains drawn. Have you been ill?"

"No. No, no. I don't like people looking in. One can't be too careful, you know." She reached for the nearest lamp and clicked it on.

China cups glinted from every table, ledge and shelf in the room. They all appeared freshly washed.

"Sixteen years and four months," Ada said. "That's how long it's been. Norman's gone straight downhill ever since. How about you, honey? You don't look like you've gone downhill, but I don't like your hair that way." She reached up to push back a long strand of hair from Maria's brow. "The girls used to wear their hair so perfect they looked like they just stepped out of the beauty parlor—now look at them. Straight and stringy. I remember when we used to work for hours to get our hair just

88

perfect. Rag rollers, permanents, beer rinses, henna for highlights. Now I doubt any of them do anything. Don't even comb it! Look like a bunch of orphans."

"Ada, you know I tried to work it out with Norman, but I just couldn't do it. He scared me. He enjoyed scaring me."

"Yes, I know you did. That boy wasn't right after the war. My brother never got over World War II either. He finally died of cancer. Of course, he had tuberculosis too—never could get rid of it either." She shook her head, lost for a few seconds with her memories.

"Who is your young man?"

"This is Mason Walker. I think you'll like him. He's a really nice guy." She gave Mason a fake punch on the shoulder as she said it.

"OK, Mr. Nice Guy. What are your intentions?" Ada said. "Don't just stand there like a piece of meat. Are you going to treat my niece right, or turn into an animal?"

That Norman's aunt still claimed her as 'her niece' brought a lump to her throat. "Yeah, what *are* your intentions?" she said. She turned to look at Mason, whose lips already had a grin on them.

"I'm just standing here being a piece of meat," he said.

"I don't want to hear about you mistreating her. Is that clear? She's been through enough with my dopey nephew."

"I promise to never mistreat her," he said, and put his right hand up in the air.

Ada nodded her head, though she had a skeptical look in her eyes.

"Do you know where Norman is?" Maria asked.

"Norman lives across town in the same house where he's always been. I have his number right here somewhere." Ada went to a table full of papers and shuffled through a few of them.

"No, we were there, and it looks like he's out of town. I thought you might know where he's gone," Maria said.

"Hmmm. It seems to me there's a hunting camp he likes to go to. I don't think anybody knows about it but myself."

"Why do you say that?" Mason asked.

"Norm doesn't know I knew he was going out there, but when he was living here a few summers ago, I heard him talking on the telephone about meeting somebody at the hunting camp. He left some of those hollow shotgun shells on the bureau in his room, in an old ashtray. I saw them one day when the door was open."

"Do you mean shell casings?"

"I guess that's what you'd call them. He went off every week after he put a bunch of gear in his car... never said where he was going, and I didn't ask. If he'd wanted me to know, he'd have told me. My daddy used to do the same thing when I was a kid. He'd pack up all his stuff and pick up his rifle and out the door he'd go. My brother went with him a lot, and Davy said they went shooting. Came back with all those shell casings."

"Did Norman stay gone very long?" Mason asked.

"Most of the day. But he was always home for supper. He loved my cooking. I don't get to cook any more... nobody around to eat it."

"Did you ever go see his house after I left? I mean, to meet his new wife and his child?" Maria asked

"Lordy, no. I don't go out any more. My cat and my TV are all I need right here. I didn't want to have anything to do with that woman he married. She didn't have any use for me. I did meet Donnie a couple of times when Norm brought him to see me." Ada crossed to the front door and checked that the locks were bolted. Then she spread out the curtain over the door window and patted it down.

All her life until she'd moved to north Georgia, Maria had been vulnerable to crime and took it in stride. Stepping back into the time capsule, she could see it now, and was so grateful that fate had led her to the other side of the continent where she hadn't thought about fear.

She felt chilled that this elderly woman had to fear leaving her curtains open, and made a mental note to find more of Ada's relatives. Perhaps they could move the old woman to a safer environment.

"The homicide detectives will be coming by to talk with you about Norman's wife," Maria told Ada. "I promised to give Detective Singletongue your address and phone number."

"But I don't know anything about that woman."

"You're the only relative Norman has. They always contact the relatives. Norman's wife was your niece by marriage, just like me."

"I suppose."

* * *

By the time they left Ada's home, Maria's watch said six ten.

Detective Singletongue's office was in the Central City Precinct. From Ada's house the route took Mason and Maria right through downtown Phoenix. The businesses surrounded by concertina wire-topped eight-foot chain link fences caused Maria to flinch.

"How many burglars do you suppose that's going to keep out?" she asked Mason, referring to one particular location.

"Probably all of them." His grin lit up his eyes as they darted from rear view mirrors through windows, toward her and back on the road.

"Yeah. Dumb question. Looks like my hometown has gone to hell. I don't remember ever seeing such well-guarded streets."

"Maybe we should go on tour of beautiful downtown Los Angeles some time."

"Have you seen anything so defensive looking in Atlanta?" she asked.

"No, but I don't go down there much. We live in a pretty secluded place."

"At least it doesn't look like a war zone. Think of trying to raise kids in this environment."

"Yeah, look what it did for you. Warped you for life."

"Come on. It didn't look like this when I was growing up. Thank God," she added.

They pulled into the guarded parking lot, Mason yanked a ticket from the kiosk and made sure the car was locked. Holiday weekend traffic was light in town. The streets had barely survived the onslaught of routine daily life and were trying to catch their breath, snoozing in the sun.

So different from where they'd been two thousand miles away, the quietude of the forested hardwoods continued to speak to Maria of a rich past in silent growth. Of a past based on warring tribes of ancient Americans fighting on its soil. Gratitude flooded Maria's thoughts.

"Maybe a few bulldozers would help this place out," she said as they made their way to the door and were buzzed in by a security guard behind bullet proof glass. "Not very friendly, is it?"

"Andy Taylor would be appalled," Mason answered.

* * *

From behind the weapons check, a steel door opened and Singletongue poked his head out. Mason waved and they were motioned into the detective's office.

Singletongue, all smiles and cordiality in his tiny office, gestured Maria into the one folding chair tucked in the corner. He smelled of a musky after-shave that defeated his earthy look. Maria expected to see Native American artifacts in his office, but there was only one bookcase unit and it was filled with what looked like policy manuals. He rolled his desk chair next to the folding chair, then returned to the other side of his desk and perched his backside on its edge, indicating to Mason to use his chair. "I've checked with a detective Livermore at the sheriff's department in Dahlonega, Georgia. He verified everything you told me about the remains found in the mineshaft. We're continuing to talk with the neighbors of the Sebastians here, to find anybody who might have seen something going on over at the house. You know, cars, unusual people, dates they were seen, and so forth. So far, we've got nothing. But that could change at any time."

"What's going to happen with the child? I really hate for him to drift into the child services system and not know how he's doing," Maria said.

"I don't think you need to worry about him," the detective said. A gold tooth glinted from the edge of his smile. "My wife, Tina, and I applied to be foster parents a year ago. Since then we applied to adopt. Tina and I talked last night." His eyebrows peaked heavy dark arcs over his eyes, asking permission. He seemed to want them to agree with the idea of him and his wife adopting Donnie. "Of course, we can't attempt an adoption until Donnie's father is found. Then there will be tribal issues. I think Donnie is Cherokee and I am Navaho. Until then, I hope we can keep him as a foster child.

Maria had a flashback of her conversation with Norman's aunt Ada. She'd said Donnie's mother was Indian, from a local reservation.

"Oh," she continued as she reached into her purse. "Here's Ada's name, address and phone number," and withdrew a scribbled-on hotel notepad. "Please give me a name to contact for elder care if you have one. I'm worried about Ada's safety. She lives alone, behind a million locks."

Dirk reached for his shelves, pulled out a huge telephone book with dogeared corners and brushed off the cover page. He flipped it open expertly, turned only a few pages and found an item. "I don't use this much any more since the Internet, but some things haven't changed." He handed the heavy book to Maria, and pointed at the already-underlined number for Greater Phoenix Social Services. "Ask for Annette at this number. She's my wife's sister. If she can't help you, she'll know somebody who can."

After they left Dirk's office, Maria called her father. She heard a buzzing noise in the background when Robert John Charles picked up, meaning he was in his work shed behind the garage. "Dad, could you take Mason and me over to the shooting range in Roman Canyon? Maybe we could find somebody who'd know where Norman might be. Aunt Ada told me he had a cabin up in the hills beyond the range."

"You're going to get in trouble looking for him, Little Girl. I told you that."

CHAPTER 12

Maria hated to argue with her father, but needed his help. He knew everybody at the firing range, had spent hours there as a police officer, qualifying with his weapons. He hadn't been retired long enough to lose his law enforcement connections.

"How am I going to sleep at night not knowing if, how, or why it was Norman we found dead in a cave in Georgia? We'll go out there, ask a few questions, and hopefully find where his cabin is. If he's not there, I promise I'll get on the plane like a good girl and go home and deal with it another way." She heard some rustling. "Are you still there?"

"Yes. I'm just trying to get this Dremel tool to clean this thing out." He sounded distracted as he fumbled with something ten miles away.

"Dad!"

"Uh? Oh. Nuts." Something rattled and thunked. Her father obviously clamored to maintain the phone, which had apparently fallen anyway. "Sorry, sorry, I dropped the damn thing. Like I was saying, those survivalist guys are all paranoid schizophrenics, and you should just walk away."

"Please, dad? One drive out and back, then it will be over."

"Ok, but you promise it's over at that point and won't pursue whatever Norman's into."

"I swear to consider it!" Maria said with her left hand held behind her back, two fingers crossed."

Mason's smile was so silly when she looked at him that her heart lightened.

Maria proudly watched Robert John Charles schmooze his way through the concrete range, nodding to people on his right and left as he was acknowledged. All wore blue hearing protectors against the sound of qualifying sheriff's deputies, county marshals, and Scottsdale and Phoenix City policemen firing their weapons.

"This place gets pretty busy with everybody having to qualify every month," Robert yelled over the din.

One at a time, men stopped what they were doing and walked over to where he was, shook his hand and asked after others of both their acquaintance. Maria was touched by the attention and admiration they showed him.

After thirty minutes of that routine, he came back to where Mason and Maria stood inside a glass room and said, "Let's go up the road a ways. Some survivalists have a camp further into the canyon. They've got sleeping cabins for overnight shoots."

The three of them bumped along the paved canyon road that became gravel then washboard dirt as it wound between the deceitfully soft looking hills dotted with sagebrush. Eyeing some of the ruts that challenged the rental car, Maria missed her four-wheel-drive.

Finally, some shacks came into view. They looked like homesteader cracker boxes built by pioneers in the 19th Century who could claim acreage merely by building anything that resembled a house.

At a huddle of the dinky cubicles, with a football field size setup of various types of animal targets, they saw man-size paper targets set on cable runners. In a makeshift arcade, rotating steel targets loomed. To their left, were some floating duck targets in a small pond covered with green scum. Everything looked well used and fully perforated. The place was deserted.

They waited for the dust to settle, then stepped out of the rental car. Her father hollered, "Hello! Is anybody about?" Maria heard a fading echo in response.

Mason and Maria followed him into two of the shacks before splitting up and checking all seven of them. Other than paper litter, abandoned cans and bottles, they found nothing to indicate recent habitation.

Mixed in with the other litter were stickers of that same cartoon bird character she'd seen at the old house where she'd lived with Norman.

"Hmmm," Mason said. "This looks familiar." He bent to pick one of the stickers off the ground.

"I was just thinking that myself," Maria said. "Donnie's pillow case."

They drove back to Robert John Charles' house in silence.

"It's just as well we didn't find anybody," Robert said. "They're survivalists, which is synonymous with 'crackpot.' I've never known a survivalist who wasn't certifiably insane."

"I know," Maria said. "I'd still like to get some answers. We shouldn't be finding dead people. I should just let Norman's world take care of itself without me."

* * *

The next morning, on their way to the airport, Maria found herself wanting to stay in the old familiar surroundings, yet wanting to be out of there at the same time. In addition, she didn't want to leave Mason, who was going to return to Florida to finish sleuthing for the lawyer in New York. Another feeling lurked in the back of her mind: she wanted to be alone.

One person can't be feeling so much emotion about four opposing things at once. God! She was a mess.

She followed Mason like a puppy dog up to his gate, wanting to keep him with her so badly she felt like crying. When she noticed she was clinging to his arm, she suddenly straightened up, embarrassed.

"What?" Mason asked as she stepped back from him.

"Nothing. I'm being a baby and it's time to grow up. Took me a while to realize it." She stared at the diamond shapes in the marble floor.

"I think..." Mason said as Maria's cell phone rang. She put up her free hand to indicate he should hold the thought. There were too many possibilities of tying loose ends up to not answer the phone.

The southern nicety of discussing health and weather before launching into the subject warmed her and it felt good to click into her professional persona. "How are you? Did you have a nice Thanksgiving? No, it never rains in Arizona. Yes, we had a lovely time with all the relatives," she said in response to the call from Tommy Larken from the Forsyth County Sheriff's Department.

He covered his end of the social questions then said, "During the holiday, the lab came up with a new wrinkle. I don't know if it makes any difference to the case, but it's interesting... the bones in the mine belonged to an American Indian."

"How'd you get that info? I thought the labs were backed up for over a year."

"Well, they are. I didn't say this was official."

"So. You've got a friend in the blood typing business."

"Yep. I've got a friend. I got the local lab to give me one of their slides and spent some time with Felix over Thanksgiving. Anyway, if it helps, the dead guy was an Indian."

"Of course it helps. Anything helps! I don't suppose you know what tribe he was from?" Maria smiled to herself. It felt good to turn the tables on Tommy the tease.

"Right. I suppose you want to know how many children he had and his wife's first name, too. All from one slide. Are you jacking me around?"

She giggled. "OK, I'll take what I can get. Good job, Larken! We're just getting Mason sent off back to Miami. I'll be into Atlanta at about 2:00 this afternoon. You take care. Give your wife a smooch for me."

She explained Tom's information to Mason, who gazed at the wall thoughtfully for a minute before saying, "That's the first clue we've had, Sherlock."

"I know. And it means there's no way the remains in the mineshaft could be Norman." A weight she didn't know was there, seemed to lift from her. The deceased person was probably a Cherokee Indian. A considerable population of Cherokee lived in North Carolina as well as Georgia, and they were not confined to reservations.

Mason hugged her. Her heart felt all melted, and she was back to thinking of clinging again. With forty minutes left to get through security and to his gate, he said, "I've got to go now. Keep warm for me." After a lovely goodbye kiss, he turned from her to stand in line at security.

Maria felt ambivalent about leaving him there. She was surprised how comfortable it was to feel independent again. She'd been alone for so long she had forgotten how one makes concessions for someone they love. As soon as he disappeared from her sight, she walked back toward her own flight gate with a great deal of relief.

CHAPTER 13

From the plane's cruising altitude of 42,000 feet, it looked like the fall ball was over. The multi-colored blanket of treetops beneath her was almost totally gray. It gave Maria a chill. As the plane hit the tarmac, it was clear all the leaves now looked like brown potato chips lying on the ground. Rain fell in a soft spit. *Welcome home.*

The Thanksgiving crush of bodies at the airport made her feel like just another ant in a city of passageways. She took the thirty minute rapid transit MARTA ride half way back home, and looked forward to some normalcy in her life, without family pressures or the thought of a child lying down with his dead mother. Without skeletons in mine shafts or a missing ex-husband. Without the responsibility of belonging to anybody.

Her Jeep Cherokee waited patiently in the MARTA station for her, and it looked so wonderful she left steamy lip prints on the window when she kissed it. The radio knew her favorite stations. And the heater worked!

The thirty-minute drive turned into a fifty-minute snail crawl, but gave her time to reflect on the conflicts lurking in the back of her mind. She still didn't know if Norman was okay, though she knew she shouldn't care. He'd mistreated her, set her life back, but she knew he was just a very sick man who'd failed to meet violent enough standards for help.

Donnie would probably need a psychiatrist for the rest of his life. She found it interesting that Dirk Singletongue was American Indian and Donnie Sebastian turned out to be the same. Dirk and his wife seemed a good fit for the little boy. A child needs parents. Maria reflected on how stable her parents were, despite the goofy extended family. What would it be like to grow up an orphan?

That thought made the corpse in the mineshaft drift to the top. American Indians seemed to suddenly pop up everywhere. She didn't understand the specifics of why the Indians had been forced to move out of Georgia. Those reasons had to be money or land, same as usual. The only things they'd left behind were names: Cherokee County, the city of Dahlonega, the Chattahoochee River, and hundreds more.

She turned onto the road to her house that lay so near the freeway, yet so isolated by forest she could forget it existed. Excitement grew inside her chest. Her house waited patiently for her, now at the end of the block. She saw as she neared, it was time to get the leaf blower out, clean the place up and trim the shrubs under the front windows before frost settled in. Why was the windowpane broken? Her heartbeat quickened.

She rolled to a stop in the three-sided carport and hurried to the front porch where broken glass lay on the window sill. Kids playing could have hit a ball or something through the window. She hoped the rain hadn't gone inside. She'd turned down the heater before she left, but it was still colder than fifty degrees outside. Her house was heating the outdoors and was going to cost plenty.

She thrust her key toward the door lock, but it wasn't secure and the door swung inward. Someone standing in the opening between the kitchen and living room turned and slammed through the back doorway. She saw him vault the deck railing and disappear. She knew better than to go inside, but was so shocked when she saw everything she owned piled, cut, ripped, or thrown into the center of the room, she wanted to find the guy and slap him silly. Intending to at least be able to identify him or his car, but knowing better than to go inside, she ran to the end of the porch, looked toward the backyard and saw the same guy she'd seen inside run through the woods wearing blue jeans and a gray hooded sweatshirt. His hair was dirty blonde. When she gained control of them, she made her unwilling legs work, trotted back to her Jeep and dialed 911 while she drove away from the front of her house. Knowing there was no road but the freeway in the direction he ran, she told the operator he may have parked on the freeway or he'd have to circle around through the woods to get to Marina Drive on the east side. She swerved into Tom & Erica's driveway across the street when she saw Tom's county sheriff's car there.

She parked in their drive and ran up the walkway, seeing Tom and Erica in their kitchen through the window. Tom hurried to open the door.

"Tom, thank God you're home. There was a burglar in my house," she said, breathing hard. "He ran off when I opened the door." Erica rolled toward her, her eyes big circles.

"What? You wait here," he said, took her hand and pulled her inside the house. "I'll go see." He jerked his pistol belt off the chair back where he'd apparently draped it when he'd come home, and charged out the door.

Maria leaned down to Erica in her wheelchair, gave her a quick kiss on her cheek and said, "I'm okay," which was partially true since she had no intention of staying put while the hero saved her, the fair maiden. She followed Tom out the door and made a dash across the street. With every step, anger replaced fear and worry. When she reached her front door, Tom was inside.

Tom was just coming back out the front door when Maria stepped onto the porch. "What are you doing over here? You're supposed to be at my house," Tom said.

"Right," Maria said. "He went that-a-way through the woods before I went to your house, the little shit."

Two blue and whites pulled into the yard. Danny McGregor rushed out of the first one while Kevin Mills jumped out of the other. Danny asked Tom if he'd found anything as he pointed his flashlight around corners and under shrubs. Kevin walked around to the back of the house.

"Nah. Scumbag split," Tom said.

Danny said, "it would have been fun to catch him." Tom and Danny grinned at each other, zoned into Copland.

Maria stood, looking into her front door. She'd gone numb except for the ache that had returned to her head. She looked at her grandmother's old rocking chair, its stuffing pouring from the seat, the carefully upholstered Indian print shredded. Her ficus tree, jerked from its planter, lay with its roots and dirt splayed all over the kitchen floor. She'd repotted that tree twice. She'd hunted for its blue pot for quite awhile before she'd found one that matched her house. Maybe blue was the wrong color. "Green would have worked," she said to Tom, who had just returned from talking with the cops in the backyard. Two men she didn't know walked toward the woods, scanning the ground.

"Green would have been just fine, honey. I think you should go read to Erica. What do you think?"

"I can get the broom. There's dirt on the floor," she said. It would take her a long time to clean, fix and repair all of her things, but if she started right now, maybe she could finish it before morning. No, she had to sleep because she had three appointments tomorrow. How would she lock her house? Her eyes got hot with threatening tears. Sitting here on the floor crying would be a big help, she thought in frustration. She rubbed her eyes, trying to accept the situation graciously. Tears leaked anyway.

"Can I sleep in my bed?" she asked Tommy, who carefully stepped over her things searching through the debris on the floor.

"No, you're going to sleep in my guestroom tonight." He looked up at her with softness in his blue eyes. Every step he took caused his leather belt—hastily thrown around his off duty jeans, to creak. His after-shave smelled like mint. Just then he was the image of her father when she was a little girl and her dad was a policeman. "You go over and read that book to Erica, OK? We'll take care of things here, and I'll help you clean this up tomorrow. Erica will want to help too."

"What did he want?" she asked.

"Money, booze, drugs. Who knows? Burglars are slimeballs. You're going to be okay." He slipped a burly arm around her and patted her back then kissed the top of her head.

A cold gust of wind rustled the leaves covering the walkway behind them.

* * *

The next morning, it took Maria a minute to realize why she awoke on the day bed in the Larkins' house. She felt her chest crush with the realization that it hadn't been a dream about her house being ruined. It was real.

She dressed in the clothes she'd worn yesterday, wanting very much to take a shower and put on clean jeans, knowing she'd have to go face the mess at her house and see if there was anything left to wear.

It didn't take her long to find a note left for her on the counter of the Larkens' house. It read, *There's coffee in the pot —get a cup and come on down to your house.* It was signed *Tom.*

She slipped on her jacket and carried a cup of Starbuck hazelnut crème royale with her out the back door. Some tattered leaves still clung relentlessly to the trees that knew they were doomed. All of their siblings lay scattered about the ground like so much of nature's rubbish, waiting to be swept away to wherever God chose.

She collected her coat around her. Not sure she wanted to see the house again, maybe she should just walk away from it. Sell it. Collect the insurance and start over somewhere else. It made her sick to think of trying to reclaim whatever would be unharmed. She wasn't sure she wanted her few violated keepsakes.

She took a deep breath when she got to her house porch. Through the window she could see a lot of activity and hear music coming from her radio speakers.

She opened the door and saw Tom in mid-stride, carry a kitchen chair over his head through the clutter remaining on the floor to the other side of her great room.

Erica diligently dusted an array of porcelain dolls. She cleaned each item with a soft cloth, then placed it inside a glass cabinet next to the fireplace. Somehow the invader missed that china cabinet.

Dena Delaney bent to scoop up some broken plates from the kitchen floor into a dustpan.

Bebe Bates danced with Maria's mop as she slopped water over ketchup goosed from a bottle that lay against the bottom of her refrigerator.

Eileen stuffed batting back inside the torn cushion fabric of the sofa, poked a big carpet needle through the fabric and bound it more or less together. The repair work looked like the stitches on Frankenstein's neck. Eileen looked up when she heard Maria laugh aloud.

"What'chy'all think I am, some kinda doctor?" she said with a big grin on her face, then went back to her work.

"You'll never make any money if you are!" Maria said as she bit back more giggles. "You guys formed a work party without me. What a sweet thing to do." Tears welled up in her eyes and she choked them back, not wanting her friends to misunderstand and think she wasn't grateful.

"Honey, y'all should see your bedroom!" Bebe said as she stood up. It looks like nothin' ever happened in there. Tom wanted to put duct tape on the mattress, but we wouldn't let him.

"Yeah. What a dope!" Eileen added, fighting with her thread.

"Here you go," Tom said and tossed a can of spray wax at her. "You can do the furniture."

Erica beamed at Maria. "It's all going to be okay. Tom even changed the locks and ordered you a storm door made with wrought iron. It's our Christmas present for you."

The huge lump in Maria's chest became a lot smaller as she watched her house come back together. She felt cared for and loved by her friends, which almost made her cry again. "You guys are the best friends in the whole world," she said.

"Gosh, Maria," Bebe said, "you'd do the same for us, honey." Bebe's eyes gleamed and her big smile made Maria suddenly feel like the disaster was just a bump in the road.

"Okay, I'm fixing you guys some tacos." She called her morning clients, changed their meeting time to later in the day and walked to the freezer and took out a package of meat.

* * *

Alone, Maria locked her new key deadbolt locks. She showered and dressed, blew her hair dry with the dryer she'd taken to Phoenix with her. She put on her usual supply of eye makeup and topped it all off with a khaki blazer that was just about the only jacket she had left since the break-in disaster. It had escaped destruction because she'd taken it to Phoenix with her.. She checked the jacket pocket so whatever stuff she may have dropped in there wouldn't find its way to the bottom of her washing machine. She didn't find money this time, only a small, soft, leather drawstring pouch.

"What the heck is this?" she asked the empty closet.

She stared at it, trying to remember where it had come from. "I can't remember ever seeing this before."

The satiny kidskin bag reminded her of infant moccasins she'd seen when she'd lived in Phoenix.

She dumped the contents into her hand. There was a tiny feather, or part of a feather—just its tip, a grassy substance *(marijuana?)* a jade stone carved into a rough animal shape, another white stone that was a smaller replica of an animal, three large aqua beads with string holes in them, and another very small pouch. Inside the smaller pouch was a clump of gold flakes. All bunched together the flakes were about the size of a marble. This stuff could have all come from Phoenix—Indian knick-knacks were in every shop in the city, especially the jewelry stores. Was the pouch something she'd brought back from Phoenix and completely forgotten? She wasn't that demented just yet.

She'd only worn it Thanksgiving day. She'd have noticed if somebody had been close enough to her to put something in her pocket! The gold flakes could not be real.

When she noticed she was going to be late for her first appointment, she shoved the pouch back into her jacket pocket, checked the windows and stepped outside, paced to the end of the porch and peered into the woods thicket. After looking in all directions, she locked the front door very carefully with the new key. Anybody wanting in would not reach through a newly broken pane and simply unlock it. Both sides of the lock needed the key she took with her. They would have to crawl through a broken window and risk getting cut on the way. And she'd want him to really bleed a lot.

CHAPTER 14

With eight messages waiting for her in voice mail, Maria took advantage of the distance to her office and made several callbacks.

She barely made one meeting after the next, running ragged, with no time to call Mason or Tom. By three o'clock, she was in Dahlonega, Georgia, to drop off a large plat to one of her clients.

Noticing the *Gold Museum* sign in front of the old courthouse, she parked across the street on the one-way road. She'd forgotten until now that the old courthouse was turned into a museum when the new courthouse was built a few blocks away. The gold, still in her pocket, could be the real thing. Somebody in that gold museum should be able to know real from fool's gold. She slipped out of her truck and hurried through the sparse traffic into the front door of the museum.

Inside the old red brick building, several people milled around the room full of glass cabinets and wall maps. The uniformed attendant whose badge said Lionel just finished with another customer, when Maria caught his eye.

"Can I help you?" he asked as he ran his eyes all over her.

Another flirt, she thought. Maria put the leather pouch on the counter between them. "Do you know what this is?"

"Sure," he said. "That's a medicine pouch. American Indian. It's kind of small to use for a purse, if you want my opinion."

Grinning in spite of herself, she said, "It's not a purse." *Dopey*, she thought.

"That's where you keep all your medicine—you know, things that have meant something to you because of what's happened to you in your life. Maybe some special herbs to burn

109

when praying. A memento from a loved one. That type of thing. It's *your* medicine bag. What does it mean to you?"

She opened up the pouch and poured the contents out onto the counter. "This isn't mine. I found it and want to know what these things are."

As he inspected the items, the grin left the attendant's face just like a train leaving the station. He picked up the green stone animal and held it to the light from a transom window. "This is jade, I think. It's a bear. The bear fetish imparts strength, introspection and self-knowledge to the owner. A good fetish to have in life. Now, this smallest one is a fox. The fox imparts humor and slyness. A reversal of fortune, perhaps. This one is quartz. Quartz is found with gold, you know." He raised his eyebrows.

She opened the smaller pouch and poured out the gold flakes into her left palm. "Gold, like this?" she asked.

He picked up a tiny piece and shoved it around in his palm before saying, "Exactly like this. Only sometimes it's found in placers too."

Feeling ignorant, she said, "And a placer would be?"

"A crook in a streambed where the gold can't quite make the turn in the current because of its weight, so it accrues. Resulting accruals make up placer mines."

Tumblers fell into place. Dead Indians, Cherokees, Indian children, gold, quartz, mines. Dahlonega, the place where in the 1820's gold was discovered in America. Where the dome on the local college was covered in gold and where, forty-five miles south, the gold on the state of Georgia's capitol dome was likewise covered in the shiny yellow metal, albeit under an inch of resin.

The attendant still talked about the turquoise beads and possible herb, becoming background music: dead guy in my listing in the woods. My ex's Indian child. That child's Indian mother. A pouch holding gold found in my jacket.

"Wait!" she nearly gasped as she held up her hand like a stop sign.

He stopped. And stared at her like she'd slapped him. "What?"

"Do you have a map of the gold mines in this area?"

"Sure. Right here," he said, pulling a map off a shelf behind him. "Not only that, but this book," he laid it on the counter too, "has the whole history of the gold mines in Georgia."

Then he cocked his head. His eyes said, *See how good I am?*

"What do these cost?" She opened up her wallet and purchased both of the items.

* * *

Leery of the approach to her driveway, Maria slowed the Jeep to a crawl. She peered in all the nooks and crannies of its architecture on her first pass.

She saw soles of shoes propped on the arm of her rattan lawn sofa in her screened-in porch. She nearly panicked before she got as far as the concrete drive and saw Mason Walker's inconspicuous, tan Honda Accord. No self-respecting detective would be caught dead in a stake-out car that was a red Corvette.

A big chilly relief wave washed over her. It was replaced with warm anxiety akin to passion. She almost cried in her rush through the screen door to get to him, and landed on top of his sleeping body. Wriggling to find a comfortable place that wouldn't keep him from breathing, she felt his arms slide around her as he laughed in surprise.

"What's caused all this?" he asked.

Smurfing answers into the curve of his neck, she mumbled, "Boy, am I glad to see you. Why didn't you call? Where have you been?" and "Hold me!" She stopped just short of adding, "Hide me!"

"If I'd known this wimpy couch was so comfortable, I'd have come sooner," he said and kissed the top of her head.

"Why are you out here? Couldn't you get inside?" she asked.

"Uh, no. You changed the locks on me. I considered taking that as a hint, but, remembering the last time we were together, I changed my mind."

"Good thinking. Sorry about the lock change. I have to explain about that. For future reference, there's a key hidden outside where all my family leaves them…under the red flower pot that holds the preying mantis statue."

When she'd finished the break-in story, still lying on his stomach, but speaking into his ear instead of his neck, she noticed his face had turned red and evil things were going on inside his suddenly cold, hard eyes. His jaw line seemed to be flexing itself. "And has Mr. Tom found the burglars yet?"

"I don't know," she sniffed. "I've been gone. Oh, oh, oh, I have to tell you what I found out today!" She clambered off of him and onto a neighboring chair. He sat up and took her hands in his. They sat nose to nose, and she explained all that she'd put together about the mine, the Indian link from Phoenix through to her ex-husband, Norman, right down to the dead guy in the mine.

"Whatever they had in common is the key, I think. Don't you?"

By then his lips had turned up at the ends, the laugh lines on his cheeks deepened and his eyes frolicked in response to every word she said.

"Why are you looking at me that way?"

"What way is that?"

"Um. Silly, I think. Like you think I'm a dope."

"Nope. That's my I-think-you're-cute-look. You're so excited and have big eyes and everything!" He rubbed her arms. "And goosebumps, too," he added.

"I guess I did get carried away," she said. "But it *is* a link to the mystery, isn't it? You're so used to sleuthing it doesn't impress you, does it? Don't you think I was brilliant discovering a link?"

"Absolutely. Now, can we go play in the bed?" he asked as peaked creases formed between his eyebrows in a parody of pleading.

"Absolutely." She planted soft kisses on his lips. Then she pulled him to a stand with her, turned, and led him through the house toward her bedroom.

CHAPTER 15

After an entire night of blessed sharing, Maria dragged herself out of bed at nine o'clock and turned on the shower as Mason sauntered out to the porch to retrieve the suitcase he'd left there the night before. She dried herself while watching him shave, then left to make coffee while he showered.

The smell of his cologne made her want to drag him back to the bedroom for carnal reasons when he showed up at her kitchen counter. She opened the medicine pouch and spread its items over the counter. "What is this stuff? Do you know?" she asked, holding the edge of the grassy lump.

He rolled it one way then another with the tip of a pencil.

"Is it marijuana?" she prodded.

"No. MaryJane mats but doesn't clump. And it turns brown instead of remaining green. Besides, the stalks are too short. This thing looks like plain old green grass. Must be some kind of herb. The museum guy said the gold was real?" he asked.

"Yes, and I've gone over the map of mines in this area. Several marked are very close to my listed proper. But if this map is correct, they're not exactly in the same place. See here— is the aerial plat from the tax files of where my listing is located." Maria spread the new paper out next to the museum map and traced the roads that lead to the property with a yellow highlighter. "Now, the red lines are the outlines of my listing. If I outline the same thing on this mine map, you can see how close they are together.

"Also, all of these mines have names. And there's a history of ownership in this book I bought at the museum. It's not a legal record, but it's pretty comprehensive, according to Lionel at the museum. I had no idea there were hundreds of gold mines in Georgia. Some of them still have gold in them too. Apparently it's not lucrative to mine them though."

"So the gold just sits there and waits for what?" he asked.

"I don't know. I suppose the value of gold would have to increase to be worthwhile mining it."

"How long has it been known there's not much gold in the mines?"

"This book was printed in 1952 and the gold was long gone by then. Maybe I should call the museum guy back and ask him that question," she said.

"And maybe I should call and find out how long the guy you found in the mine has been dead. It would be interesting to see if there was a possible link between those two dates," Mason said.

"Even if these mines are accurately marked, they're still no closer to my listed property."

"True, but can you trace back the ownership of the listed property? Maybe the dead guy was one of the previous owners. Perhaps, if we trace the rest of the owners, we could determine if one of them had ever gone missing."

"Good idea!" Maria said. "Rats! Since this is Friday and I'm scheduled all day, we have to wait until Monday when the courthouse will open. Do you have time to try it on your own?"

"I've got people to meet at the boat about waterproofing its top, then a conference call that might take a couple of hours."

"I'll try to get time today to go by there. All it takes is time to do the ownership traces. It'll take a lot more time to try to find all the previous owners. But then, I suppose that's what detectives do, isn't it?" She fluttered her eyelashes at him.

* * *

On the way to show houses all day Friday, Maria called Tom Larkin's office early to invite Tom and Erica out to Mason's boat for drinks that evening.

"Sorry, Detective Larkin's not here. His files have been moved to Detective Moran. I can transfer you," the phone service said.

"No, this is a personal call," Maria replied, wondering what in the world was going on. "Where did Larkin move to?" She asked.

"I'm sorry. Detective Larkin's files have been moved to Detective Moran. I'll transfer you." Click.

"This is Detective Moran's desk. Please leave a message and I'll get back to you as soon as possible," the recording said.

Maria hung up, leaving no message. She called Tommy's cell number. "This number has been disconnected and there is no forwarding number," another recording said.

She dialed his home number. "Tom Larkin," Tom answered.

"What's going on? I called the department and they tried to transfer me to somebody named Moran."

"Hey, Maria. I've been accepted at the GBI. It all happened yesterday, so I haven't called anybody yet. I've been talking to them for a while, but there were no openings in town until now. When they told me I wouldn't have to move, it was cinched. I start Monday morning."

"The Georgia Bureau of Investigation. Wow. You're coming up in the world. I'm glad to hear that," Maria said. "Where's your office going to be?"

"Gwinnett County. Close to the Mall of Georgia."

"Congratulations. How does Erica like the idea?"

"She's all for it, just as long as I'm not getting shot at."

"Absolutely. Mason says there's going to be beer on the boat after one o'clock tomorrow, if y'all want to come out. I won't be back until after two, but can catch up when I get there."

117

"Put us down for two beers at five, after I get off work. I'll pack up the mama and we'll be there. And, thanks for the congratulations."

* * *

The Jeep Cherokee slogged its way north toward Dahlonega, windshield wipers droning out a rhythm. Maria parked in the new Lumpkin county courthouse lot and tried to not get drenched on her way to the records room. Squirts of water permeated her umbrella fabric, misting over her hair and face like spray from a waterfall. Saturday's house showings had netted her a sale that she thought would work out. Today a little rain wasn't going to slow her down.

She found the public records of ownership and traced the mineshaft property back through several generations of owners. She quickly realized that it had been consortiums, corporations, groups of people that had been the owners, and she'd have to look up those ownerships to find out who the principals were in each organization. For the time being, she simply listed the ownership as far back as she could follow. She reached an impasse and contacted a clerk for instruction where to look next. The clerk said some records had been lost due to a fire. She wanted to scream.

Instead, she went over to the gold museum across the street to talk with Lionel, the representative who sold her the mine location map. She parked her draining umbrella in the corner of the foyer and stomped water off her shoes.

He appraised her dampness with a grin. He said, "Aha, I knew you couldn't stay away long."

"Yes, it's true, but I need more information. And I think you are just the one to ask."

118

His ears seemed to perk up, and since no other gold information seekers seemed to be out on the rainy day, she had him to herself, she thought with misgivings.

"Can you tell me how the American Indian, the Cherokee, was affected by the discovery of gold? It seems to me, after reading the book I purchased from you last week, that the Indians were removed from the whole State of Georgia because they lived on lands that held gold. Am I wrong about this?"

"No, you're not wrong. That's essentially it."

"But, I thought there had been a treaty."

"Yes, ma'am, there was a treaty, totally ignored by Andrew Jackson. Apparently he didn't care much for American Indians. The only thing the treaty actually accomplished was a tenancy for those American Indians who turned over their land. They could stay on the land where they lived for ten years if they gave up title. If not, they were displaced immediately."

"So, we're talking blackmail here."

"The thing you have to remember is, they never paid for it originally. It was never claimed by them, recorded or deeded to them."

Her America, the land she loved so much, committed this atrocity. Bile rose in her throat. Through teeth she didn't know she'd clenched, she said, "So it was just stolen from them. We made the laws and they didn't live up to them."

"At that time, the land ownership was granted by lottery."

"If Indians happened to be living on the property when it was granted, they were out of luck, right?" Maria asked, knowing the answer already. "Why do you suppose they didn't get in on the lottery?"

"There were eight lotteries, actually. The politicians had already said Cherokees couldn't own land. Not only that, but they couldn't buy it, sell it, or develop it. But, in some cases, they could continue to use it. And, the fact is, some Indians

119

mined land that wasn't titled to them, even though they couldn't sell any gold they may have mined."

"OK, let's get beyond this because it really makes me mad, which is unproductive. Could a mine have existed and not be on this map that I bought a copy of last week?" She stabbed the map with her finger.

He took a step back from the counter between them.

"No, I don't think so. Our maps are not legal documents, but we've tried to be as accurate as possible. The title to every piece of land had to be recorded. If it had gold on it, the owner could mine it or have somebody mine it for him. Those records were very meticulously kept. Our maps show what the records show."

"So it could be possible for a mine to have existed, but not have gold in it," Maria asked.

"I suppose. But if land title had to be granted for them to have it in the first place, what purpose would there be in not declaring the gold they'd retrieved from it? If that's where you're going with this."

"Yes. I see what you mean." Maria's idea bank ran out of ideas. "How long did people find gold in this area?" she asked.

"From about 1827 to 1933 gold was actively mined, and then remined. New techniques caused them go back and try again at the beginning of the 1900s."

"So there were Indians around all that time? Sort of as displaced persons? What did they do if they couldn't own land and their land was waltzed out from under them?"

"They were sent to Oklahoma on the Trail of Tears." Lionel looked down at his feet.

CHAPTER 16

Dead ends. Maria knew there were answers right under her, tied to the land. If it could just talk, there'd be no more mystery about the pile of bones in the mineshaft. No more questions about an unauthorized shooting gallery on the property. The previous owners' names would be available and those people might be able to explain the chain of title clear back to the lotteries. Like, why gold exploration was stopped and just what that mine was used for afterward.

But the land was silent, waiting, as always, for justice. A line of poetry came to her mind: Justice wines and dines with luck to collect an IOU, and Retribution sits in back, watching what they'll do.

On her drive back to her office in the drenching torrent of rain, she mulled over all she'd learned. She was spending valuable time becoming frustrated over something that wasn't even her business. And why, exactly? Why should she care if a guy died in a mine? What difference did a dead woman in Phoenix make to Maria's life? Who cared about a child in Arizona who could have been her child? He'd never miss his mom, being too young to remember for very long.

Maria looked for a place inside her where all the unfairness could be boxed up and forgotten, but it curled up like a snake in her stomach and hurt.

Wait a minute. Back up. A child who could have been her child. Norman's child. Where is Norman, anyway? But she couldn't let herself care about that either. Her only obligation was just to market a piece of land, and only half of her responsibility at that. That's the end of it, she thought. She was going to forget about it, starting now. Dirt is dirt. Period.

121

Her phone rang, and was glad to have something else to think about. "This is Maria."

"It certainly is," Emily Louise Tandy said on the other end. "My showing is going to be in ten days, Cuz. And I want you to come to it."

"No hello, how are you?" Maria said.

"Oh yeah. Hello, how are you, my showing is going to be in ten days and I want you to come to it."

Something has got to go right today. "Boy, you sure put that together fast. I thought it took at least a year to get all the clothes made."

"Not for me, *moi* partner of DNA. It's going to be at the Hyatt in Roswell. On December 18, just a few days before Christmas. We hope to sell my designs for Christmas gifts. Please tell me you'll come."

"Of course I'll come, Em." *What a time waster.* She knew she wouldn't buy any of Emily's designs. They were just a little off kilter. She'd seen the drawings.

"All Knowing, cuz. That's my design name, my professional name, my business persona name. Now I must insist that you use it. How will people know when you talk about me if you don't use it?"

"Why am I going to be talking about you?" Maria asked.

"Because all of your friends are going to want to wear my designs, of course."

I seriously doubt that.

"Besides," Emily continued. "I want you to bring all of them to my showing. Oops, gotta go. Remember, December 18, I'll call you with directions and times." Click.

* * *

Two hours after she returned to her office and was buried in paperwork, her cell phone rang. "This is Maria," she said.

"Hi, Babe. It's me. I've got some good news for you."

"Mason." She felt a warm smile plaster itself on her face, thinking about last night.

"Tommy, our newest member of the GBI, and investigator extraordinaire, made a discovery. Sebastian's wife was American Indian, Cherokee tribe. Her maiden name was Aiwinita Navarro Arrowkeeper. The child is half Indian, probably Norman's. His name is Donnie Salali Sebastian, which, of course, we knew. What we didn't know is that Donnie is therefore one-half Cherokee. When they find Norman, they can complete the testing.

"Tom sure works fast," she said. "I called him this morning to see if he and Erica could meet us at your boat, like we planned, and he said he'd just been hired for the new job." She looked at her watch, discovered it was already five thirty.

"Yep, he's here now, working on his first beer. I thought I'd find out when you'll arrive. Apparently he has a friend who was already working on the names through Phoenix."

"Well, I'm glad somebody got something today. My trip up to Dahlonega after I finished with my clients today was a bust. I couldn't follow the land ownership records because the names are under corporations, consortiums and so forth. Also some of the records from that far back—before 1890—were destroyed in a fire."

"Maybe there will be records of the mine ownerships somewhere. They're registered, right? A gold mine registry?"

"Hmmm, there must be somewhere. Actually, I got pretty disgusted and started wondering why I care."

"You want to drop it? Let the bad guys win?"

Maria burned at that comment. "Maybe they're all bad guys."

"Boy, you are disgusted! Well, we'll talk about it later tonight. Speaking of which, does it rain like this very often? I'm starting to feel like a duck."

"Haven't you ever heard the song called 'A Rainy Night In Georgia'?"

"This is day time, I'm talking about. I thought I was under Niagara Falls. It laughed at my umbrella—a minor encumbrance—filled up my shoes by running under my collar and down my back. I thought the weight of rain pouring on my boat was going to just sink it right out of sight under the marina dock. I think the lake level has risen about one foot since yesterday," he said.

"Something has to knock the rest of the leaves off the trees so they can be good and dead till spring."

"Well get finished and come on out. We're about to grill up some salmon steaks.

She began piling up papers in categorized stacks — two new listings, three new clients looking for various property. She stapled each client sheet to properties of potential interest to each of them. Just before she shut down her laptop, she typed in "white pages, Oklahoma."

When the prompt came up for a surname, she typed in "Navarro Arrowkeeper" and got 11 hits. Now short of time, she saved all the listings in Word and stashed everything else in her computer bag.

* * *

The following morning they rocked on the water and watched snow settle onto the lake surface from Mason's houseboat bed.

"Not to change the subject, but how are we going to get information from Norman's mother-in-law in Oklahoma, this Navarro Arrowkeeper woman, even if we get lucky and find her? And, are you still interested in finding your ex after all?" Mason asked.

"Well, if we could find something out by making a phone call...."

"Yes? So you are still interested?"

"I don't want to be, but I guess I am," Maria answered. "As soon as I get out of here and finish showing a couple of farms to Mr. Jordan then meet at my house with the insurance adjuster, I'll see which Navarro Arrowkeepers I can eliminate from my list. I suppose I'll just have to call all of them." She turned onto her stomach and stuffed a pillow under her shoulders. The bed smelled like Mason. He was all over her, just where she liked him to be.

He twirled strands of her hair around his finger as he stared out at the lake. "I don't think you brought enough clothes to be going out in the mess today."

"I don't think I own enough clothes to go out there. But Mr. Jordan won't care. He wants to buy a farm. And I want to be just the person to sell it to him," she said. "I like to eat."

"Maybe four people will decide to buy your land with the mine, and you'll make lots of money."

"Absolutely." Maria turned to him. "I like the way you think." She gave him a big kiss while he grabbed for her. She scrambled backward out of bed and laughed. "Does the shower work, or do I have to go home?" She didn't really want to wash the night away just yet.

"According to my plumber, it works perfectly. If the water heater didn't go out during the night, I mean."

"Oh," she said. "I almost forgot — do you want to go to a fashion show for Emily's clothing line in two weeks? Please say yes. I can't face it alone."

"No, I absolutely don't want to go. But I will." He pulled on a pair of jeans from the floor. "First I'm going to do you a favor.

125

I know a guy, and think I can find your Navarro-Arrowkeeper woman in Oklahoma. But you're going to have to contact Tom Larkin and see if he can get her first name from the Phoenix PD. Hopefully they've contacted her about her daughter being dead by this time."

Maria clenched her teeth. *How am I going to talk with this woman I've never met about another wife my ex had?* She pushed the on button to her cell phone while she waited for the warm water to start in the shower. There was a phone message from Dirk Singletongue. "Hello. I just wanted you to know the authorities have located Donnie's relatives, so I guess he won't be available for adoption after all. We're happy for them but very disappointed for ourselves. Call me when you get time."

During the shower, she mulled over her plans for the day. With the two-hour difference in time, it was too early to call Singletongue in Phoenix.

Maria showed small farms to her client during the morning hours and went home. She arrived thirty minutes before her appointment with the insurance adjuster assigned to her house burglary/break in, and pulled her Jeep across the icy driveway into the open carport. She'd just ducked inside when a car pulled into the driveway behind the Jeep. A short man dressed in a heavy overcoat and scarf got out of the car and very carefully walked over the icy walkway to the front door.

The insurance adjuster agreed to cover eighty percent of the damage to the house. It would cost her about fifteen hundred dollars to get everything repaired. She'd learned from the phone calls she'd made, it would take about a month to get everything done. She felt glad she had two closings coming up soon so she could make it through Christmas without tapping her savings and retirement accounts. This morning her client seemed interested in a farm she'd shown him too.

Finally she had time to call Dirk Singletongue. "I was sorry to get your message about Donnie," Maria told Dirk. "It's possible the grandmother won't be able to keep him, I suppose," she said.

"She won't want him to live with a Navaho," Dirk replied, his voice full of sarcasm.

"I'm not sure what you mean," she said.

"It's the old tribal soft shoe. I'm thinking the Indian Council will place Donnie with a Cherokee family if his grandmother can't keep him. At least I think that's what the Navaho Council would do.

"Meanwhile, our guys rebuilt the answering machine messages from Sebastian's house and found a call that traced back to a Wanda Navarro in Oklahoma City. They've got the guys in Oklahoma going out to her house to see if she's the right Navarro."

"The poor woman. If she's the right Navarro, that means her daughter is dead." *Would the woman herself be in danger if she's the right Navarro?*

CHAPTER 17

Maria ferried her papers, utility case and purse through her door to a beep tone on her phone. She dropped everything she carried onto the couch. Her purse bounced once and landed upside down on the floor. A lipstick tube, two pens and her business cards skittered under her coffee table. She pushed 77 to dial into her voicemail.

"This is Wanda Navarro in Oklahoma," the message said. "I got your name and number from the police. They said you wanted to talk to me about my daughter, Nita." Her voice broke off at this point, and there was nothing for several seconds. "I don't know how I can help you now that she's dead. You can call me back if you want." She left a number.

Maria sank onto the nearest barstool to think. While she did want to immediately call the woman, she really didn't know what she could say. *How does a person discuss something as brutal as the death of their child?*

To delay, she called Mason.

He picked up on the second ring. "Hi, good looking."

"You know, if you didn't have caller ID, you couldn't answer the phone like that," she said. "You could become very embarrassed, unless you only have women callers."

"Exactly!" he said.

"Something interesting happened. My ex's mother-in-law left me a message. She asked me to return the call. She said the police gave her my number. That doesn't sound right. I didn't think they'd do that."

"At least she's been found. And they've let her know about her daughter. Have you called her yet?"

"No. I'm chicken."

"But she might know where Norman is," Mason said. "Something else. That cartoon character your dad worried about?"

"Yes?"

"He was right. It's a logo for a subversive paramilitary organization called ORCA. I'm not sure what that stands for yet. I suspect they're a real piece of work."

"How did you find out about them?"

"Can't talk right now, something has just come up here and I've got to run. Sorry. I'll call you later." He hung up.

"Well, damn!" Maria said to the hum in her phone.

She worked up her nerve and called the phone number Wanda Navarro left.

"Hello."

"Ms. Navarro?" Maria asked.

"Yes."

"This is Maria Sebastian, calling from Georgia. I'm so sorry about your daughter."

"Yes," The woman said with a tremble in her voice. "I understand you found her in the house. I would like to know what happened. Why it happened."

Maria sighed. *This is so awful.* "Well, I can't tell you very much. My friend and I went into the house because the boy, Donnie, looked terrible to us. Not hurt, but neglected."

"They said I can pick Donnie up right away. But I don't know if I'll be able to do that. Please, tell me about Nita."

Oh, no. "She was in her bed. She'd been shot." She died peacefully in her sleep, not knowing she would never wake up again, never hold her baby again. Even Norman wouldn't have done that to her. A warm storm formed behind her eyes.

"In the head?"

"Yes." Maria felt tears run down her face.

"Had she been beaten?"

"No." She grabbed a tissue from the box nearby, caught the drips starting from her nose and eyes. "She didn't look hurt otherwise. At least to me. The coroner would know more about that than I." *What can I say to this poor woman?* "She just looked like she was asleep."

She heard a big sigh then soft crying over the phone. She wished she could wrap her arms around Wanda, to comfort her somehow. "I'm so sorry. The little boy's appearance caused us to go inside to investigate. That's when we found her and called the police." She didn't say Donnie thought his mother was asleep. She didn't say he was obviously hungry. There was no point.

"Donnie wasn't hurt?"

"No, ma'am. He's fine."

"Thank God for that, at least." Her voice thick with grief, Ms. Navarro said, "I spoke with Detective Singletongue. He's a nice young man. Too bad Nita couldn't have met him years ago."

"Yes," Maria said. If Norman treated his second wife as badly as he'd treated her, she totally understood this woman's feelings toward her ex.

"You were married to Norman before?"

"Yes. He wasn't a very good husband for me."

"Or for Nita either. He probably killed her, you know."

Maria said, "He was mean to me. I left him ten years ago. Do you know where he might be now?"

"No. I'd kill him myself if I did. The police asked me the same question."

Maria hoped Wanda hadn't told the police she'd kill Norman if she could.

"I did forget to tell them he stayed with his friend sometimes. Nita told me that. I don't know how I forgot about it until just now. She used to send me pictures of Donnie on my son's computer. He travels a lot and left it here with me. Nita was teaching me how to use it."

Maria tingled with anticipation. "Where does Norman's friend live?"

"I can't remember. But it's in my saved mail in the computer. I'll have to go through and look for it. I can email it to you if you'd like."

Maria scrambled to get a pen out of her purse. She gave her email address and said, "Let me have yours." She wrote it down twice to make sure she had it right.

After she'd finished the conversation, and promised to call if she learned anything new, Maria assimilated the sparse information she'd gathered. It had all really started with Emily thinking the body in the mineshaft was Norman's. What would have happened to Donnie if she hadn't been alarmed enough by her cousin's thought to stop by Norman's house to set her mind at ease?

But that had only caused more worry when she'd found Nita dead with Donnie free to run around in his house. *In fact, in her old home.* At least she knew the Native American remains in the mine could not have been those of a northern European of Jewish descent named Norman Sebastian.

Welcoming an excuse to not think about death, Maria turned her attention to making some money for a change. She was only one quarter of the way through her old client call list, so she settled in to get some of that done. She combed the newspaper classifieds' For Sale By Owners in case they were tired of waiting for buyers.

Several hours later, organized for the week ahead, Maria turned off her lamp and reached to shut down her computer. Hearing, "You've got mail," she sat back down to tidy up the last thing for the day.

Wanda Navarro's email included the last time she saw Norman Sebastian which was over six months ago, and a general address in Nevada for some long lost cousin of his, whom Maria never heard of.

Maria hit "save mail" to spend more time with it later. Four hours of planning and thinking were enough for one night.

Before going to bed she noticed there was an email from one of her cousins who lived in Casa Grande, Arizona, and was tracing genealogy on Maria's family. She always took a lot of time to read new information from Yvette, as it was usually tied to their family tree and had become very complicated to absorb.

As she crawled into her bed and grabbed her pillow, she didn't care where Norman Sebastian was. She could finally put him out of her life forever.

CHAPTER 18

Maria wanted to stay asleep. *Still dark outside, it can't be morning yet*, she thought. But the digital numbers on the dresser read eight oh nine. She peered at the thick layer of fog. It pressed down on the earth as it pressed on her mind. She turned over and tried to ignore her beeping phone. But her mind began its race and she knew there was no hope of more sleep.

She ran to her thermostat, turned it up, and jumped back into bed with her cell phone.

The message from her genealogy-tracing cousin, Yvette said, "This is Y. Whoa, Maria, have I got news for you. Call me."

What now? She remembered the email she hadn't read last night. Clever technicians had put lights inside her cell phone for reading under the covers.

She hit autodial. A groggy, "'Ello! Uhhh, who dares to wake the ogre this early?" followed from the other end.

"Y. It's me, cousin Maria. Please don't eat me."

"Hiya, Cuz. Glad you called me back. Have I got news for you. You're half Apache!"

"Right. And you're Bozo the Clown," Maria said.

"Don't be nasty. It's true, I swear. I traced your father's ancestry through the census bureau for our family records. His name is not Robert John Charles Walton. Or at least it wasn't his name at birth."

Maria closed her eyes. *This is only a dream.*

Yvette continued, "His birth name is Bobby Wahkinny, born March 2, 1943, to Joseph and Juanita Wahkinny who lived on the White Mountain Apache Reservation at that time. It's in the census records. He has two brothers, I forget their names, since

I'm technically still asleep. It IS six-ten here. Congratulations. I'm going back to sleep now."

"Wait, Y," Maria nearly yelled. "What are you talking about? This is nuts!"

"Aw, Maria, I thought it was kind of cool. I didn't mean to upset you."

"No, no, no, I'm not upset. There's a mistake. Look at me. I'm blonde! My dad was in the army! He was a cop! He didn't live on an Indian Reservation!"

"Maria. Your mother is blonde, your father is not, consider the DNA issue. I could have made an error, but it looks pretty plain in the records. I emailed them to you yesterday. Your dad never mentioned it to you?"

"No. That's why it's nuts. He would have told me about my own heritage. His parents died before I was born. He doesn't have any brothers. He was born in Arizona, he joined the Army early and was a lifer. Then he joined the police department and retired after twenty years."

"If you want to know for sure, ask him where he went to school."

"If I want to know for sure, I will just ask him if he's Apache," Maria snapped. Angry that someone would think they knew more about her own father than she did, she tried to remember exactly what she knew. Her memory was very hazy about that topic.

"Okay," Yvette said. "Obviously I shouldn't have mentioned this to you."

"No, Y, don't think that. I really appreciate all you do for the family. We're all grateful. I think something is wrong with the records if they say my father is Apache Indian, though. Since he's not on the Tandy side of the family, how did you happen to research it in the first place?"

"Your mom's been married to him forever, and whenever I can, I put in the spouse's history as well. He's mentioned anyway on your mom's page. It's simple to follow up. I'm just so sorry I've upset you."

Maria felt like all the air had been knocked out of her. What possible reason could her father have had to not make her aware of her heritage? They were so close. At least she'd thought they were. Would he lie to her about something so basic?

"Records from 65 years ago could have errors in them."

"Errors that I find are generally with names being different than birth names. People spell things differently, women marry and change their names. It happens. But the fact is, Robert John Charles Walton didn't materialize until he joined the military in 1957."

"Okay, I'll get it straightened out. I'll let you know what I find. Thanks again for all your work." Maria hung up, which left her in the pitch dark. Bobby Wahkinny? 1957? Dad had been what? Only 14 years old. Much too young to get into the military.

Now that the house had warmed up, she showered and dressed. Then bent forward to put the lipstick in the right place and took a good look at her face. There were strong features, dark blue eyes, not particularly high cheekbones. An almost straight nose with a clearly prominent forehead made her look again. Blonde hair. No chance she was Apache. Her dad would laugh the accusation off and that would be the end of it.

* * *

Mason showed up exactly at the time he promised, wearing perfectly creased slacks, a blue silk sweater and camel sportcoat.

"Tell me again why we're going to Emily's fashion show premier?" he asked.

"Because somehow my mother will find out if I don't go to support my only neighboring cousin and will make life hell for me. You are kind and don't want to see me living in hell. That's why."

"Yeah. That's what I was afraid you'd say."

The trip south to Roswell in Mason's Honda was a nightmare of taillights and swerving traffic. Maria remembered why she avoided night trips in this direction.

A brass revolving door hustled them into a lobby lined in brass. Pretty girls wearing old-fashioned usher hats busied themselves behind the counter, and a potted jungle fooled everybody who hadn't been outside that day.

They walked through the hotel lobby to the last conference room door on the right. A short man with oddly purple hair brushed straight up met them at the door with a program which he handed to Maria. "Have you see Ms. Knowing's design's before?" he asked.

"Only some of her sketches," Maria answered as she reached for the door.

"You're going to be amazed," he said as he stepped in front of her and opened the door.

She wanted to tell him she'd appreciate never being amazed by her cousin, Emily, again in her lifetime. But she held her tongue and proceeded into the room with Mason close behind.

An aisle formed by sets of chairs to the right and left of the entrance resembled theater seating. A raised stage and small runway lay at the front of the huge room. Maria looked around for seats.

Mason said, "What the hell?" and pulled her closer to him. She looked to see what had his attention. A huge man with a bald head and three huge hoop earrings worn like stepping stones up the side of his ear glared at them. She noted the far side of his head covered in swirling tattoos, which continued down his face and neck, and into the leather vest he wore as a shirt. Next to him stood a tiny blonde with the largest bouffant hair Maria had ever seen. Obviously augmented breasts screamed, "I'm Dolly Parton!" as did her whole self, sans the beautiful face of the namesake. Dressed in shimmering blue spandex, she somehow managed to stand, sit and walk while wearing four-inch high platform sandals.

"Eek," Mason said.

Maria turned to look at him, found a grin.

"Do you think this is the right place?" she asked.

"I really don't know." He stood back and surveyed the room. "I'm seeing impossibly pink eyes, um, lots of spandex, green hair over there, orange hair over here." He craned his neck in every direction. "Are you sure you want to be here?"

"The doorman, or greeter, whoever he was, mentioned Emily's stage name when we came in. It must be the right place. Let's just sit in the back row. We can leave if it's not."

Lights flashed and the roomful of people dispersed to seats. A hidden orchestra played a Gershwin show tune Maria couldn't remember the name of. An announcer dressed in a red tuxedo spoke in a breathy voice of the amazing All Knowing and her spectacular couture designs.

A model appeared from out of darkness in a spotlight that followed her unnatural gait across the stage to the far end of the runway. She wore a skin-tight black or navy blue pant suit with a lacey blouse, which was entirely too strange. Maria felt like she was seeing another dimension.

The announcer talked steadily over the mumbling crowd. "Marcy is wearing a lovely suit, gorgeous mauve lace blouse with fluttering wrist tips, and jewelry by Mainstay..."

"Is it a bodysuit?" Maria asked Mason as others around them continued to murmur through the announcer's description.

He had his hand over his mouth. She looked at him.

"What?" she asked. He was laughing so hard he choked when he tried to answer.

"It's a bodysuit all right."

"What's the matter with you?" She felt like pinching herself to see if she was dreaming this whole thing up.

Tears welled in Mason's eyes. "Look very closely when she turns around again."

Maria stared at the model. The back of the pants were so tight she could see the cleft in her butt. Then she could see the cleft in the model's crotch in front.

"She's only wearing paint!" Maria said too loudly, and people turned to look at her.

"Absolutely!" Mason said, breaking out in loud laughter. She grabbed his hand and pulled him up the aisle and out the door.

"Do you mean my cousin's clothing line is nothing but paint? All the months she's been planning a fashion show of nudes? Where did she get models willing to be naked on a stage in front of hundreds of people?" Maria ranted all the way back to the parked car as Mason grinned and shook his head.

"You've got to admit it's original."

"We drove all the way down to Atlanta for a farce!" They got in the car, backed out of the parking lot, paid the attendant eight dollars and zigzagged back to the freeway entrance.

"I think we should stop to have something to eat and a lot to drink," Mason said.

"That sounds like a brilliant idea. Maybe I can forget I have relatives," she groused.

"Maybe after a couple of margaritas you'll take me home so I can have my way with you."

Her stomach tingled. She looked at him. "Do we have to wait for a couple Margaritas or do you want to remember having your way with me?"

His teeth gleamed white in the passing headlights.

* * *

Maria sat working on the showings for maybe her last customers of the year. Her fax machine dinged and started grinding. She saw the fax was from Wanda Navarro. An article had been cut from some newspaper, or possibly a magazine. It was incomplete, as if it was the second part of a continued story.

"The act was categorized as terrorism due to the way it was executed, the organization's stated motives and the trauma suffered by the Wells Fargo security guards," Maria read. She scanned down to the bottom of the email. It was apparently a note from Awinita Sebastian to her mother, Wanda.

Maria read further, a computer-written letter immediately following the newspaper article: "He is part of an underground conspiracy to interfere with commerce and has drafted many of our people, including Jaime. The main group is in Puerto Rico."

Now she was totally confused. Who is the "he" Nita referred to in her note to her mother? Norman? Norman was neither Puerto Rican nor American Indian. What could this have to do with him?

The email went on and on and on. Maria printed the whole thing out. And she was pretty sure she was going to need it.

CHAPTER 19

Three faxes from Wanda churned out of the machine.

A close-up of a jade bear with a diagram showing a metaphysical properties chart, a description of how a bear is significant to some people, and then the same thing for each of the items Maria had found in her blazer pocket. She wasn't sure what it all meant, but intended to study it.

"You've got mail!" called the computer. Maria turned from the papers to the screen. Wanda Navarro's email said she'd sent the fax and hoped it explained the things Maria had asked.

My son, Jaime, once had these items in his medicine bag, though I'm sure his is a much larger bag after all these years. I remember he once wore turquoise belt buckles because he had the stomach evils when he was a child. When he discovered the green stone made that better, he always wore them on his belt. I hope this information helps you find whoever the skunk person was that killed my daughter.

Jaime has been gone from me for a very long time. About ten years. He wanted to change the world and found a crowd of white people that wanted to use him to organize our people to be like them. I told him he could not be part of the earth if he was willing to drown it in blood. Our people have been through enough. He left and never came back. I am

```
alone now. It is how I came to the earth.
Now it is how I will return.

   I've got some old fetishes that
belonged to my husband. I have no need
for them now. I will send them to you by
mail. Please give me your address right
away. I am going to the post office
tomorrow.
```

Maria felt terrible for the woman. She sent another email that included her snail mail address. She added that she would keep Wanda in her prayers.

Before going to sleep, Maria settled down to read Wanda Navarro's entire story, which had to be a figment of a mother's nightmares. The woman began by saying that Jaime's middle name was "Tsula," the Cherokee name for "fox."

The white fetish was a quartz fox that caused the bearer to approach life with amusement and cleverness, but would impart invisibility to its bearer when he was in a tight situation. Wanda felt her son would have used an icon of this sort to deal with the negative aspects of whatever he was into, in order to achieve the overall goal of the group.

Likewise, the feather inferred the magical power of an eagle that allows one to fly above the shadows in life and could render Jaime invisible to his enemies when necessary, whereas the Jade bear would give him clarity on introspection as well as superhuman strength where he needed it.

Curious about how she could use this information, Maria called the phone number Wanda gave her. There was no answer, so she left a message on the answering machine.

What the information had to do with anything, Maria had no idea, but the fetishes were definitely in her pocket so she needed to figure it out. *Dreaming sometimes helps with such things*, she thought wryly as she yawned. Her eyes closed as visions of colored stones rolled across the inside of her eyelids.

* * *

In the morning, Maria called her father.

"Dad," she said, "What's this I hear about you maybe changing your name?" It sounded diplomatic enough to her.

"What the hell are you talking about?"

"It's in the census records that you changed your name."

"Well, it's a screw-up, isn't it?"

"I don't know, dad, is it? I don't know anything about your family. You've always been very quiet about your background, your parents, your siblings. I figure you'd like to fill me in about them since the census is wrong. We should straighten the records out."

"Definitely. Where did you ever hear such a pile of crap. And why are you looking at the census records anyway?"

"You can thank the Tandy family researcher, Yvette. She apparently researches spouses as well as the Tandy blood. She says your real name is Bobby Wahkinny. And that your parents' names were Joseph & Juanita Wahkinny of the White Mountain Apache Reservation in Arizona. You were born on March 2, 1943 and you had two brothers."

Silence. Then the phone at the other end of the line clattered into a cradle. Her father hung up on her.

Maria's hand poised over her cell phone to call her father back, when the phone rang. Frank Denning's voice said, "Did you see the Atlanta Constitution this morning?"

"Um, no. I'm not out of the house yet today. We've got a lot of ice on the trees."

"Check out the first page of the second section. Emily had a fashion show. Were you there?"

"Unfortunately. Look, I know my cousin is eccentric, but I have no idea how she got into the paper." She couldn't imagine what Emily had done now.

"Apparently the local Cherokees are incensed at her for using her fashion show, which, by the way, was only paint covering some poor desperate models who were crazy enough to model paint," this he said with an emphasis on the word 'paint' that made it sound like a gunshot, "and some of them were painted up like Indians. You know, with feathers on their heads, war stripes on their faces, quivers on their backs, carrying bows and arrows."

God! It must have gotten worse after she and Mason left.

"Somebody is upset about it?" She asked from under her hand covering her mouth.

"Well, yeah. The Indians are on the warpath about it, no pun intended. Not to mention those women were absolutely nude under all that paint. It's all there in the newspaper. The article says she belittled Native Americans. Made a mockery of Cherokee culture. Then, they referred to Ms. Tandy as finding a dead Indian in the mineshaft on our land."

Maria flinched. "Oh, ouch. I'm so sorry. I'll get the paper right away and catch up, then call my cousin and get her to straighten it all out." *If I can.*

"If I'd known her fashion designs had nothing to do with cloth, I don't think I would have loaned her the money. Well, Mr. Duke is plenty angry about this," he continued. "I tried to tell him Emily is just artistic and doesn't see things like you and I."

Or anybody else, Maria thought. Frank Denning had actually financed the disaster. She'd give Emily a piece of her mind when she got the chance.

146

"He's plenty angry about it, and says he doesn't want anybody going anywhere near that property. He wants to cancel the listing immediately."

"That seems hasty." Maria cringed inside. That listing was her only tangible hope for income in the foreseeable future. "Let me see what I can do before you make that decision. We could be closer than we know about a buyer." That was quite a stretch, but until she actually checked with other agents, she wouldn't know if it was getting attention or not. She hated to lose the listing, and she hadn't spoken to Bonnie since she'd seen her at a caravan meeting two weeks ago.

Lighted snowflakes and poinsettia blossoms were already up on power poles as Cumming's nod to the Christmas season. Maria hadn't noticed them until now—only a week after Thanksgiving was over. She didn't even want to think about Christmas.

Still knee deep in a sudden envelopment of Indian culture, she didn't know if her father would ever speak to her again since she'd accused him of not being honest with her. And he was the most honest person she'd ever met.

The information she'd obtained from Wanda Navarro suggested her son had been involved with a subversive group of radicals wanting to overthrow the government. Thankfully that had nothing to do with her. But the woman did have a dead daughter who was found right before Christmas, for all intents orphaning her son, Wanda's grandson.

Where was Norman? Why hadn't Wanda answered the phone? Too much was happening too fast, and each issue leapt around in her brain like popping corn.

Maria threw on her jacket and rushed to find a newspaper. Leaving her truck in the parking lot, she stomped through rain to the grocery store. She picked up an Atlanta Constitution newspaper, and went to check out.

Back in her Jeep, she tossed aside the first section, looking for the article Frank Denning called her about that morning.

In the upper right hand corner she read, POSSIBLE LINK TO WEATHERMEN, which she didn't understand, but she did understand the picture of Emily smiling out at her from the newsprint.

Buckhead. In an unprecedented spoof, a local scam artist/exotic dancer/garment designer by the name of Emily Louise Tandy, aka stage name, All Knowing, had a showing Saturday night of her alleged line of couture, at the Ritz Elan Hotel, to the bafflement of her investors, spokesman Grant Halloway said early Sunday morning. "Ms. Tandy showed us her designs several months ago and hired appropriate manufacturers to produce the line of clothing. I really don't know what happened to the clothing line we thought we were financing," Halloway told this reporter.

Halloway knows of no reason why the clothing line materialized as body paint. "I couldn't believe those women were wearing nothing but paint," referring to the alleged models.

Many of the outfits were themed as historical Native American dress, for which George Allanwold, attorney representing the Cherokee Nation, states were an "affront to the dignity of all Native Americans. No Native American could possibly have condoned the caricature of Tontoism expressed by the designs exhibited by Ms. Tandy in the name of couture."

Native Americans are calling for a formal apology from Ms. Tandy.

Ms. Tandy is linked to the discovery of an unidentified body found in an abandoned gold mine in Auraria, Georgia on November 15 this year. It has been determined that the body found in the mine is that of a Native American.

According to an unnamed source, ownership of the Auraria property is related to a subversive group known as ORCA, which as late as 2005 has been tied to a cell originally established in Puerto Rico. The Los Osos organization under Puerto Rican, US and international law, was responsible for terrorist activities led by a string of bombings categorized as terrorism due to the way they were executed. The criminal charges filed against the participants in the various robberies include: *Aggravated Robbery*, *Aggravated Robbery of Federally Insured Bank Funds*, *Armed Robbery*, and *Conspiracy to Interfere With Commerce By Robbery*.

Maria nearly ended up on the floorboard of her Jeep. Thank God her name wasn't mentioned in the paper. She looked around to see if she had been seen in the parking lot by any of her former clients. Now she understood why Frank Denning was so angry, though to her way of thinking, he'd been used as a dupe as well as helping to finance the disastrous showing.

But how could that mine shaft property be linked to a subversive group of militants? Her head spun from information

149

overload. She would have to get to the bottom of this, or she'd lose the listing and along with it, a good share of her next year's income.

Maybe Bonnie knew something that would explain the misinterpretation by the press. As for Emily, Maria wanted to wring her neck for bringing down unwanted publicity on an innocent piece of land.

Or was it an innocent piece of land? Lost in thought, she drove back home.

* * *

Finally able to look at the email from cousin Yvette, the first document Maria saw was an outline of a census report, which, as Yvette told her, listed her father's parents, surnamed Wahkinny, of the White Mountain Indian Reservation, Arizona. Both parents and two siblings listed had "deceased" written next to their names, with some dates scribbled in.

The next attachment was a birth certificate for Bobby Wahkinny. It had frayed edges and filled in lines written by hand, which anybody could have jotted down. The only thing making it look legal was the seal by the state of Arizona. Who ever heard of the U.S. Government Department of Health & Human Services Indian Hospital?

"Certificate of Live Birth" was printed with a flourish across the top of the third page. A birth certificate stating Robert John Charles Walton was born March 2, 1943 to John Charles and Juliette Walton, of Maverick, Arizona.

Maverick, Arizona? Her father always lived in Phoenix. Except when he was in the army. Maria didn't see the connection Yvette made between Wahkinny and Walton.

The next page was Robert John Charles Walton's DD-214 file showing his service record, followed by two Commendations for valor and an Accommodation letter to his parents from his Commanding Officer informing them of his outstanding integrity in carrying out his duty during training.

A note at the bottom of the page, written in Yvette's longhand, said, "Look at the dates of death on the census report, then look at the date your dad went into the army."

Census report dates of death for *all of Wahkinny's parents and siblings* were the same: August 8, 1957. The DD-214 date of her father's entry into the army was August 28, 1957, just about two weeks after the murder of his entire family.

CHAPTER 20

How to separate fact from conjecture kept Maria up late into the night, rereading all the information she'd gathered. She tried calling her father again, but now he wouldn't answer the phone. She'd have to get a cousin to go over to her parent's house and at least talk her mother into calling her.

Maria's hand paused over her cell phone, ready to call her Aunt Minnie in Arizona. If anybody could get in to see her mom it would be her sister.

Her cell phone rang before she pushed the first button. Mason's name was on her screen. "Hi. I see you called me earlier. I was under my car and couldn't get to my phone," he said when she answered. "I took it to the shop to be serviced. I had a taxi drop me off. Now I'm standing on your front porch."

She dashed to her front door and tore it open, dropping her cell phone on the couch as she ran by. She grabbed him around the middle and hugged. "God, you feel wonderful."

"Whoa," he said. "Not as good as you do." He hugged her right back.

They segued into the living room, holding onto each other.

"Would you like a drink or something?" she asked, as she looked up at him from under his arms.

"Okay. You got any coffee?"

"Absolutely." She led him by the hand toward the kitchen and pulled out a barstool. "Now tell me about your trip, and the case you're working on."

"Same old stuff. Bad guys with black hats and me with my white one." He smiled, etching dimple lines down the sides of his mouth. "What's up with your mine adventure?"

"There goes talking about you. Now we're talking about me."

"Well, your stuff is much more interesting, so you go first," he said.

"Oh boy, you're not going to believe it. You've only been gone for four days, and so much has happened, I don't know where to start." She poured two cups of coffee from the pot she'd brewed this morning. After checking to see if it was still hot enough, she slid one cup toward Mason.

She pushed the creamer and sugar bowls over toward his cup, and handed him a spoon. "The synopsis is: I may be Apache Indian. Emily has covered herself with glory once more, ergo, I may lose the listing on the property where the mine is, and I've spoken with Norman's wife's mother in Oklahoma."

He swirled his coffee with the spoon, tapped it on a napkin, then set it down. "Not such good news about the listing, but maybe the owners will reconsider after a little time passes. How'd you find out about the Apache thing?" His face bore a look of intensity Maria hadn't seen before.

"My cousin the family historian."

"How many cousins have you got anyway?"

"178 this year." To his look of incredulity she added, "Not all first cousins, of course. And since we lose track of who's an aunt and who's a second cousin, we just simplify by using 'cousin'."

"I see. Good thing I'm not prejudiced against other cultures, huh?" He flashed his killer smile.

"Hmm. I didn't think about that." She looked in his eyes for signs of brewing problems. Seeing nothing there, she added, "We don't have to worry about that one."

He laughed loudly, pulled her to him and sat with his arms around her and his face pressed into her shoulder. "God, I've

154

missed you. It sounds like you've gotten into a heap of trouble in the short time I've been gone."

"I know." She held his head against her chest and ran her hands through his hair.

"I'll give you twenty minutes to cut that out," he said.

"Don't be getting frisky right now. I've got to go see Bonnie at the office. She'll only be there for a few minutes. Why don't you ride with me and I'll explain everything that's happened. After I talk to her, we can go have lunch at your favorite place.

"Shucks. Just when I was getting frisky," he said, mimicking her tone of voice.

They left for the office immediately, Maria feeling regretful about that decision as soon as she got in the Jeep. She wanted to be home, with Mason in her bed, drinking hot chocolate with marshmallows, between bouts of making love. Which brought her to another question: just how many bouts might that be?

Focus.

"What did Norman's mother-in-law tell you about him?"

"Not much about her daughter or Norman, unfortunately, but she did tell me about the fetishes I found in my jacket. I'm still wondering how they got there. The bottom line is they're like the ones her son kept that she thinks may have caused him to abandon her."

"Her son. That would be Awinita's brother?"

"Yes, poor woman. She hasn't heard from her son in over ten years, she said, and now her daughter turns up dead. How awful!"

"The fetishes could have been dropped into your pocket any time. But the coincidence of both the daughter and the son being taken away from her is strange. Maybe they were both into something they shouldn't have been. And maybe your ex was in it too?"

"Of course, I wouldn't put anything past Norman. But if the son has been gone for ten years... I mean, Nita would have only been in her twenties ten years ago."

"Just because her son abandoned his mom doesn't mean he abandoned everybody. He could have still been around, just not around his mother. Lots of families are split up."

"A split-up family is an oxymoron to me. And besides, the woman still had some kind of relationship with her daughter because they talked sometimes." The possibility of her dad having another life drifted through Maria's mind.

"Your family is very unusual, Maria. I have a brother I haven't spoken to in two years. No reason, it's just a fact."

Maria pulled up to a gas pump at the Country Cupboard.

"That's so strange to me. Even though I have no brothers and sisters, my cousins have been with me all my life. I can call any of them any time and pick up where we left off as kids." She had turned and faced him from the driver's seat.

"Like I said, it's really rare to have a family where everybody knows everybody. By the way, I'm too chivalrous to watch you pump gas. I'm doing it." He opened the door. "What does this critter take? Diesel? Unleaded?"

"Regular unleaded. I'm cheap." Unused to riding around with a gladiator, she got out of the truck anyway.

"Yeah, I'm cheap too," he said as he grinned at her, "and I can be had. Pull that gas cap access hatch for me."

"Gas cap access hatch?" she asked as she reached back inside the truck and found the lever.

Uncomfortable with watching him do her job, she handed Mason her charge card and walked inside the Country Cupboard.

She returned with a Diet Coke, as he was hanging up the pump handle. She handed the drink to him. "White knights should be rewarded."

Mason accepted the Coke, grinned at her, then opened the door and sat down on the passenger seat. "Now we have enough gas to get to San Diego and back."

Entering and starting the car, she said, "Good for us, since we're going about another half mile. By the way, do you remember when my dad got all upset about the toy I found in the mineshaft?"

"Yep."

"Do you think he really had something there?" The truck swayed on the rain-slick road. She watched for ice.

"As a matter of fact, I've been doing some research in my spare time about that toy. It's a logo for a subversive group of guys and gals who dally in munitions exchanges with underworld types."

"Why didn't you tell me?" She took her eyes of the road for two takes to read his face.

"I just did."

"I mean, before now."

"What did you do with the toy?"

"It's in my purse. I never got a chance to give it back to Donnie."

"I think you should give it to me and maybe pretend you never saw it," he said.

She saw a shadow cross his face out of the corner of her eye. "I'm asking questions, here, and you're not answering any of them."

"That's because I think you may be getting into some serious shit, and it's time to walk away."

"All of the things that have been happening around me are becoming things I cannot walk away from. It isn't you whose father may have been lying all your life. It isn't you whose heritage may be as yet undiscovered. It isn't you whose cousin has been a trial for almost forty years. And it isn't you who

157

found the remnants of a body in the mineshaft of the only thing between you and going hungry.

"So, kindly don't tell me to walk away from the roadblocks in my life." She thumped her chest with her left hand. "That logo may be the key that could unlock some of this crap." She jerked the steering wheel right, into the parking lot of the shop repairing Mason's auto, anger swarming through her veins.

"I didn't say burn it. I said I'd really appreciate it if you would let me hold it for you, please. As it turns out, the dudes whose organization it represents are third-world radicals. ORCA is a terrorist organization run by a bunch of mercenaries who think they can overrun polite civilizations who aren't as violent as they are. You may have fallen into their focus. You have no idea what that can mean."

"So it's this ORCA group who killed the Cherokee guy that we found in the mineshaft? How can you be sure of that?"

"Maria. I'm not sure of anything. All I know is you need to distance yourself from anything resembling ORCA."

CHAPTER 21

Maria stomped through the office door after dropping off Mason.

Bonnie sat at her desk, talking on the cell phone. She swiveled her desk chair around so her back was to Maria. Maria wanted to grab her rolling chair and sling her across the room. She moved the side chair as close to Bonnie's phone conversation as she could, just for spite. Then she pretended to be eavesdropping on everything Bonnie said into the phone while she made a mental list of questions she wanted answered.

Bonnie closed her phone and glared at Maria. "What is it that's so important?"

"Death, Bonnie. I think that's pretty important, don't you?"

"Who died? Oh. You mean the guy you found in the cave?"

"You found him, as I recall. We had other things on our minds, like your ankle."

"Yes. And I already told you how much I appreciate you taking me to the hospital and calling my family."

Yeah. She appreciated it so much she ran right out and tried to bull me off of the listing.

Maria instantly decided not to tell Bonnie anything about Phoenix. If Bonnie wanted secrecy, as she relayed when Maria first arrived, then secrecy is what she'd get. There were a million real estate agents just like Bonnie—scared to death somebody would steal information from them. "I want to know if Daniel Duke said anything to you about the mine being on the property. Or about the shooting range being on the property? As a matter of fact, how did you meet Mr. Duke?"

Bonnie's eyes opened wide, her lips pursed slightly.

"No... he didn't tell me anything about that." She tugged at the hair behind her ear and blinked several times, looking over Maria's head.

She's lying through her teeth, Maria could hear her father's voice regarding lying "tells."

Frank Denning had told Maria that he'd overhead Mr. Duke tell Bonnie about the shooting range. If he knew about the range, he doubtless knew about the mine as well. Even though it was very old, the access road to both was shared. One passed the mine to reach the range.

If he knew about the mine then he surely knew about the dead guy inside it, Maria thought. The consortium had owned the property for only two years. Tom told her it takes a lot longer than that for a body to become only bones. *Hmm. I wonder why he didn't tell us about that mine.*

"As a matter of fact, Maria, Mr. Duke is angry about the property's notoriety due to your cousin's, um, indiscretion, shall we say. He wants to cancel our listing."

"Then what? He's going to relist it with you alone?"

"Well, one of us should do something with it after all this mess." She gestured toward her walking cast.

Maria's phone rang. She hated to stop the conversation with Bonnie, but she didn't recognize the number that popped up on her phone's screen and it could be too important a call to ignore. "I'll talk to you later," she told Bonnie as she walked toward her desk to answer her cell.

"This is Maria Sebastian."

"Hello, Maria. This is Donna James with Adamson Realty. I have a contract for your 95-acre tract of land in Auraria, Georgia.

Maria held her breath. This is too good to be true, said her bad fairy.

"Do you have the latest Disclosure Statement on that land?"

160

"You mean the one about a mine being on it?" the woman asked.

"Yes, ma'am."

"No, but that doesn't matter. My buyer is an investor who wants some land he doesn't have to do anything with except wait for it to grow money."

"I just found out it has a shooting range on it. Do you think he'll care about that?" Maria asked.

"Is that a problem? Is it a public range? Does it have anything that might upset the EPA? Need cleaning up?"

"Not as far as I know. Since it's a consortium that owns it, the client that filled out the disclosure didn't know about the other items. In fact, he's never seen the land. I apologize for that —I didn't know it until recently."

"By the way, where is the mine located that is causing so much chatter down here in Atlanta?"

So they know about the whole tie-in with the insulted Native Americans. Some people are just attracted to notoriety is the only reasoning Maria could conjure. She blathered on as if it were the finest opportunity in town. "From what I can tell, it's up on the hilliest part of the land. I have a topography map I can email to you. Of course I don't know how the mine turns into the hill, but I know approximately where the shaft opening is located and will mark that on the plat and send it with the topo. It's in the upper right hand corner, opposite of the road easement. Of course you know there is no real road to the property at this time."

"No, I didn't know that. I do know the mine doesn't bother him, as he doesn't intend to build on the property. He doesn't care what's on it, as long as it's sellable. He's seen the plat. He wouldn't care if it had been timbered. It's all about money. He likes the price."

Relief tempered with curiosity swept over Maria. If she could get a good offer and the property had only the original listing on it, then the seller would have to honor the listing agreement with both herself and Bonnie as dual agents. The co-owner's distress would be smoothed over with a contract in his hand. But she'd had perfectly sanitary pieces of property be milled scrupulously through microscopes for every detail. Now here was one that was so prime for questioning she was expecting an exasperating due diligence obligation of all parties to get the property finally closed.

She hovered over the fax machine as it hummed out the contract from Donna James. She walked back to her desk and settled in to read the whole thing. The offer was within ten percent of the asking price. Terms were subject to financing from three one-year CDs that would all come due within six months. Earnest Money was $25,000, to be paid when the purchaser's first CD matured. Donna was right. This contract offer was better than Maria had seen in over a year. Having no stipulations was the best part. *I love land deals.* But her bad fairy was laughing hideously in her left ear.

Under the signature of the buyer was a corporate seal. The hair on the back of her neck stood up.

It was the outline of a Striped Tanager, with its name running around the border of the seal.

* * *

She put Donna's name and phone number in her BlackBerry, her heart beating much too fast for her chest. She considered calling Donna back to ask her the name of the corporation represented by that seal. But why should she care who bought the land? It was just a toy.

That property was perfect for a corporate investor. It was located on highway frontage that would some day go commercial. There were no ravines or natural runoff problems, no areas where water could pool. It lay on the high side of the road and was covered in gorgeous dense hardwood trees and backed to National Forest, which made it ideal for any investor. The mine could be an issue because it couldn't be built over, but with it being in the steepest part of the land, she doubted anybody would need to build right at that location.

Donna's call was made in heaven. It would be good to have the property sold before anything else could go wrong.

She called Frank Denning, but got his voice mail. "Frank, this is Maria Sebastian. I've got some good news about the Auraria property. A contract just came in from a real estate company in Atlanta. The buyer wants investment land. And I believe it is an excellent offer. Call me as soon as possible. Thanks."

After filling out seven forms for the First Multiple Listing Service on a tiny property south of town, she headed over to the courthouse before midday traffic became too congested.

Just as Maria started to pull her truck out of the parking lot, Emily honked the horn of her red mustang and pulled into the lot. *Nuts!* Maria had locked eyes with Emily just before the honk. She couldn't pretend she hadn't seen her. She stopped and opened her truck window, motor idling. Emily did the same.

"Oh, *ma cherie*; did you come to my showing? I couldn't find you afterward. I wanted to hear how you liked my designs!"

What could she say to her idiot cousin? "As a matter of fact, I'm still mad about that so called showing, Emily."

"Mad? Why, whatever do you mean?"

She just doesn't get it.

A car swung into the driveway, trapped by Maria's Jeep and Emily's car.

"I have to move for this guy." She continued out of the driveway, turned right because of relentless traffic and drove around the block. When she could turn left to get to the freeway, Emily pulled up behind her and tapped her horn. She drove into the nearest parking lot of the nearest hotel. Emily followed.

"What's the matter, Cuz?" Emily got into the front seat of Maria's Jeep.

"You just don't get it, do you?" Maria said.

"Get what?"

"That a fashion show of nude people wasn't a fashion show at all. Mason and I drove eighty miles for a farce."

"Oh, good. Then you did come after all." Emily's dark eyes were gleaming. "Didn't you love the feathers and arrows?"

"We left after the first model. She was naked, Em."

"Wasn't she beautiful?"

"No. Just naked. I was embarrassed."

"But you should have stayed to see the Princess Tatiana collection."

"Do you know how mad Mr. Duke and Frank Denning are? They're going to pull the listing from me because the American Indians are angry about the caricature you made of their culture! And Mr. Duke is furious that you drew attention to the land. He wanted a nice quiet title transfer. Instead he's blaming me for your notoriety. You didn't have to tell the newspaper we found a dead guy in the mineshaft. But there it was in black and white."

Emily cringed against the passenger door. Steam clouded the inside of the windows. Raindrops dripped down the outside.

"Land deals are private," Maria continued. "Agents don't have loose lips. If somebody wants to talk about their own property that's their choice, not yours. How do you think I make my money? I can't make money with you screwing up my listings!"

164

"But Maria," Emily tipped her chin down and rolled her eyes up in a parody of guilt. "It was I who told Frankie you could sell the property for him." She blinked twice then ran her eyes over to the outside of the Jeep. Her lips puckered slightly.

God!

"Yes, I know you did, and I appreciate it. But I thought you realized the importance of buying and selling land. I thought he was serious. Now the deal may be gone." She didn't mention the contract.

"No. It won't be gone. I weel fix it for youuu."

A gleeful look overcame her face. "Do not worry. I swear on my pinkie," she stuck the little finger of her right hand into the air. "Frankie will keep the property listed with you." She hopped out of the Jeep wearing black tights and brogan boots, dashed over to her idling Mustang and slid inside. Flashing Maria a big toothy smile, she drove out of the parking lot.

Maria banged her head against the steering wheel.

CHAPTER 22

When Maria checked her voice mail, Frank Denning's voice said, "I'd like to see the offer on the property, but I'll be tied up all day today. Our investment group's regular meeting is tonight, so can you email or fax the paperwork to me? We can discuss it at the meeting and I'll call you tomorrow."

Closer to the office than home, she stopped in to fax the contract. She preferred to present the contract in person, but her choices were to crash their meeting tonight, wait a day, during which another disaster might strike, or get it over with. She pressed SEND.

A potential listing client also left word she could meet with Maria at six o'clock. After the comparable paperwork was accumulated for that listing, she had three hours to kill before six. Her father didn't answer her call, so she called Aunt Minnie.

"Hi, Minnie, this is Cousin Maria."

"Oh, Maria, I'm glad you called. I'm worried about your mom."

She held her breath. "What's wrong?"

"I don't know, but Elizabeth won't come out of her house. We were supposed to go together to bingo last week but she cancelled it. And book club. She told me she didn't read the book and wouldn't go to our regular meeting Saturday morning. This isn't right. She loves bingo because she usually wins, and she doesn't miss book club either. She chose the current one herself."

Her parents weren't supposed to have the problems of mortals. First dad, and now mom. Anger lurked in her chest. Suddenly exhausted, guilt misted her brain. "I think it's actually my dad that's the issue. He's upset with me. Maybe he's stressing her out. He gets moody sometimes."

"I haven't seen your dad since Thanksgiving. Can you tell me what's wrong?"

"Cousin Yvette is doing the genealogy chart for the Tandy's side and she found information on my dad's family. It wasn't very clear, so I called my dad to ask him about it. He wasn't happy."

"Why, forever more! What bothered him?"

"There's a dispute about his name and his heritage. It's not important to me what his real name is or if his parents were American Indian. But if it's true, I don't understand why he's keeping it a big secret."

"Oh, my. Your dad... he's an interesting character. I've known him for forty-something years, and I've never really known him."

"I thought I knew him, but I guess I don't either.

We always lived in Phoenix, where he said he was raised. I've never met any of his family—no cousins, no siblings, nothing. And we were always so busy with the Tandy family, I never really thought about it before."

"I know, dear. Our family has taken on a life of its own. When Elizabeth first met him, he'd just gotten out of service. They actually eloped, and none of us were at the wedding. It seemed okay at the time—I mean for an elopement. But my parents were certainly not happy about. He'd been in the war, so I figured he just didn't want to talk about the past. None of those boys did, though. It was a terrible war."

"Since they won't answer my phone calls, I can't even talk to my mom."

"I can tell you my parents wouldn't have been happy if they'd found out that Elizabeth married an American Indian."

"My grandparents were prejudiced against Indians?"

"Oh, yes. They thought all of them were lazy and worthless. There were gangs, you know. Hate groups, really." Minnie sighed. "People don't seem to be able to get over injustices and want to retaliate. I guess I can't blame them."

"Left over from the 19th century? That's kind of small-minded."

"No, dear. Left over from the 20th Century. I'm talking about Viet Nam."

"But what's that got to do with American Indians?"

"Some of the Indians here in Phoenix identified with people overseas fighting America and started movements against civilians right here in our country. I remember when they converged on the Capitol Building downtown. The 'Winged Victory' statue up on top of it had a Black drape around it for two weeks. I have no idea how somebody could reach it. It's over 200 feet in the sky. They took that black shroud down with a helicopter."

"That couldn't have anything to do with my dad. I'm not sure how long he was in service, but he joined in 1957, according to the information Yvette found."

"Probably not. It's a good thing my parents never found out, if he really is Indian, though." She paused in thought. "I can go over to your parent's house and talk to Elizabeth. I'm sure she'll call you if I ask her to."

"I'd really appreciate that. I'm so worried, I may have to get another flight out there. If you think it would help after you talk to them, I'll do it."

"Now, you don't worry about anything until there is something to worry about. I'll let you know."

Maria closed her cell phone, then blinked when she realized she was at the office, as her mind had been far away. What could be so bad about being American Indian? She gathered up her purse and papers and started for home. It's not as if he just found it out himself, if it's true.

* * *

Maria felt desperate with Christmas only a week away and a possibility she would need to go to Phoenix again. Despite the bad weather, she put on her down jacket and drove to town anyway. She found the smallest tree on a Christmas tree lot and bought it for five dollars. She stopped at LePage's used bookstore, bought six copies of *Loving Frank*, six colorful bird-shaped bookmarks, and returned to the Jeep. Ice covered the windshield and hung in three stalactites from her side mirror. She rustled among the emergency equipment box in the back of the Jeep, found the scraper and scraped ice from the windshield. Huffing from the exertion, she climbed into the driver's seat.

When the phone rang, she used her teeth to pull off the glove on her right hand and pushed the green button.

"This is Maria Sebastian."

"Where are you?" Mason said.

"At the Ferris shopping center. Why?"

"I need to talk to you."

"Sounds serious. I'm going home because I think we've got an ice storm forming. Where are you?"

"Almost to the boat. I can go to your house instead."

Warmed by his voice, she said, "What a good idea!" Suddenly, Christmas might turn out okay after all.

The phone rang again with Tom's name showing on its face. "Hi, Tom," she said. "If it hadn't been you, I wouldn't have answered this call, in case you want to know that."

"Then I guess I should feel privileged. I'm wondering, do you know what Mason is up to?"

170

"You know as much as I do. He's doing Private Eye things. I think he's finished with the Florida job, but I don't know what else is on his plate. I'll see him before long. Do you want me to find out? Anything in particular?"

"He's doing something else besides that."

"What do you mean? Like another job for the FBI? I thought he was through with them." Maria remembered an undercover job he'd done some consulting work on a few years back.

Tom laughed. "Yeah, he's some consultant alright. Interesting that he knows stuff before we do, isn't it?"

Maria's thoughts went somewhere else while she continued to drive. Just a few minutes ago she was so hyped over seeing Mason, and now she felt like a shot bird. "What kind of stuff?" she managed to ask.

"I don't know whether to be pissed off or pat him on the back. I called Dirk Singletongue in Phoenix, and he tells me our Mr. Walker found Wanda Navarro deceased. Now, isn't that interesting. What the hell was Mason doing in Oklahoma? Maria? Are you there?"

CHAPTER 23

Maria swerved to avoid a car sliding toward her. She knew it was a mistake to jam her brakes on ice, but the SUV heading straight for her side door gave her no choice. Her Jeep slid across the roadway. She knew what was happening, but had no control over the spin. She counted passing the stop sign twice as she spun around. Centrifugal force threw her against the driver's side window and pressed her face against the cold glass. On the first rotation, time slowed to a crawl a turtle would appreciate. Breaking the window glass became paramount in her mind. Her purse and paperwork careened across her lap, hopped up to the dashboard and slammed into her head.

She felt her shoulder belt cut into her clavicle and could only pray it would hold her tight. Her arms were useless.

The airbag came at her like a basketball goal shot, punching the free side of her face harder into the window glass. In an explosion of shimmering glass chunks, everything went black.

* * *

With groggy awareness of clanging metal, scrambling people and soft but urgent voices, she tried to yell that she was okay, but discovered she had no breath, even though the window was no longer closed. *This is a hell of a way to die*, she thought. *Being killed by life saving devices*. Night fell for the second time.

When she opened her eyes again, something was over her face whooshing air into her lungs. *Thank God*. She felt rumbling, heard dinging, whirring, and voices talked around her like she was invisible. *Ah, this is what the inside of an ambulance is like*. A slab of meat being kept alive to be handed off to a hospital. She wanted to kiss the guy running the machines.

"Hi," he said. "You're fine, just a little beat up.

Shouldn't drive on ice, you know." He winked. Yep, it was instant love.

* * *

The hand holding hers was kind of small, but it was warm, so Maria chanced opening her eyes. Her friend, Dena sat next to the hospital bed, a deep wrinkle between her eyebrows, and red rims where eye makeup used to be. "Good morning."

"Ouch," Maria said. "I'm trying to smile, here, but I bet it looks more like a grimace."

"Nobody cares what it looks like."

"Did I live? Are all my toes still with me?"

"Yes, everything is present and accounted for. You could take inventory with cautious wiggles, I suppose."

"I'll do that. Thanks for coming to my rescue, so to speak. It's nice to hear I'm all here from somebody I love." The smile only hurt for a second.

"We couldn't find your cell phone. Your Jeep was upside down in the ditch at Sanders Road and Buford Dam Road," Dena said. "Your purse was closed, so it only got banged up." She picked up the purse to show Maria.

"Upside down? I don't remember that part. I didn't hit anybody did I?" A chill poised to run down her back.

"No. The cops said you spun out when you tried to stop for a guy who was already sliding."

"I was on my way to my house. Oh, gosh! Mason was supposed to meet me there. I need to call him." She tried to sit up, but that turned out to be a bad idea.

"Just stay where you are. Your head got banged, then wedged between the driver window and the air bag. It also punched you in the chest, so you couldn't breathe for a while. That was the scary part. When your head broke the window, some of the glass cut your skin, even though it was safety glass. The doctor said that much pressure would have cut you, even if it hadn't been glass.

"I've got a contract, a mad father, mother, boyfriend, and hundred questions to get answered, so I can't stay in here." Maria looked for answers on the ceiling of her room.

"They'll probably throw you out in a couple of days, the way hospitals work. I'd stay as long as I could, if I were you. I think the big scare was loss of oxygen, and possible concussion. But you seem to be your same naughty self and you don't look too funny to me." Dena moved over the bed right in front of Maria and peered at her face. She moved her hand to Maria's cheek and gave it a short poke with her finger.

"Yikes!" Maria yelled.

"See? You're not done yet. Better stay in bed awhile."

Maria couldn't sleep even though pills quelled the aches and pains. After friends had come and gone, after plastic food had been somehow swallowed, after people wearing white pants and colorful hospital tops had stuck thermometers in her mouth and wrapped blood pressure cuffs around her arm three different times and her assigned doctor rushed in to assess her progress and told her she could go home tomorrow, Maria hobbled out of bed and searched the maw of her purse for her BlackBerry. How could she work without her clients list and phone numbers, her reference sphere list, her friends and family phone numbers? She'd be out of business. It would take a couple of weeks to rebuild critical phone numbers. *Shit!*

Okay, what did I do before BlackBerries were invented? She'd kept everything on a calendar, made phone calls from the office and home, had an answering machine, and a financial calculator. She smiled to herself as she remembered all her stuff in her old attaché case was still under her bed. People would think her wicked stupid to use antiques, but they'd work until she could replace the crucial BlackBerry.

She was just dropping off to sleep around ten thirty when someone knocked. Tom popped his head around the door.

She pretended to not have seen him and said, "If it's anybody but Tommy Larken, go away."

Tom's face broke into a smile from ear to ear. "You don't sound very sick to me," he said. "One of the guys at the sheriff's department called me."

"I would have called you myself, but my BlackBerry disappeared. It's probably under water in a ditch.

"Check your homeowner's insurance. Maybe they can do something for you."

"You haven't heard anything from Mason, have you?" she asked.

"Tom shook his head. "I was hoping by this time you'd know what he was doing in Oklahoma."

"I wish."

"The guy's a spook, you know."

"CIA? Mason? The guy who rebuilds houseboats?"

"You told me a couple of months ago that he worked for the FBI."

She scooted up higher on her pillows. "But I thought that was consulting."

"And it was just coincidence that he helped us?" Tom sat down, shaking his head. "Mr. Walker is multitalented, as it turns out."

"Why was he doing a job for the FBI if he's CIA?"

"Nobody seems to be able to answer that question. There are lots of other organizations who have him on their payroll as well. But not a payroll you'll ever see. He tends to show up in venues all over the world. Mysterious things happen then he's gone. Like a magician. First you see him, then you don't."

"There has to be a reasonable explanation." She remembered that instead of answering her questions, Mason always turned the conversation around, made it about her.

"Yeah, there's a reasonable explanation... he's got a network organization that's for hire. He probably changes his identification like I change my socks. He's a bit too far under the radar, Maria."

"I think you're getting some bad information. He'd never do anything illegal. He hates for bad guys to win. Okay, when you told me about him finding Wanda Navarro, I did think he'd deceived me. But would he still be around if he has what he wants from me? It's not like I'm arm candy for somebody like him if he's so cosmopolitan." Maria looked at her reflection in the mirror over the sink. From where she sat in a hospital bed in the north Georgia woods, she didn't look sophisticated at all.

"I don't want to see you get hurt by some player who's full of lies."

"I can take care of myself."

Tom glanced at the hospital room, her patient chart, all the bandages that belied her statement.

"Right," he agreed. "You're just here for the food."

CHAPTER 24

Dena drove Maria home after the doctor had released her. She showered carefully and sat down gingerly to figure what her next move should be. At least she still had the desktop computer. Maria spent the day combing electronic files to rebuild information lost with her BlackBerry. Since computers crashed all the time, nobody on her phone/address list would question her emails requesting addresses and phone numbers due to an accident.

She also found her pile of old electronics and made several calls from her home phone to reinstate them. As soon as she could get a rental car, she planned to shop for batteries to activate everything else.

With not much else she could do, she organized her home office desktop, making file folders for each topic she was working on. A fax she didn't remember was next—from Wanda Navarro. A wave of sadness strengthened the ache in her head. The date she's printed it was only two days ago. Yesterday Tom told her Wanda was dead.

She remembered a fax had come in while she was madly emailing Wanda, calling her father, and trying to contact Mason a few days ago. She hadn't taken time to read it. She picked it up then tried to overlook the frosty feeling that the fax had come from the world beyond.

It read:

```
The fetishes in a medicine bag are only
important to the one who owns the bag. The
feather likely was to give power to the
owner, as it looks like an eagle feather tip.
```

The animal carvings could represent some
incident that occurred to the owner involving
those animals, or they could be to protect
the owner from the natural prey of that
animal. The white one is tsula, a fox. the
green one, yo-na, a bear. They're probably
quartz and jade. The beads are turquoise. The
gold could be there for many reasons. The
grassy substance represents healing of some
type and is likely a herb. I don't know what
type of herb, but I can find out.

Maria's eyes stung. The fox, with its power of invisibility
hadn't done Jaime much good. She walked to her bathroom and
shook out a couple of aspirin, swallowing them with water from
the glass she'd left on the counter. She lay down on her bed until
her headache subsided, and went back to her desk.

The fax continued:

The pouch itself is very common. Many men
prefer the soft leather because it can be
worn around the neck without irritating their
skin. But it couldn't have belonged to an
older person because it's so tiny. Most
Native American bags that represent someone's
life are much larger.

"Thank you," Maria whispered.

The phone rang, but Maria didn't want to pick it up.
However, her basic home phone did not have voice mail, and
she didn't want to miss any more calls.

Tom's voice said, "Hi, kid. How are you and your headache
doing?"

"Hi. We're fine."

"Yeah, you sound fine."

"I'm just down because I found a fax I hadn't read. From Wanda Navarro."

"Oh yeah? What'd she say?"

"She just told me what the fetishes probably mean. It's very general. I emailed her pictures of the fetishes I found in my pocket." Another thought sent a chill over her scalp. "You don't think it had anything to do with her death, do you?"

"No. Still. I'd like a copy of it. And I'm going to need a copy for the feds as well."

"Sure."

"I've had a message from Walker asking where you are. He's going to camp on your porch if I don't call him back."

"I lost his number with my BlackBerry now somewhere in the Georgia swampland. Give me the number from your cell and I'll call him. Or maybe his tent will appear on my deck."

"Atta girl." He gave her a number with an odd area code. "It's a Skyphone. Um, satellite phone, I believe they're called. Actually, probably *Spyphone* is more appropriate."

"I told you, I think you're wrong about that, but we'll see. Anyway, thanks for calling me."

"You get well."

"I'm already well, except for no electronic devices hanging from my head, and the guy who slipped into my ear to play drums on my brain."

"Oh, and let me know what Mason's excuses are so I can use them in the future myself."

"Yeah. 'Bye." Excuses, she thought. Was Mason playing her? She could learn to live without him. She'd done it before with men.

* * *

An image of Mason aiming a sniper rifle at a man two miles away from him with Badguy printed across his t-shirt entered

Maria's dream. A red laser dot appeared on the badguy's chest. Then a bullet hole appeared there. He clutched his chest and fell to the ground, writhing in agony. For some reason, no blood came out of the hole. When she yelled, she woke herself up, hearing the lame shout as she came to.

She got off the couch and found her aspirin bottle. Her head throbbed.

Then she remembered the headache that had crept up on her. Instead of calling Mason, she'd fallen asleep. She looked at the pain killer prescription she'd had filled at a pharmacy on the way home from the hospital. Deciding to save that for serious pain, she slid it back beside the faucet of her bathroom sink.

The mail truck's squeaky brakes announced its arrival. She shrugged into her jacket, slipped into her waiting shoes and trekked out to the mailbox. The blast of icy air seemed to lift a weight off her face. Waving at the mailman who was at the neighbor's box by time she got to the curb, she retrieved the envelopes and fliers and perused the mail as she ambled back to her porch.

A legal-sized envelope with her father's handwriting grabbed her attention. She hurried into her home office, grabbed her razor letter opener, slit the envelope seal and slid the opener into her pocket. It read:

Dear Maria,

I haven't wanted to tell you about my past because it's not a pretty story. You and your mom mean everything to me, but the truth is, I should never have married or had any children, and in fact, didn't plan to. It's just plain accidental that you are here today, that I am married to your mother and that I'm even here to tell you any of this.

I suspect that my mother was pregnant with me when she married my father, who was a widower with two young boys.

It was never discussed, and I have no proof of this except that I never looked like my family, who were all Apache as far as I know.

My parents had fallen on hard times, as they say. We lived on the reservation and beginning during the Korean Conflict, there were a lot of dissidents who routinely came to the rez to recruit activists.

With nothing to do but get in trouble, my teen brothers fell in with one of the gangs and spent their time going to meetings, and wearing various icons and armbands, among which was a version of the walking bird toy you had with you in November. And by the way, that walking bird is a Striped Tanager, the state bird of Puerto Rico, where this hate group originated.

The brothers weren't overt about it, but I know they were using rifles and other destructive weapons. They left every morning in their precious red coats and returned some evenings, only to go out to meetings after dark. They were training for some big event that I was too young to be involved with at the time.

The nearest school was fifty miles to the north, as there was not one on the rez, so my mother arranged for me to live with a family named Walton off the rez during the school year.

One day a gang who felt my parents and brothers knew something they shouldn't came to our home and assassinated all of them. If I had been there, I would have been killed with them. Our home, which was really a glorified shack, was burned along with whatever evidence could have been obtained at that time.

Then these raiders came looking for me. Since the Waltons lived unobtrusively, it wasn't well known that I was with them. Fortunately the people they accosted really didn't know who or where I was. John Walton, to whom I owe my life, taught me to drive well enough to get a driver's license with an altered age, and gave me his Social Security Card. He used parts of his transcripts and certificates to give me another identity. Though I was very young, I was a big kid. John Walton took me down to volunteer for the Navy. He signed documents as my parent, and my old life was gone forever.

Please humor me and burn this letter immediately. I have spent most of my adult life working to clear the world of anything having to do with ORCA, which is a group whose goal it is to murder innocents as well as their own. I thought they were gone now, but all it takes is one radical to find low income bored youngsters and give them a purpose for their lives, even if it means only learning to fill that void with hate.

I never thought you would cross paths with them. I will re-contact friends who may still have information about this pile of crap, and assert whatever pressure I can.

In case you've not figured it out yet, it was me who put the murdered boy's medicine bag in your jacket pocket when you were home for Thanksgiving. After Norman's wife was killed, I recognized ORCA's handiwork and had to give your local authorities a link to them. Norman left that bag with me years ago. I'd almost forgotten it until you got involved. I knew you'd not rest until you knew the truth.

Watch your back, little girl.

Always,
Dad

Maria felt like she held a piece of her father in her hand. Then it was all true. All those years not knowing her true heritage—not knowing her true father. Nausea crept up her throat. She gingerly sat down on the floor and put her head on her knees. Now she didn't even know who she was.

More questions crowded her head. Why did her father have the Indian medicine bag? Why did Norman give it to him?

She quickly dialed her parents' number.

"Hello," her mother said.

"Mom. Thank God you answered. I just got...."

"Maria! So good to hear from you."

"Mom. I just got a —"

"Are you coming out for Christmas?"

She gritted her teeth. "Mom, you aren't listening."

"I'm always listening, honey. Now, your father isn't here right now, or I'd put him on the line."

"Oh," Maria said. Where are we going with this? "Will he be back soon?"

"No, he's gone hunting. He'll be back when he gets a doe, he said."

Hunting? Her father never hunted in his life. "But, Mom, I didn't....."

"So, are you coming for Christmas? I sent you some cookies and wanted to send a jacket I found at Nordstrom's, over in Phoenix, but wasn't sure of the size. You said you've lost weight."

I did not. Her father is gone, her mother suddenly wants her to come for Christmas. Something was wrong.

"Minnie came by a couple of days ago. She mentioned she'd talked with you. The Tandy Family Calendar is going to be ready at Christmas, you should receive it in the mail right away."

Whatever it was, she'd have to find out from Minnie.

"I don't know if I can get off work yet, Mom."

"That'll be fine, honey. We'd love to have you."

Her mother knew she wasn't employed by anybody, but sounded like the lie was a truth.

"I should know by Tuesday. I'll call you then, okay?"

Frustrated something was wrong with her mother, she wondered if somebody was there, or worse, somebody was threatening her.

After she said good bye and hung up, she called the Phoenix Sheriff's office and asked for Dirk Singletongue.

"Singletongue," Dirk answered.

"Hi Detective. This is Maria Sebastian. I met you when Nita Arrowkeeper Sebastian was killed.

"Yes, I remember. How can I help you?"

"I just had a very weird conversation with my mother. The short version of the story is, something is wrong at her house. Either that or she's suddenly come down with Alzheimer's Disease. I'm here in Georgia, my father is off somewhere and my mom may have some psycho in her house. My mother lives in Scottsdale actually, do you cover that area?"

"The city normally handles that," he replied. "Your father was one of our own a few years back, I think. Am I right?"

"Yes, sir, he was Phoenix P.D."

"I'll check the district patrol to see if they're on a call. I'll let you know what they find."

Relief swept through Maria, taking the headache with it.

Now, what was she doing? Oh yes. *Burn the letter.*

CHAPTER 25

"Walker here," he answered the phone when Maria called.

"Mason, Tom said he told you what happened and why I didn't call you back."

"God, Maria! I'm on my way over to your house. I waited on your porch most all night. I had no idea where you were. I figured you didn't want to talk to me.

She could see his smile in her head, but it didn't have quite the gleam it did before. "I understand you were in Oklahoma and found Wanda dead."

"Yes."

She walked into the bathroom and retrieved the washcloth she'd been using on her forehead. "What were you doing in Oklahoma?"

"That's why I want to talk to you."

"What happened to Wanda?"

"I can't explain all of that on the phone. I'm almost to your house."

"You've been using me, haven't you?" she asked.

"Using you? No."

"Then why didn't you tell me you were working on something that involved Wanda?"

"I do a lot of things I don't tell people about."

"Like what, for instance? I thought I ranked more than 'people'."

"Are you listening? I can't talk about that. When I get there I'll tell you what I can, but only if you let me in."

"Definitely. Good bye."

"Good bye."

Why do I believe what he tells me? Because I want to believe him. Because he's got cute dimples. *What a dope I am.*

When the doorbell rang, she veered into the kitchen and tossed the washcloth into the sink. "Who is it?"

"Let me see. I'm not the pizza delivery guy. Oh. I must be Mr. Walker."

She opened the door and stood back so he could walk inside. He stopped on his way past to look at her eyes, the bruises. He brought his fingers to her chin and gently tilted it toward the light. He examined the area that had hit the window of her Jeep. His eyes misted. Then his eyes hardened as anger flashed across his face.

"Okay, I'm listening." She sat down at the end of her couch.

He shed his black overcoat and unzipped a down vest before he sat at the opposite end. "Wanda was shot with a .45. I found her in the hills behind her home on the Cherokee Reservation in Oklahoma. Somebody apparently chased her, shot her, and left her there. Nobody heard anything. Nobody knows anything. If I don't miss my guess, she was shot by some element of ORCA, probably because of her son's affiliation with the group."

"He's been gone for ten years. Why would they shoot her now?" Maria said. "And what were you doing there in the first place?

"Because she had something they wanted, I'd say."

"And..."

"And that's the part I can't talk about."

"Why? It's the most important part. It's the part where I understand you're not using me to get to this subversive group I've fallen into."

"You have to trust me, Maria. We have to have a relationship based on trust."

"Did your wife trust you? Did she understand that you just pop up all over the world and find dead bodies? Did her path and yours just happen to cross like mine and yours did—with people getting killed because of it? Was she an American Indian woman? What about her family? Did they understand what you were? What you are?"

He stared at her with chocolate eyes that held absolutely no expression. "You found out about your dad, didn't you?"

She drew her legs up into the seat and hugged her knees with both arms, anger starting its slow boil inside her bloodstream.

"And how do you know about my father? You knew before I did? Who are you, anyway?"

"Okay, look. I'm an investigator. For your information, I had no idea your father would show up related to the ORCA group. My job is to find where weapons are coming from, why people are dying. It isn't just him, it's hundreds of other people. "Are you all right?" he asked, moving next to her, not touching her.

"No. I'm not. I feel horrible." Tears rolled out of her eyes. "Poor Wanda! My poor father!" She looked up at him and said, "Why? Why would someone do those things?"

"Those are questions I can't answer. It seems your father's brothers, who were quite a bit older than he, may have been involved with the same group as Wanda's son, ORCA. Until recently, we really believed ORCA was disbanded for lack of support."

"I think they were half-brothers. How did you find all of this out?" She wiped her eyes with the sleeve of her sweater. When she saw stains of mascara smear the sleeve, she walked into the kitchen and pulled a square of paper towel off the roll next to the refrigerator and returned to the chair while he answered.

"Newspaper articles mostly. And some file records that I have access to. How did you find out?"

"My cousin sent me my dad's DD-214 file. God! If she could get that paperwork, can't the ORCA guys?"

"That was in 1957! I'm quite sure nobody is around today who remembers that particular incident. It may be they didn't even know your dad existed. I have to say ol' dad is a pretty smart puppy to carry off something so extreme, and not get caught by either the bad guys or the U.S. Army."

"But he was only fourteen years old!" she said.

"Ah! I also found a copy of your dad's basic training photo." He shuffled around in his wallet. "I saved it for you." He handed her a picture.

She stared into the black and white eyes of her fourteen-year old father. "He looks like a kid trying to look old. He was so thin!"

"They all look like that coming out of basic. The old Class A uniform hat made them look even younger. Seventeen-year-olds could get in the army with parental consent. He doesn't look all that young compared to the other guys. A guy went in with me who was 5'5" tall. Eight weeks later he was 5'9" tall. After Training School, four weeks later, he was six feet tall. Kid was a weed. Apparently your father was already 5'9" when he lied his way in."

"I still can't believe nobody noticed."

"Well, it worked. He's still alive."

Those words rang in Maria's ears so loudly she didn't hear the rest of what he said.

"....so he's probably only half Apache," Mason was saying when her ears came back to life.

"Uh. Say that last part again. I didn't hear you."

He looked at her for two beats. "I said, your dad's mother married your dad's father not long before his birth. She was his second wife, the first wife wasn't legally married to him and was the mother of the two other sons. Let's just say she came into the marriage pregnant with some white guy's child."

Her father had just written this information to her. How could Mason have received it? She wasn't going to tell him anything. If he wasn't going to be forthcoming, she wasn't either.

"Now, wait just a minute," she said. "How can you sit there and tell me my dad came from a mess like that?"

"Maria. Grow up. Shit happens to everybody. Half the world wouldn't be here if everybody was legitimate and they had to have two parents. You're not getting what I'm telling you. Your dad is a genius. And that genius is alive today, not dead up on some reservation mountainside like poor Wanda Navarro."

"I've always known he is a genius. His inventions are so useful—he's got a couple of patents on better mousetraps. But I feel like I hardly know the man," she said.

"Actually, you know the man today—what he has become. You just wouldn't recognize the man he used to be."

"I thought we stayed the same person through our lives, constantly adding wisdom, knowledge, experience. Like growth. Not cutting out parts like sections of grapefruit." She walked into the kitchen and opened the refrigerator.

"I think it's more like a shish-ka-bob," he said, following her, and settled on a barstool. "A person adds different lives together with their old ones, so they're many different people combined in one body. Depending on when you know them, you have one perspective of them."

She poured a glass of wine and handed it to him. Then she turned to start dinner. When she placed two dinner plates on the bar she asked, "Just what do the letters ORCA stand for?"

"Organized Retaliation Citizens Association."

"And their goal?" She laid out silverware and napkins.

"They're just a hate group. A catchall subversive group of people against everything. It originally had roots in Puerto Rico. They were among the huge numbers of Junta groups formed to overthrow governments. Financed by drug money. Where you have drug money, you've got armaments. They never got into suicide bombings, but wear better armor than our military, strut around in red jackets in their off hours. Every once in awhile they find an excuse to kill off the latest regime, heads of state, and politicos. Their height of membership was in the 60's. Here came the drug cartels with no agenda but money and ORCA was just in the way. They came to the States to horn in on the drug money and were annihilated. Or so we thought."

She spun from the stove, leaned her forearms on the counter and looked in his eyes. "And who is we?"

"Yeah. Well, if I told you that then I'd have to kill you."

"Very funny. Why is it that you didn't find the time to let me know that my mineshaft listing was connected to your Junta subversives?"

"Because I didn't know it. Very nasty people. They showed up again in San Juan in 2005. One thing and another, a cold, cold trail to Jaime Navarro. Not in my wildest imagination did I think it would ever lead me to Wanda Navarro in Oklahoma. You mentioned that name to me and I knew where to look. By time I got to her, it was too late."

"Now back up a bit. That part about I mentioned Wanda's name to you. Why didn't you tell me there was an issue? Maybe I could have saved her life."

She pushed her plate aside and turned back to heating tortillas on the burner of her stove. Sautéed beef waited to be put inside the shells she formed with her hand. Tomatoes, lettuce, cheese, and salsa sat in their individual bowls.

A tear splashed onto the tortilla. She considered throwing it into the garbage disposal but reconsidered that Mason deserved all the bacteria her tears could supply. Another one plopped down. She used her sleeve to sop up the next one before it fell.

"Honey. If I had known for sure that your Wanda and my Wanda were the same person, I would have done things differently. But anything I do, anything I know, puts anybody else I know in jeopardy. You absolutely will never learn anything from me, because I value you way too much."

He got up from his stool, and walked over to the stove. He wrapped his arms around her, nuzzled his face into her hair and mumbled, "I am so sorry."

She flipped the tortilla she was now burning onto the counter top and turned into his shoulder. She cried for Wanda. She cried for Jaime wherever he was. She cried for Norman for being so stupid as to be involved with ORCA, no matter how peripherally. She cried for her father's lost family. She cried for her father.

"Oh my God!" she said. "I forgot to call Minnie."

She wiped her face and hands on a napkin instead of Mason's chest , and went to her desk phone. Quickly dialing her aunt's number, she looked at her watch.

"Hello?"

"Minnie! This is Maria. I talked with my mom earlier today and she scared me. It was like somebody was in her house and she couldn't talk to me. I called the police in Phoenix and asked them to drive by, but I don't know what happened after that."

"Maria! I'm so glad you called. Your mom is here with me, and we're going to George's cabin for a few days."

A wave of relief rolled through Maria. "And, how's my Dad?"

"Just a minute. I'm putting Elizabeth on the line."

"Maria?"

"Mom! I'm so glad you're okay. I was worried when....."

"That nice policeman you sent over brought me over to Minnie's house. Your father told me not to talk on the phone to anybody."

"Well, where is he, Mom?"

"He put on his old fatigues, took a bunch of gear out of the attic, loaded his rifle and another gun and told me he was going to become smoke, dear."

CHAPTER 26

Maria missed the chance to talk to her father before he'd taken off for God knows where. What could he be thinking? She replaced the phone in its charger and turned to Mason who had helped himself to a cup of coffee from the pot in the kitchen. He held the cup out to her. It felt comforting in her cold hands.

"Are your folks doing okay?" he asked.

"My Mom's family is taking care of her while my Dad has become 'smoke' according to Mom."

"It's just a term, honey."

"A pretty scary term, if you ask me. You probably know about these things, since you're a 'spook'." She looked up from her coffee.

"Spook? Me? Who have you been talking to?"

"You. Mr. 'I can't tell you that.' Mr. 'You found out about your father, didn't you?'"

"Ah," he said.

"How did you find out about my father?"

"Records." Mason walked back to the kitchen and poured another cup of coffee then brought it to the sofa and sat down.

"But how did he come onto your radar screen?"

"One thing led to another. Discrepancies appeared—like the amount of time between his family's death and his joining the Navy. You realize, of course, at that time he was suspected of killing his own family."

"Are you out of your mind? A child, to kill his own family?" Maria's face burned and her headache returned with a vengeance.

"Of course he was. Family members are always the first suspects."

"If people like you had been involved, he'd probably be in jail," she fired at him.

"Okay. Truce. I'm out of here." Mason stood, reached for his vest and his overcoat and headed for the front door.

She'd felt good when she said it. "Can I take it back?" she asked.

"Nope. Not just now. I need to go find a brain eraser. I'll let you know when it's gone." He stepped out the door and closed it carefully, finally. She wanted to throw her coffee cup at him. But he was gone.

* * *

When Maria answered her ringing phone, Michaela said "Hi. Are you coming to the office Christmas party tonight?"

"Do you think I'm in good enough condition for a Christmas party?" She shook a couple of aspirin into her hand from their dispenser.

"We sent invitations to your clients as well as everybody else's. Of course we didn't know you were going to get in a car wreck. You can get Mr. Beautiful to bring you though."

"I guess if you put it that way I have to come. My clients won't know anybody there but me. And Mr. Beautiful may be a thing of the past."

"Maria! What did you do? What did he do? Honey, listen to me. I know what I'm talking about. You can't let Mason go. We have to fix this right now."

"He's using me. He won't tell me what his job is, except it's very underworld crime something or other."

"Does he do drugs? Is he an alcoholic? Does he have three ex-wives and fifteen children to support? Does he beat you? Does he have a criminal record?"

"Mikey. I haven't even thought about all that. And the answer is I honestly don't know. He tells me nothing, except I know he had a wife who died. He definitely doesn't beat me."

"Well, you're not doing your homework, girl. It's about time you find out. He's too delicious to turn loose. And I swear, if you do turn him loose, I intend to get him."

"What time tonight?" She sighed, took one extra aspirin then lay down to take a nap.

* * *

The headache was gone. The nap was good. The memory of the morning and Mason was awful. Maria stayed under the blanket staring at the ceiling, thinking about how mean she'd been to him. She couldn't deal with his secretiveness. But there still was no reason for her to be so rude to him. After all, he'd come over to her house and given her a darling picture of her father. He'd tried to comfort her, said he was worried about her. She'd been snide and sarcastic to him in return. She'd probably ruined the only real relationship she'd had since her fiasco marriage to Norman. What a dope she'd been.

She got off the bed and looked into her closet to see if anything would work for a Christmas Party. It was pitiful. She'd been in the woods so long, there was not one dress hanging in that closet. There were eight pairs of useful jeans hanging where the dresses should have been. There were some black slacks stuffed against the wall, the part hanging over the hangar's crossbar white with dust. If she could get the dust off them, iron out the wrinkles, wear black boots since all her shoes were sandals, and find some kind of a top, it might work out.

She headed into the bathroom and turned on the shower. Then looked in the mirror. Shock and awe! Her face, more swollen than yesterday, looked angry in its new shade of pink, and was dotted with scabs. Her black left eye looked like a cartoon character should slap a steak over it. She still didn't have a top to wear even if she could reconstitute the black slacks. The only good part was she had three hours to get ready.

While she piddled with makeup to disguise her bruises, she noticed the mirror reflected the toy she'd brought back from Phoenix to return to Donnie. It still sat on the top of her dresser in the bedroom, its bright orange bird breast incongruous with her mood. She crossed the room and picked up the toy. She wound its stem and sat it down on its miniature feet. After two steps, it quit walking. A push didn't help, so she made a mental note to see if she could find somebody to fix its springs.

It was possible she'd be back in Phoenix soon, but she had no idea where Donnie would be found, now that his grandmother had been killed as well as his mother. Dirk Singletongue would probably know, however, and she smiled to herself. In fact, maybe with no other relatives alive, Dirk would be able to adopt Donnie after all. Of course, Norman might show up, not that he'd ever be a poster boy for fatherhood.

She couldn't pull the back of the toy off to find out what was wrong with it, so she hunted up a nail file, stuck the point of it into a seam and pried down.

The whole toy crumbled and fell to the floor in pieces. A square white thing bounced a couple of times when it landed on the carpet. *Hmmm,* she thought, *a wind-up toy with a battery. Boy am I not keeping up with the electronic world.*

She picked the battery up to examine it. It was a flash drive, not a battery.

The flash drive wouldn't open when she put it in the port on her computer. "Password" blinked on the screen.

Maria leaned against the back of her chair. It could be so many things.

She typed in "Donnie." "Password" blinked back at her.

Well, that was a dumb idea. The kid didn't make this flash drive. Who did?

It had to be Norman, or Awinita. She tried their names one at a time anyway. "Password" blinked back at her.

She tried Norman's first, middle and last names, then the same for Nita's. She tried Norman's date of birth didn't know Nita's date of birth, but made a mental note to get it. She didn't know Norman and Awinita's anniversary date either. There was really so little she did know about their lives.

Her computer screen clock said six twelve. She'd have to come back to this later.

The thought occurred to her that it could be because of the flash drive that Awinita, her mother, and possibly her brother were killed. ORCA had shown no mercy in the past, as evidenced by her father's family being murdered, so the drive could be exactly what they were looking for. She looked at the innocuous piece of plastic and saw a venomous snake.

What do you do with a snake? She gingerly pulled the flash drive out of the computer and thought about putting it in her sugar bowl. Instead she got a baggie from a kitchen drawer, gathered up all the broken pieces from the toy and put the pieces and the flash drive into the bag. Tomorrow she'd take it to her safe deposit box at the bank. She put it in her purse, finished dressing in a red sweater she'd forgotten she owned, the black slacks and a black leather jacket.

Michaela's Volvo pulled into the driveway just as Maria walked to the front door to flip on the porch light.

She waved through the window, picked up her purse, locked the door behind her and hurried out to ride with Michaela.

As she stepped off her porch she noticed a car parked across the street that she hadn't seen in her neighborhood before.

CHAPTER 27

Cars jammed the entire parking lot in front of the real estate office, so Michaela pulled down the street, turned around and parked at the curb two business doors down.

Giant Christmas ornaments dangled from the ceiling of the office foyer, glittering in the moody light Michaela had created out of lampshades and crepe paper.

Maria recognized Mannheim Steamroller's version of "Deck The Halls" as she made her way through the crowd toward the food tables. Stopping to hug each agent as she passed them, she was reminded of how bad her face looked. Some of them actually flinched.

"Maria. You forgot to duck!" James Breen said.

"Aww, honey, I bet that hurts," Bebe Bates said, blonde hair swirling.

Maria responded to banter with her own, and searched for faces of her clients.

She jumped when someone poked her ribs.

"Hiya, Cuz," Emily said.

Maria tried to walk away but Emily grabbed her arm.

"Are you still mad at me?" she asked.

"Yes I am," Maria answered while nodding to an agent from another office who had crashed the opposition's party. "Did you come all the way up here from Atlanta to ask me that?" She turned to face Emily. "I notice you aren't wearing paint." Her cousin was, in fact, dressed in spiked heels, fire engine red spandex slacks and low necked white Cashmere sweater that clung to her like tape.

"I'm really sorry. I didn't mean to embarrass you. Anyway, Mr. Chic Walker won't hold me against you. You don't have to worry about him." Emily beamed as if she actually had a brain. "I brought Frankie and his friend, Danny Duke, with me tonight,. But I also brought you a present. So you can't be mad at me any more." She batted her eyelashes.

"Where's Mr. Denning? I need to talk to him. I didn't know Mr. Duke was invited."

"They were just over that way, talking to that Bonnie woman. She's a bit of a bitch, if you ask me, Cuz." She tossed her head to indicate where she'd left the men.

"You got that right," Maria mumbled. She followed Emily's head toss and found the two men in conversation with Bonnie who was sitting at her desk. Emily trailed behind her.

"Mr. Denning," she said as she held out her hand. "It's so nice to see you this evening, I'm glad you're here."

"The road was clear all the way. Your office looks good tonight. I believe you haven't met Daniel Duke."

"No, I haven't. We've missed each other." She offered her hand to Duke, who gently shook it.

Denning continued, "We've been talking with Bonnie here. It looks like she's recovering well."

Bonnie looked up at Maria like a cat. "Hello, Maria, how are you after your mishap the other night? We're a pair, aren't we? Both injured in the line of duty." She looked from one man to the other.

Duke said, "I certainly hope there are no more mishaps for you women. We're glad to have the property sold at any rate."

Maria wondered if she'd just been verbally smacked. Emily grabbed Denning's arm and said, "Frankie, I think we should get a plate of that delicious looking fruit salad." They took off toward the food tables. All the men in the room turned to watch Emily sway by in her kiss-me-catch-me stilettos and amazing pants, black hair falling below her shoulder blades, big eyes missing nothing.

202

"She's really stunning, isn't she?" Daniel Duke said.

"Yes, sir, she always has been," Maria said.

Bonnie laughed too loudly, then stood. "Daniel, why don't I get you a plate? The caterer really is exceptional."

He nodded at her. Maria doubted she'd be inspired to get food for him if he couldn't bring himself to talk. But Bonnie waddled off toward the table.

Duke said, "I understand you were with Bonnie when she fell through the top of the mineshaft. You found the body in there." His beady gray eyes bored into Maria.

"Yes. Evidently there've been questionable things going on in that old mine long before you bought it. Did you know there was a mine there?"

"Of course not!" he retorted.

Aren't we touchy? Not exactly party conversation.

Clients of Maria who'd bought a house from her approached and she stood to talk with them. She noticed several more of her clients milling about with drinks in their hands.

Bonnie returned with two plates, set them down on the desk and filled the chair, looking like she was encamping for the evening.

Maria excused herself and began to mix.

Emily poked Maria in the ribs, making her jump again.

"Will you cut that out?" she said between smiling lips and gritted teeth.

"Oh, Cuz, don't you want to know what your present is?" Emily asked.

"Not really."

"I left it at your house."

"Okay, what is my present?"

"Roland."

"What—who is Roland?"

"He's your new bodyguard."

203

"Right." Maria hoped she was hearing wrong.

Emily turned to a man standing nearby and said, "You have the most beautiful smile I've ever seen." She stuck out her hand to shake his.

Maria said, "Who is he?"

Emily asked the man, "What is your name? I'm Emily Tandy, and this is my cousin, Maria Sebastian."

"James Brody," he responded, then he shook Emily's outstretched hand.

She leaned back toward Maria and said, "James Brody."

Maria smiled at James Brody. Emily turned and wiggled her way through the throng of people. James Brody stood looking expectantly at Maria.

Maria sighed inwardly. Typical of Emily to inject her into something and then walk away from it.

Andrea Falstaff, another office agent, who was standing nearby, turned to Maria and said "Oh, Maria, I heard about your accident—I love your sweater."

Maria said, "Thank you, Andrea, I'd like you to meet James Brody, James, this is Andrea Falstaff—she's an agent in our office." She smiled as they greeted each other, then made tracks.

Another hour into the party, Michaela said to Maria, "I've got to leave soon. Will that be okay with you? Or should I see if Bebe can take you home?"

"I would so love to leave. You know how good I am at schmoozing. And, I forgot to ask you earlier. What's the name of the repairman who fixes the office computers? I have a problem with my PC."

"Sure, I'll get it for you, just a sec." She strode over to her office area and looked through a Rolodex file. She wrote on a post-it note and returned to Maria. "Okay, I've got to tell Donovan I'm leaving, and pick up the extra boxes of decorations from the workroom. Here, take the car keys and bring the car up to the front for me.

Maria went back to her desk, tucked the PostIt note into her purse, said good night to Bonnie, who was still there, talking now to Mr. Denning and Emily.

"I hope you like my present," Emily said as she waved good bye.

Roland, Maria thought, has to be some kind of burglar alarm contraption. She left out the front door and walked down the street to pick up Michaela's Volvo.

As she passed the first business building next door to her office, she heard an engine roar, and moved closer to the cars parked along the curb, watching for headlights. When something crashed behind her, she jumped up on abutted bumpers of a SUV and Donovan's Cadillac, just as a black sedan tore her shoe off her foot as it screeched by.

Spread out on the hood of the Cadillac, her foot aching, she looked to see if it was still there. Her heart raced as she looked at the car speeding off into the night, down the opposite way from town and onto an unlighted access road. She rubbed her foot and looked back toward the SUV. The driver's side mirror swayed from hanging wires, dangling into the street.

CHAPTER 28

"Maria!" Michaela yelled as she ran from the office entrance. She raced toward Maria, who sat on the ground next to Michaela's car. Puffs of misty breath poured out of her mouth as she said, "Are you all right? I came out on the porch, but the car was still down here. Then I saw you on the curb. Oh my God! Should I call 9-1-1? What happened?"

"I'm okay. I just can't drive right now. My foot hurts. Some dumbass tried to hit me with his car. But he missed." She rubbed her foot.

"I heard a crash." Michaela said as she stooped down in the dark to peer into Maria's face.

"I think he hit something on that SUV. Do you know who owns it?" Maria said.

Michaela stood and cautiously looked around the street side of the vehicle. "No, but they must be at the party if they're parked here this late. The driver's rear view mirror is torn off and dangling by its wires. I'll take care of that. Is your foot okay? Do you want to go to the hospital? I'm calling 9-1-1 to report this." She took her cell phone from her purse and punched in the three numbers.

"I don't need a hospital, but probably my boot does. I can't believe the whole thing got torn off."

"You're lucky your foot didn't get torn off." Michaela clacked her phone shut. "One of the cops will be here in a couple minutes." She picked up the car keys lying on the ground next to Maria and opened the Volvo's back door, grabbing a sweater from the seat. She sat on the curb near her friend and wrapped the sore foot up with the sweater. "At least it's not bleeding."

"It's really okay," Maria said. "All the toes bend and my ankle works." She stretched her foot out, flexed it, moved it in an arc. "See?"

A police car with its lightbar lit up like a Christmas tree ran up the freeway off ramp a half-block away, siren whooping, and turned right toward the women.

"Good," Michaela said, "maybe we've got a cute young rookie." Maria saw her friend's teeth gleam in the police car's oncoming lights.

The cop ran his unit up onto the shoulder, saying something into his radio mic as he opened the door and stepped out. "Hi, ladies." He pulled a spiral notepad out of his shirt pocket and aimed the beam of his flashlight at first Michaela then Maria. "Are you hurt?"

"No," Maria said quickly. "I don't need a hospital—all that happened is my boot got jerked off my foot."

"You were really lucky." He squatted down to look at the ankle more closely. "You should go have it looked at anyway."

"I'll call my doctor tomorrow and have it checked. If it gets bad, I'll go have it x-rayed."

He stood up and scribbled on his notepad.

The box on his shoulder began to jabber in code and static as Maria told the officer what happened.

"We'll check out the SUV and go inside to find its owner," he said, then asked, " Did you see the driver or recognize the car that hit you? Could you tell what color it was or possibly see the license plate number, anything outstanding that would help identify the driver?"

"I didn't even see him coming. I heard the crash behind me when he hit the SUV and jumped as far as I could away from the road. I ended up on the bumper of the Volvo.

"That's when my shoe got torn off. I was busy looking at my foot instead of his license plate." She mentally kicked

208

herself. "My father always told me to stay alert and gather all the information I could when something like this happened. He was a cop."

Michaela walked back over to the office entrance where many of the partygoers spilled outside, and located the SUV's owner.

Cards, names, addresses were exchanged, insurance companies alerted, and Maria was told to pick up the report on Monday.

On the way home in the Volvo, Michaela said, "I like the young ones."

"You just like the uniforms. You don't even care who's in them," Maria said.

"Not true. Cute is cute. How about if you come home with me, since somebody has decided to eliminate you from the planet?"

"I'll see if it's too creepy at home. If it's not, I'd rather be there. But thanks, Mikey." Maria felt her eyes heat up with tears, which she made herself control. "You're a treasure to me."

"When do you get your Jeep back?"

"Probably not for about a month. I'll have to rent something on Monday. I sure hope my insurance company helps with that."

Michaela pulled into the driveway and Maria stepped out of the car onto frozen concrete. Michaela got out of the car, moved to her headlights where she hugged her friend. "I'll walk you in."

"Mikey, I think I can walk five feet to the door by myself," Maria said, and limped across the porch, stepped inside and waved to Michaela from the lighted open doorway, as her friend backed out of the drive.

She shut the door and turned around. A man was sitting in her rocking chair.

209

"Wait," he said as she threw her purse at him. "I explain." He held out an envelope to her. "I wait outside, but I get cold so I come in here."

She was out the front door and halfway to the mailbox.

"Honest," he said. "Just read note."

"You read it," she yelled as she stopped and turned toward him.

"Okay." He fidgeted with the envelope. "Dear Cuz?" he read laboriously. "This is your present I promised you. His name is Roland." He looked up and smiled, revealing a gold tooth. "He's your new bodyguard. Love, All Knowing."

Maria crept back toward the house, took the note from Roland and read it herself, relief flowing through her. Yet another vow to kill her cousin tucked itself inside her brain.

Roland stood six inches shorter than Maria and had black hair tied behind his head in a rope down his back.

He looked like a human fireplug.

"You want to see my gun?" he asked.

"Where did you come from?" she said.

"Guatemala, lady."

"Well, go back home."

"No, lady. I stay." He sat back down in the rocking chair and looked thoughtful. "I bring you car." He looked at his watch, then closed his eyes and looked asleep.

"Roland. You can't stay here."

Roland snored.

* * *

Maria had never locked her bedroom door before. With Roland in the living room, she not only locked it but jammed a chair under the doorknob as well. He was gone when she woke up Sunday morning. She checked the other bedroom and bath, and the closets. She looked in the backyard and the front of the

210

house, but no Roland. Feeling better than she thought she would, she took a shower, made some phone calls and had a Slimfast for breakfast.

She thought about making some cookies for Christmas, like she used to do back home in Phoenix before her trainwreck marriage. She looked in her cupboard for flour, found about one cup left in the bag. While looking for sugar she heard a couple of clunks and muffled yells come from the front of her house. She closed the cupboard door and snuck around the corner to the back door, adrenalin pumping on high alert.

"Maria," sounded from the front porch. It was Tommy's voice, so she went to the front window and looked outside.

Tommy was hugging her corner porch post. She opened the door. Then she saw Roland on the other side of Tommy with a roll of duct tape. Tom's hands were wrapped around the pole, hands on his opposite shoulders and silver tape wrapped four times all around his body. Tom's revolver was tucked into Roland's pants.

Tom was red faced and kicking toward Roland as the shorter man wrapped Tom's legs up with more tape, running around the post.

"Roland!" Maria yelled. "That's Tom, my friend." She ran over to Tom. "Are you hurt?" She felt his arm and shoulder, looked at his legs and feet.

"You son of a bitch!" Tom yelled. "You're gonna be so dead, your mother is gonna be dead, and I'll tear off your arms and feed them to alligators." He glared at Roland.

Roland tore the tape roll strip in two as he finished up and patted Tom's leg.

"Who is this pint sized moron? Get him off me so I can kill him," Tom continued.

"You look like a mummy," Maria said. She giggled at first, then struck at how completely immobile Tom was, no matter

211

how much he squirmed, said, "I need some of that stuff, In case I have a burglar."

"I repeat," Tom yelled, "who is this idiot?"

"Shhh, it's okay. That's Roland. He's my bodyguard."

She looked at Roland, who stood back, admiring his work. "You've got to let him go. He's a good guy."

Behind Roland, parked in the driveway was a brand new fire engine red SUV, a Ford Escape. She looked at the road in front of her house. A flat gray primer color 1953 Chevrolet squatted, its undercarriage below curb level.

Roland's head hung like a chastised child

"Whose car is that?" She looked at Tom.

"Would I drive a piece of crap like that? Get me down from here before somebody sees me."

Maria looked at Roland

"Lady, that your new car," he said as he gave a jerk on the duct tape encircling Tom's legs.

To Tom, she said, "We're going to get you unstuck, but no fair going after Roland. He doesn't know you."

"Is he going to tape up everybody who gets near your house?"

"No, he's going to be gone right away. I'm just humoring him. My cousin was worried about me I guess. She hired him."

"Emily?"

"Yep."

"Figures." Tom tore off the last of the tape from his pants leg. "My watch commander just called me about your incident last night, so I came over here to see how you're doing. He said you weren't hit, but I was worried." He stomped his foot on the porch. His jeans that had been crunched against his legs righted themselves and slid down over the tops of his running shoes. "You be sure to stop over to talk with Erica. I had to tell her

212

about last night. She's really upset. Any idea who tried to hit you?"

"No." She shook her head. I jumped out of the way, but my foot was banged."

He looked her facial bruises from the first accident over carefully. Then looked at her with a question in his eyes when he saw her foot wrapped in an Ace bandage.

"The foot is fine, just sore. I haven't put makeup on yet today, so my face probably looks pretty bad."

"I can put a patrol on you. I'm thinking maybe the first accident wasn't an accident."

"I already have Roland." She looked around for him, but he was nowhere in sight. "Why do you think the first time wasn't an accident? Nobody knew I was going to be at that intersection exactly at that time." She looked for Roland's car, but it was gone too. "Did you hear Roland's car leave?"

"Hmm. No. The sneaky little bastard." Tom looked over his shoulder at the red SUV in the driveway. "Where'd that come from?"

"I don't know. More of Emily's doings I suppose. Roland said he brought it for me, whatever that means."

"Well, Roland is more of a clown than a bodyguard, so I'll get a patrol officer assigned to you."

She didn't think this was the time to bring up the gun Roland said he carried. "Look, I can't have a trail of people following me around. I'm trying to work."

"No. You stay at home today. I'm thinking that fellow you found in the mine is tied to what's happening to you. Somebody doesn't want you to finger them. It could be about the guy in the mine, or that woman in Arizona. Now it could be the woman in Oklahoma. And where is Mason in this? It's pretty coincidental that he just happened to find a dead woman who was related to the Phoenix woman."

213

"I've been thinking the same thing since last Thursday. Last night I dreamed about the guy driving the car that tried to hit me. The driver was Jaime Navarro in the dream."

"Who is he?"

"He's the missing son of Wanda Navarro, the woman who Mason found in the woods in Oklahoma. She's also the mother of Awinita Arrowkeeper Sebastian, the dead wife of my ex."

"So this Jaime is the Arrowkeeper woman's brother?"

"Yes." Maria felt something in her mind pull a string. "Jaime Navarro has been missing for ten years."

"He's a Native American?" Tom asked.

"Cherokee."

"Like the dead guy in the mine?"

CHAPTER 29

"Whoa. I didn't see that coming." She stared at Tom while her brain reran all the events since her encounter in the mine.

"You need to lay low. Now go back inside and stay there until I call you," Tom was saying .

"Right," she said as Tom went back across the street to his car and started it up.

As soon as he was around the corner, she quickly put on her makeup, grabbed the stuff she'd removed from the back of the Jeep and put it in the back of the new red Ford.

The leather interior smelled like a new car she'd sat in once. There were no empty plastic water bottles or paper coffee cups in the cup holders, no foxtails or hitchhiker pods on the floor mats. No red Georgia clay stared at her from the floorboards when she put her purse and notebook behind the front passenger seat. She never imagined having a vehicle that screamed, "Look at me!" She felt ostentatious driving it.

After stopping across the street to reassure Erica that she was in decent health, she got back in the new SUV and set out to take care of business.

She knew she was missing something to do with the mineshaft. There were too many unanswered questions. Now that Tom had more or less pointed out the remnants of the body could be Jaime Navarro, it followed the medicine pouch her father had put in her jacket could link Jaime's American Indian heritage to something in that mineshaft. She would have to go to that mineshaft and do a complete search, perhaps map the whole mine out, which should have been done years ago. If there had ever been a schematic, the paperwork was lost because it hadn't been attached to the property deed.

The thought of wandering around in the dark under the earth made her a little queasy. She'd overcome her fear of the dark when she was four years and needed to use the bathroom in the middle of the night. She'd considered lying there, just peeing in the bed but couldn't have faced the humiliation in the morning. She asked her father to shoot his gun under her bed once. He told her that was ridiculous and to go to sleep.

A mineshaft didn't have any beds in it, she reasoned. You can see everything in a mineshaft if you have enough light.

Enough light was the real issue. The limelight her father gave her would solve the problem.

She drove to Gwinnett County to pick up a plat from the courthouse on a commercial site a client wanted her to consider listing for him. He'd bought the lot when prices were beginning to skyrocket and hoped its value had doubled since that time.

After doing a search and making a copy of the plat and recorded deed, she headed back to the freeway, but remembered an Outdoor World was only a few miles away. She turned in the opposite direction from home and drove to the huge warehouse building, parked in the lot that seemed to be about two acres in size, and locked the fancy SUV with a click of the automatic remote. Everybody in the parking lot stared at the red vehicle. She felt like Emily wearing gold lame. Or Emily wearing anything.

She made her way to the back of the store, found the hands-free light area, and noted the great variety of head lights, chest worn lights, cap bill lights and free standing lights. The one that got her attention was a fifteen million candlepower spotlight. With her limelight and the big Brinkman flashlight Mason had given her, she could light up a whole warehouse. She bought the spotlight then cruised over to the rifle and gun section. After looking through the arms, knowing she'd have to learn how to shoot it before she could feel comfortable with it, she moved over to the pepper spray area and purchased a canister. Next she stopped at the bug spray area and picked up a variety of long-distance wasp killers. She tossed all of her supplies into a shopping basket and went to checkout.

She stepped outside of the store and noticed a commotion in the general area of where she'd parked the SUV. She hoped nobody had scratched it because she wasn't even sure who owned the thing, and hadn't remembered to find out about insurance either. Her heart sank when she saw the color red in the center of the men and vehicles gathered in a clump.

When she finally reached the yelling crowd, she saw three men handcuffed to parking lot light posts, all jerking their arms and yelling obscenities. Two other men stood out from the group and talked on cell phones. Just then a Gwinnett County Patrol car pulled up. A deputy jumped out of the driver seat, walked over to the handcuffed trio and spoke softly to them. They stopped yelling but all talked at the same time. Maria heard, "Sonofabitch left me here and got in my car and moved it over there"—he pointed with both trapped hands toward his car. "I thought he was going to steal it, so I swung at him. Faster than I could see him do it, he had me over here fastened to this effing pole."

The next guy said, "Yeah, I saw the little shit trussing this dude up and pulled in next to the red SUV to scare him off. But he practically tore my door off, grabbed me and tied me to the same post." He moved my car over there—that green Toyota.

The third man said, "I came across the parking lot and yelled at the man. He pulled a gun on me and then tied me to the post too."

Maria quietly got into the SUV and pulled away as the officer opened a pocket knife and cut the men free of the nylon ties that had been used to fasten the men to the light pole. She looked around for a 1953 primer-color Chevrolet, but it was nowhere to be found.

The uneventful trip home made Maria glad to be driving such a beautiful vehicle. She forgot about all her problems and daydreamed about driving across country to visit her cousins some day. They really weren't as crazy as she had once thought. Since she'd moved to Georgia, she'd found that all families have crazy people in them.

At home again, she emptied the car, taking her purchases into the kitchen and out of their various boxes and hermetically sealed plastic cocoons.

Roland appeared at her left shoulder and she dropped a can of bug spray on the floor.

"Cut that out!" she yelled at him.

"Si, lady. What I do?" He backed over to the sink.

"You give me a heart attack when you materialize out of nowhere."

While he was in front of her, she said, "Does the SUV have insurance on it?"

"Si."

She walked to the trashcan on the back porch and dumped all the packaging inside, then returned to the kitchen counter. "Is the SUV a rental?"

"Yo no se."

"You don't know?"

"Si."

Maria scratched her head. "I don't suppose you followed me when I went out today."

"Yo no se."

"Never mind. I don't want to know either."

"Si."

"I am planning to go out for a while, and I won't need you to go with me. So you can stay here. Then tomorrow, I think you can go back to Emily or wherever you came from, because Tom said he's going to have a patrol officer watch my house. Okay?"

"Si"

"Fine." She took all of the lights and bug and pepper spray out to the SUV, then found the plat of the Consortium property, her 100 foot tape measure and grabbed her purse. As soon as she started up the SUV her good fairy started nagging her. "Have you lost your mind?" it said. "Every time you get on that property some disaster happens. Even though you've tried to cover yourself with all the equipment in the backseat, you are asking for trouble. Something is going on out there and you're going to be right in the middle of it."

"But I have to see the property. I don't have any money coming in and I'm low on listings. The only way I can make money is to sell, not list right now. I don't have any choice. It's my best bet."

"Yeah," said her bad fairy. "You know what you're doing and you can take care of yourself. You'll sell that property if you know every inch of it. Go show them you're in charge."

She started up the Ford, backed out of the driveway and waited to see what Roland would do.

"How many times have you been hurt lately?" asked her good fairy.

"I don't want to think about that," she answered,

"Emily gave you Roland to guard against trouble. Why not ask him for help? He's going to follow you anyway," the good fairy said.

"Oh, phooey," its counterpart answered. Roland is as big a bozo as Emily."

The good fairy got right next to Maria's ear and whispered, "Roland stopped Tom, which nobody else has been able to do. And, his car would never be noticed in the bare woods."

219

Maria waited for Roland to run hippity hop out to his car before he noticed she'd stopped at the stop sign at the end of her block. She got out of the SUV and walked up to his driver window. "How about we go in your car. It's not as conspicuous as this red thing you got for me."

He stared at her for thirty seconds. "Si." He swung the door open while she parked the SUV, then transferred her equipment to his backseat.

Forty minutes later, Maria found the marker that indicated the turnoff through the woods to the mineshaft and made sure it was marked appropriately on her plat. Roland pulled in off the road and proceeded down the ancient dirt path.

At the end of the drivable road sat a black Lexus that had a cracked right windshield and huge gouge that ran down the passenger side along the top of the windows. Roland was already backing out the way they'd come as a reenactment of being sideswiped played through her mind, and her heart pounded.. Two miles further down the pavement, they looked for another entrance to the landlot where her listed property lay. When she saw an old logging road run into a pine thicket that was overgrown by giant wild azalea bushes, she motioned for Roland to stop while she stepped out of the car and into the woods a few yards. She knew the bush branches would not hurt the car, and the ground was high and firm, so she motioned him to ease the car into the woods beyond the shrubs. She called Tom's cellphone and left a message for him that she'd found the car that had tried to run her over. She trudged through the woods wearing the backpack with her equipment, intent on at least getting the license plate number off the Lexus, which she'd forgotten to notice when they'd first driven up to the car. Maria couldn't see through Roland's jacket whatever arsenal he doubtless carried with him.

CHAPTER 30

Oak, hickory, and sweetgum branches danced lightly overhead, pretending they were dressed. The musty smell of moss and lichen mixed with damp frosty air. Nothing was happening among the fauna and brambles. From a hundred yards north of the Lexus and behind a giant red oak tree, she peered at the license number of the car through small binoculars. Binoculars, a roll of fluorescent tape, hammer, screwdriver, pliers, and compass were part of the land walking bag she kept in her Jeep. She could just make out the license number which she scribbled on a PostIt note pad she carried in her pocket. Whoever left the Lexus there wasn't doing any shooting, so probably was in the mineshaft. She felt the woods' silence. Then noticed Roland had vanished.

Right when I need you the most.

Full of adrenalin gushing through her veins, Maria was in her element. If it turned out she was half Apache, she'd finally understand why a deep forest was total comfort to her. Damp leaves lent new meaning to sneaking around back as she made a wide girth from the mine opening. Circling low to her right, through a bunch of rhododendrons camped on the edge of bottomland, she climbed back up the outside of the shaft to the now infamous air vent where Bonnie had disappeared. Breathlessly, she listened.

Voices echoed through the woods, maybe 200 yards south of her. She squatted abruptly, wondering why people would be near the shooting range yet not shooting.

Knowing the Lexus was up the hill behind her, she felt uncomfortable. She couldn't make out what the people were saying but the swell of the hill between them kept her from being seen as long as she stayed low. A body loomed suddenly to her right. She dropped to the ground and kicked out before she noticed it was Roland.

"Ow, lady. But, silencio," he rasped out., then whispered, "That was not nice, lady."

"Roland, I swear, I'm gonna kick your ass," she whispered back.

"No, no. I have a big gun. You cannot do that." He reached down and rubbed the knee she'd kicked.

She sat up, rubbed mud and leaves off her jeans, and said, "What...."

"Shhhh," he reminded her. "There is men over that hill," he said.

"No shit." She stood up.

"What you doing? I think this not so good. Who is those mans?"

She went back to the air vent, listened, but heard nothing. She started slowly along the top of the mineshaft, back toward the entrance As she stepped carefully up the the rise, she saw two men over the hill. She flopped back down on the ground, and turned toward where Roland had been. He was gone.

She slithered further into the mulch pile then peeked beyond the rim of her hillock. The voices were louder now they were out in the open. Two men were headed back in the direction of the Lexus.

The guy on the left looked familiar from the back, but she was sure she didn't know the other one. Then she felt silly hiding like a ground hog. If she hadn't seen the Lexus, she'd think they were probably just curious. After all, if the one man was Daniel Duke, as she suspected, he had every right to be out there on land that he co-owned, stomping around, checking for gold, whatever. Was the other guy with the Lexus one of the other owners? She couldn't just stand up and wave at them, say,

"Hi, I was just out looking around, thought I'd drop by and see if there was any gold left in your mine." Not after she'd nearly been killed by that car.

Yeah, but how could Mr. Duke walk right past the mine to go to the range, without noticing it?

She watched them walk out of sight and hearing range, then dug herself out, adjusted the pack she'd brought, and made her way off the roof of the mine shaft around to the main entrance. She stayed back far enough to not be seen, then heard their car start up

She walked back to the mine entrance, disgusted with herself. Before starting inside, she looked around for Roland, but didn't see him. Now she wondered where he'd gone.

"Roland!" she called out not very loudly.

"Si."

She had no idea where his voice was coming from, and didn't want to spend time looking for him. Moving into the blackened mine shaft, she took off her backpack to don her lights. The spotlight draped around her neck on a strap to be chest high. She turned it on and nearly fell backward in the burst of 15 million candle light power. The now superfluous hat with light, she put on her head anyway, stashed the flashlight in the pack, the pack on her back and left the limelight in her pocket.

The "Raiders of the Lost Ark" video game came to mind as she moved along the corridor, getting a good look at the source of the gold trinkets in her jewelry box at home.

Tools were slung on the ground as if all the miners had suddenly thrown them down and vanished. She wondered about that. When she came to the place where the bones had been found, she eyed it, but everything involved had been removed except some old crime scene tape remnants and some spray paint outlining what had been found. Footprints in the silt dust were everywhere.

She followed some cart tracks, thinking they'd go to the last place gold had been found, at the maximum length of the shaft. Funny. Where was the cart she'd seen? Maybe the law had removed it.

And that led to wondering whether, during the mine's heyday there had been burros pulling the carts. She made a mental note to look for dung. The notorious air vent the size of Bonnie's butt was on her left, where a shaft of daylight crept in from above.

About two hundred feet inside, a branch of the shaft peeled off to the south.

She shined her lights down that tunnel, which looked cleaner than the main route she was on. The cobwebs seemed less dense, the ground less obstructed with loose rock. She took some neon pink surveyor tape from her pack and lay a strip of it at the corner where she turned, and placed a rock on it. She followed that tunnel another 150 feet until it turned deeper into the hillside. Opposite the turn, yet another tunnel went off to the left. This one had light at the end of it, only about 50 feet away. She headed toward the light, following a new set of cart tracks, even though the tunnel narrowed considerably. She came to a sheet of plywood that appeared to have been placed over the opening, but wasn't large enough to cover the entire hole. She forced it open by shoving her body weight against one edge to make it slide sideways. A huge slab of steel fit directly behind the wood. When she stepped around it, she realized the steel was actually a target covering another entrance to the mineshaft. She was on the shooting range. And ever so grateful nobody was firing just then.

After taking time to sketch the tunnel route onto her notepad, she turned around and went back to the corner where she'd left her surveyor tape, and turned into the new part of the tunnel she hadn't yet explored. Here she saw evidence of earth crumbling around the huge posts placed there to hold it back. Footprints through the loose dirt made it look like a lot of activity had recently taken place there. Further on, the massive posts were shored up with copious greenwood six by sixes put there to reinforce the original work. She wondered just how old this mine was. If it was dug any time around 1829, then the wood wouldn't have been stamped as pressure treated pine.

Maria noticed that miners had made attempts at coziness by carving niches every so often in the earthen walls where small articles, oil lamps, maybe lunch boxes could be placed. There were occasional seats jutting out from the consistent walls. Made sense to have a place to sit after hacking at earth for hours on end. She turned around to sit on one of them, seeking ambience. As she turned around, Roland's form lit up like a deer caught in headlights.

"Yerp!" she yelled as she fell sideways and her light extinguished. With an onset of panic, she fumbled to find the switch and turn it back on. Despite the icy temperature of the cave environment, sweat formed on her forehead.

Roland stood in the same position as before lights out.

"What you doing in here, lady?"

"Why don't you go haunt somebody else?" she asked, her heart rate lowering from its spike. "For your information, somebody needs to know just how deep and wide this mine is. The buyers really don't know what they're getting into. I don't want to be in here all night, so please be quiet so I can finish what I'm doing." She stood and began down the opening maw.

She heard a sigh and a "si."

After another one hundred fifty twisting tunnel feet, a man-made wall stopped progress. "This is interesting. Maybe they put this up because something dangerous happened on the other side." She pushed on the substantial barrier. Then she noticed the quantity of footprints she'd been following seemed to proceed as if that wall was not there. Partial back halves of prints were cut off from the toes.

"I think this wall must open," she said as she looked over at Roland.

He took a push at the wall as well. Then the two of them began pushing, touching the edges and sections of the potential doorway.

"I guess not." She gave the wall a final shove and turned around.

Roland slumped against it. "I can..." he began, but the wall rotated in on a central pivot reminding Maria of a resort hotel's revolving entrance door.

"Ha!" Maria exclaimed, and gave Roland a pat on the shoulder.

The two of them continued down the connecting corridor that remained seven feet high and ten feet wide with the same earthen walls.

Fifty feet further they entered a chamber of about twenty feet square and twelve feet high, but this area was stacked full of crates and boxes of various sizes.

Maria tried to open one of them. "Can you tell what's inside these?"

"I cannot read the language on the outside."

She took note of letters stamped on the crates she'd never seen before. "I can't either."

CHAPTER 31

Maria backed toward the opposite wall of the cavern room, looking up at all the stacked crates, some of which bore the colorful picture of a bird's head.

She took another step and felt a poke in her back. She turned around, throwing light on the object. "Here's the long lost cart. It must be how they got the stuff back this far."

"You know what's in the boxes?" Roland asked.

"Something heavy," she answered as she tried to lift a small one.

"Is rifles. The small ones is bullets. Always they are stored this way."

"All of these?"

"Si."

The only reason she could think of for having such an arsenal was total anarchy. Mason was probably right about her apparently stumbling into the midst of an ORCA cell. For her ex-husband to be involved was so far fetched she couldn't get her mind around it, though. "That's an awful lot of rifles." She turned back to the area beyond her sight that held the rest of the cart, and wiggled through between the wall of clay and the cold steel.

"Holy cow. This room is twice as big as that one." The walkway was just that, for stacked on both sides of the cart path were more box crates approximately twenty feet high, stretching about forty feet to the next passageway. She paced over to the next opening quickly, peeked into yet another room of the same size, Roland right behind her.

Roland released a long wolf whistle. "Lady, this is enough guns for a whole war."

Maria realized her mouth was hanging open.

"Yes. I believe it is." She ran her hand over the face of a nailed down box. "I don't think we can open one of these. We need to tell the authorities about this. I think we better get out of here before one of those guys comes back."

She took the new Wal-Mart disposable phone out of her pocket before she remembered it wouldn't work underground.

When she looked back up again, Roland was gone and someone much taller stood where he'd been five seconds ago, a silhouette against the huge white wall. She reached for the huge Brinkman light she'd slipped into a strap on her hiking pants. As she turned into him, light flooded his face.

"Mason? What are you doing in here? You scared me."

"Hey, do you think you've got enough wattage on that thing?" He'd threw his hands against his forehead and backed up two steps. He looked past Maria's right shoulder. "Hey, bud."

Maria turned to see what that was about. Roland stood within an arms length of her.

"Hola, Señor."

She dropped the flashlight back into its strap and directed the chest light on the floor. "Is somebody going to enlighten me about this cozy gathering?"

"I followed you, Sweetie Pie," Mason said as he walked past her to the wall. He had a big duffle bag strapped to his shoulder. " Very clever using Roland's car."

Roland turned around, stepped to the wall and felt the left side of it, where he'd slouched earlier when it had opened. After rearranging his body against it, the left side of the wall began moving backward while the right side moved forward.

"Well, what do you think of that?" Mason said.

He reached over, grabbed Maria's hand and pulled her into an embrace, gingerly avoiding her chest light and his duffle bag.

"Oh boy," Roland said.

After nuzzling her hair, Mason stepped through the opening. "Do you know where the trigger is on the inside?"

"No, amigo. Not yet."

"Shine that light back up here. Let's see what's at the end of the tunnel."

At the end of the third room, Mason banged around in the duffle bag and pulled out a short crowbar. He pried the lid off the closest crate that had the look of a small coffin. Inside she could see shredded newspapers filling into the corners of the box.

Mason dug down with his right hand, then pulled it out and peeled back a thick layer of the shredded newspapers.

"AK-47, the insurgent's choice this year to overthrow governments. How did I know that's what we'd find?" he said. He stuffed the rifle back into its nest and carefully repacked the stuffing around it. Then he replaced the crate top, pulled a ball-peen hammer out of his bag and tapped the nails back into place. He picked up some loose stuffing from the floor and stuffed it into the right pocket of his jacket. "What do you want to bet this newsprint is all in Chinese?"

"I'll take that bet," Maria said. "It's gotta be Russian or Polish." She shined the light up higher onto crates closer to the cave ceiling. "See that print on that crate?"

"Ha! You mean the one with the bird face on it?" Mason asked as he craned his neck upward. "Ohhh, I see," he said immediately. "Definitely not Chinese. Not perpendicular enough." He followed that with, "Okay. Roland, my man, if you'll stand guard at the entrance and whistle if you see anybody coming, I'll proceed with my task here. Maria, I'll need your light to lay these things out." He slung the duffle bag to the ground and extracted some square boxes and long tubes. Together with tools he stuffed into his various pockets, he used a crate to climb into a darker alcove in the cave wall.

"What are you doing, if you don't mind me asking," Maria said.

"Hand me that screwdriver," he said. "This one is too small. I'm installing battery-powered video cameras with motion sensors up here in this hole. We're gonna watch these guys break the law."

"How did you know all these weapons were in this mine?"

"We didn't. But I knew there was some kind of link because you keep having all these accidents. And the only dead person tied to you was the guy in the red coat you found here. Of course, that was before Norman's wife and mother-in-law got killed." He checked the batteries with a charger, tucked the whole thing back into the bracket he'd installed, and climbed down off the crates.

"Do you think the dead person was Jaime Navarro? She held him in her light beam.

"Probably. If we can find some DNA that we know is from Jaime, forensics will be able to make a definite ID. They can likely use his mother's DNA for a partial analysis too. Now come along, my little acolyte, we've got work to do."

"How many of those are you going to install?" she asked.

"Six more, I think. I only have six more with me, three for in here and three for the second entrance." He winked at her and picked up his duffle bag.

"How did you just happen to bring video cameras with you, not knowing what was in the mine?"

"We knew ORCA had a cache of weapons some place. There's more I can't tell you, but I think this mine is a temporary holding facility."

"Are you going to take all the weapons out of it? It's under contract to sell. Your bad guys are going to have to move the weapons before it closes. Otherwise the buyer will find them."

"Nope. We're going to let them do that for us. The cameras will not only tell us who they are, but when they start moving weapons, we'll tag along, incognito, so to speak."

"You guys are pretty sneaky."

"Yep."

"How do you know Roland, anyway?"

"Emily told me he was with you. I saw his car parked in front of your house. I spoke with him. After he checked my credentials, he agreed to cooperate and tagged your car for me. But the cell phone you bought at Wal-Mart has a GPS in it. My people traced you."

"Who are your people?"

"My people are your people," he said on the way up another set of crates.

"US Government?"

"Yep."

They made their way back to the trick door and pushed it closed. As an afterthought, Maria looked at the footsteps in the dust, but couldn't tell theirs from the ones already on the ground. At least she could understand now why the sheriff's deputies didn't search further into the mineshaft when they'd come to investigate the body being found. Because the second entrance had not been used for years, the whole place appeared to be abandoned and rickety. What were the chances a primary entrance to a cache of firearms would lay at the other end of the tunnel?

Mason, Roland and Maria went back to their automobiles in separate directions. On her half-mile walk through the woods, Maria wondered where her father was and what he was doing. She wanted to call and tell him the ORCA cell, at least in Georgia, was about to be annihilated. What would he say if he could see the massive supply of guns and ammunition accumulated underground in a tiny county in North Georgia?

Now he couldn't even call her because her phone number had changed. When this ORCA issue was settled, she'd call relatives and leave her phone number with all of them. At least then her dad could find her.

She drove straight to the office, pulled the contract on the property she'd just left, and found the name and phone number of the real estate agent who'd brought the buyer. She called the number she found for Donna James of Adamson Realty. After three tries, hearing the same recording, "The number you have called is no longer in service and there is no forwarding number at this time," she gave up and looked for another number in her address book. But the only information she'd had was in that BlackBerry, probably talking to frogs.

She Googled "Adamson Realty." No listing. She pulled her hard copy of the Atlanta Yellow Pages from the bottom file drawer. No listing for Adamson Realty. She Googled Donna James. No listing. She called the Atlanta Board of Realtors. No listing for either of them. She looked up the Atlanta Board of Realtors on line to find the Adamson license numbers. No listings. She leaned back in her chair and wondered if she was losing her mind. The only thing else she could think to do was to call Bonnie.

CHAPTER 32

Maria called Bonnie's house and left a message on her answering machine, then called her pager. She didn't understand how Bonnie functioned in real estate with no voice mail on her cell phone. But then, she realized, life continued without the latest and greatest electronic equipment. After all, she'd found her old devices worked just fine after the loss of her BlackBerry. She'd been having fun using her antique financial calculator, remembering what a time saver it had been when she first starting using it.

It was a nostalgic stroll through her past. She liked calculating mortgage payments, interest rates and attrition percentages. Intrigued with re-familiarizing how to work the thing, she noticed a half hour had sped by when her phone rang.

Bonnie said, "Maria, this is me. Your number is in my pager."

"Hi Bonnie. I want to know if you called Donna James at Adamson Realty. The phone number on the contract isn't right."

"Nope. That was your baby. I haven't talked with the woman."

"Before our deal, had you ever heard of the company or agent? I can't find a listing through the board of realtors either."

"Do you mean the contract on the consortium property is a fake?"

"I mean I don't have an accurate phone number for either the agent or the company. I called to see if you'd heard any other name either of them could be listed under."

"Is it a chain agency?"

"Not as far as I know, but that gives me an idea. I could try the national company's headquarters and see if they have

233

listings under Adamson. Maybe Donna James recently changed her name or is a brand new agent from another state."

"Fine, Maria," Bonnie's voice dripped with sarcasm. "You brought in a contract from a company nobody ever heard of? Did you bother to check the fax number? It was faxed to the office, right?"

"Good idea. I'll see what I can find from the fax number." She clenched her teeth, then spat out, "I'll let you know what I find."

"Yeah, you do that." The receiver slammed down on the other end.

Maria sat staring at her cell phone, feeling her cheeks flame with embarrassment and alarm. She looked through the file once more and found the fax number. Still chagrined, she dialed it. The fax on the other end didn't pick up.

Maria wrote a note and cover sheet, and called the agent's office to let her know a fax would be on its way. A recording told her the number had been disconnected.

Since she really had nothing to tell Bonnie and didn't care to be humiliated further, she avoided calling her.

Fifteen minutes later, while Maria was doing a computer search for small residences, her cell phone rang.

"This is Daniel Duke. I understand you've lost the numbers to the buyer's agent on our property."

"They're not lost, Mr. Duke, they've been changed. Rest assured I'll get to the bottom of it."

And I'll kill Bonnie as soon as possible.

"Well, this is the icing on the cake. You find those numbers and straighten this out. If it's not right by tomorrow, I'm going to sue. Then I'm going to relist the property with Blakestone Realty."

"Look, it's just an oversight on the part of the purchaser's agent. I'll get it straightened out." Maria prayed that was true.

"I'll let you know right away when it's settled. The agent will call during her routine due diligence. Please don't worry. I understand your concern, but this is a minor setback."

"Bonnie told me I should sign with her and I should have listened. I expect to hear from you immediately."

He hung up on her.

Maria dropped her head onto her desk. How did this happen? Could she have prevented this?

Her head pounded with unanswered questions.

* * *

Maria returned home, planning to swallow a bunch of aspirin. She found Mason there, hanging equipment on her house.

"What are you doing?" she said as he ran across her porch roof. His maroon sweatshirt clashed with the adobe-colored shingles.

"Connecting to the satellite so I can get reception from the cameras in the mineshaft. I'm not sure I can receive images from the cell towers to my PDA. I don't have reception at the houseboat, so I volunteered your house. I hope you don't mind." He swung from the roof to the roof's post and slid down to the deck.

"After I grab some aspirin for my headache, I'll pour us some wine. This is Christmas Eve, after all."

He stood up after landing softly on his feet. "Your friend left you a present."

She didn't want any more presents. "What friend?"

"Roland." He gestured her attention to the end of the porch where a huge Christmas tree lay.

"Hmm. I guess he didn't care much for my tree."

He took the key from her hand and opened the door for her. After he followed her into the house, he looked at the three-foot tall tree haphazardly strewn with ornaments and tinsel.

"I'm thinking it was a good idea." He grinned.

"The only good idea is to get rid of the battering ram running into my skull from the inside."

"Okay, go drug yourself. I'll pour wine. We'll make popcorn and string it for your new tree." He stepped back out onto the porch, lifted the tree upright and brought it into the house. Its top bent over against the ceiling. Its sides dusted three pieces of furniture even though Mason placed it as close as possible to the emptiest corner of the room. He went out to his car and retrieved a hacksaw and an old towel from the trunk.

Maria called to him from the porch, "Where is Roland, anyway?"

"I told him I'd babysit you for awhile so he could go home for Christmas eve."

He came back into the house and cut two feet off the lower part of the tree with the hacksaw. "It's still too big for the room, but what the heck." He set it down on the old towel, leaned it back into the corner and said, "Voila! Your Christmas tree, Madam," and swooped into a bow.

Maria swallowed two aspirin. "Christmas Eve and I haven't got a thing to eat in the house."

"Oh, yes you do," he said as he took a package of Orville Redenbacher popcorn out of a box and stuck it into the microwave. "I suppose Jesus won't care if we have breakfast instead of dinner on his birthday." The popcorn began doing its thing.

Maria opened the refrigerator and there was a ham, a dozen eggs and a bottle of buttermilk. "Hey," she said, "the food fairies have been here."

While Mason fiddled with his PDA to the tune of popping corn, Maria sat down and put a wet washcloth over her eyes.

"How will cameras broadcast in the mineshaft if cell phones won't?"

"I put a battery-powered repeater at the entrance to toss the signal to the nearest tower. When somebody enters the cave, the cameras will start recording and I'll get a phone call on my PDA. If I miss the original call, the PDA will record it and save it like a message for me. It'll come through as a video on my screen."

She pulled the washcloth off her face and looked at him. "I didn't know you could do that."

"Technically, you can't. I mean only Star Wars technology allows it. I know a guy."

"Yeah. You know a guy." She plopped the washcloth over her eyes once more and leaned back into the chair. "What if the bad guys see the transceiver or the battery before they go into the mine?"

"With all that rubble outside, I don't think they'll notice it. The unit is less in size than a matchbox. The battery is half that size. It's up on an overhead post beam, out of sight."

Maria mentally calculated the miles from her house to the mine.

"While we're eating our ham and egg breakfast, what if the bad guys go into the mine? How are you going get thirty miles north before they finish and leave?"

"They're move all those rifles soon. I expect it to take them quite a while. Too many people are finding out things about that mine. And you've got it sold, so they'll have to do something soon," he repeated.

She took the washcloth off her eyes and looked his way.

"Feeling better already?" he asked.

"A little. But that's the thing I want to tell you. I can't find the agent or her company that sent us the contract. I don't know if it's sold or not."

"Didn't they give you earnest money?"

"Nope. They agreed to deposit earnest money when the loan was approved."

"Your seller agreed to that?"

"Sellers, plural. I tried to talk them out of it, but they said earnest money doesn't mean anything anyway, so they took the deal."

"Who's the lender?" he asked.

"Don't know. They didn't have one as of the time of contract. Their agent was supposed to contact me when they made application for the loan and give me all the data. All the phone numbers and fax numbers were dead as of this afternoon. The Board of Realtors has no listing for them."

"What do you do in a case like this?"

"You pray there has been an error instead of fraud, and hope the agent calls soon."

"But what if she doesn't?"

Yeah, what if she doesn't?

CHAPTER 33

"Hey," Mason said after their dinner. "How's the headache?"

"It must be gone, since I haven't even thought about it for a while. I feel so good, you'd think I would have noticed." Maria stood up and turned around, searching inside her head for some remnant of pain.

"Good, because I have plans for you and me now." His eyes danced across her. Warmth charged down her legs and arms as he reached for her. He lifted her onto the kitchen counter. Now she was lip level with him standing between her knees, kissing her eyelids, her forehead, her neck. She melted against him. Her shirt came off, the light went out. A stray thought surfaced in her head. Something she was supposed to tell Mason, but it drowned in the river of heat flowing between them.

The cold hard countertop somehow became mattress, as she submerged into rolling waves of security and adoration.

"My skin wants you painted on me," he said and pressed her to him.

She could stay there forever, nestled under him, his weight a cocoon for her soul. "I'm having an out-of-body experience," she said, "so how about if I just borrow your body." She explored his neck with her lips.

"Good idea, take any part you want," he answered.

* * *

She read 4:30 a.m. on the clock face. Maria tunneled out of the pile of quilts and found Mason snuggled up against her back, breathing softly. She thought about going back to sleep and didn't know why she was awake at that hour. Cold air licked her head and shoulders. She heard a very faint beep she didn't

239

recognize as one of her appliances. Incredibly thirsty all of a sudden, she gently pulled away from him, placing a pillow under his head. She streaked into the closet to get her cozy robe, then padded barefoot into the kitchen for a glass of water.

She turned to the sound of another soft beep. It had to be Mason's cell phone, still attached to his pants which were lying in a heap on the kitchen floor. She smiled, remembering how they got there. She reached for the cell phone as it announced, "beep," indicating a message was waiting.

She carried her water glass and the cell phone back into the bedroom. She lay down face to face with Mason. "Hello?" She couldn't see them, but knew he'd opened his eyes when his head lifted off the pillow for a second.

"Crazy woman, what are you doing?" He threw the pillow aside and reached for her. "It's dark outside."

"Your phone was talking in the kitchen, so I brought it to daddy. It's too complicated for me to answer."

"Okay." He rolled over, took the phone she held toward him and pushed a button. "Uh, oh." Mason sat up suddenly and fumbled around the lamp for a light switch. Light flooded the room as he pushed some more buttons on his phone. "The message came in about forty-five minutes ago. Somebody's been in the mineshaft."

Maria wrapped a blanket around him while he looked at the phone screen. She walked to the central heating thermostat, pushed some buttons then returned to the bed. As the room warmed, she snuggled up to his shoulder and watched the silent video show that held Mason's attention. A single silhouette showed first.

"Is he alone?" she asked.

"So far, yes."

"Can you tell what he's doing in there?"

"Not from this angle. I'll check the other cameras as soon as I lose track on this one. Another should pick him up. I wish he'd brought more lights with him."

"He's wearing cammies—look at the squiggly print on his sleeve."

"Yes, the ambient light at the mine entrance works well with these cameras. He's wearing a floppy-brimmed hat—I can't see his face."

Maria felt eerie staring at a figure from a remote position, watching an ordinary person in a place he shouldn't be. "What's he doing?"

"He's carrying coils of odd-looking rope into the mineshaft. Maybe it's coils of hose—something kind of stiff."

"What's it for, I wonder?"

"Have to go to another screen to pick him up on infrared if he's inside the arms area." Mason pushed buttons on his cell phone. "Here he is, just getting inside the storage caves. Oh, crap!"

"What?"

Mason grabbed Maria's house phone that sat on the night stand and dialed briskly.

"What?" Maria said again.

He said into the phone, "Code alert. We've got a guy inside laying DET Cord. He's going to blow the whole mine."

Mason had his shirt buttoned by time he reached his car, grabbed his hooded jacket and ran back into the house. Only ten minutes passed before a thumping engine sounded outside and a little helicopter appeared in the street in front of her house.

At the first sound, Mason grabbed Maria in a one-arm hug, kissed her, said, "Ciao," and ran for the street.

CHAPTER 34

"Hey! I want to go too," Maria yelled too late. She was still in her robe, throwing clothes around, trying to find the necessary layers in the proper order to dash out the door behind Mason. Anger hid right behind insult that she wasn't included in the possible showdown. Mason had taken off like a giant mosquito, leaving her slightly panicky, suddenly full of adrenaline despite the short night of actual sleep. He didn't know anything about the deep woods.

Finally dressed in long johns, jeans, boots and a warm coat, she jumped into her rental SUV and headed north to Auraria. In the sweet aftermath of lovemaking, she had only distantly noticed the man in the video had been wearing a hat similar to one her father used to have. If Mason's resources could trace that type of hat to its manufacturer, maybe it would help to profile him. She tucked that thought into the back of her mind to discuss with Mason later.

Since it was still dark and freezing outside, she watched for ice on the road, though without stars she could only assume there was a cloud cover. The thought of three to five more months of cold drizzle gave her a chill in the fogging car. She readjusted the heater dials and vents, willing warm air to begin flowing.

To keep from going crazy with worry, she parsed out her feelings for Mason as she drove. There was the lust factor, which was on the plus side of her imaginary scale. He made her feel cherished and beautiful, two things she hadn't thought about for a long time. There was the love factor that she knew from experience she couldn't trust.

Then there was the trust factor itself. In this case, blind trust, since he couldn't share details of his work with her. And truly, she pictured herself needing him and he'd be in Bangladesh. She slipped that onto the negative side of the scale.

When she spotted the mileage marker in her headlights that was near the drive entrance to the listed property, she pulled the SUV onto the muddy woods road and made her way through dark trees.

She reached the end, found several other vehicles left helter skelter in the woods, and parked. She stepped out of the car, checked her compass since she couldn't see landmarks, and grabbed the Brinkman she'd tossed in the back when she'd taken all her equipment out of Roland's car.

The shooting range was on the left and the mineshaft entrance was straight ahead. She pulled the collar of her jacket up against the chill.

Suddenly the ground shook so hard, she nearly fell. Immediately a monster fireball flashed a heat wave that whooshed through the woods. Deafened, she fell to the ground. In slow motion, silhouetted branches, bark pieces, pine needles, and still-clinging dead leaves popped off their main trunks and shot to the ground. They rained around her as she huddled against the base of a sourwood tree

Maria checked herself for burns. Dark surrounded her again. Her ears throbbed and she could hear nothing but she was grateful to find no burned skin or clothing.

Mason was her only thought.

Where is he?

Is he okay?

Did ORCA orchestrate a trap?

She circled off the direct path to the mine entrance. She kept her flashlight confined in the sleeve of her coat and hopped through the woodsy litter lying over every inch of the woods floor.

She didn't understand why there was no fire. An explosion like that should have set tree branches on fire or started the ground cover smoldering.

Silhouettes of men came into view, light and smoke behind them. They darted back and forth with flashlights like flickering fireflies. She hid behind a twenty-four inch white oak and peered around its side.

In the distance she heard the steady whump of rotary blades, and now the faint sound of sirens. She could barely hear over her ringing ears.

Right now, Maria had to find Mason. She left her tree, dodged ground litter and headed into the cloud of dust and smoky fumes.

"Hey, there's a hell of a hole up here," a man yelled from the top of the mineshaft.

"Reminds me of a volcano I looked into once. Everything's on fire down in there."

"Watch out for more explosions. There's probably a ton of gun powder spread all around the place," another man answered.

"Yeah, get out of there, Dean, we don't need your ass roasted too," a third man said.

Two others started digging at the mouth of the mine with shovels.

Mason Walker emerged from the mineshaft entrance just then. "Let's wait for the bulldozers, men. I doubt anybody was inside there. He had it on a timer of some sort unless he had a death wish. And you'll never get through all that rubble."

Maria was woozy with relief.

The man called Dean came around to stand in front of Mason. "I wonder why the explosion didn't blow all of us up and start a forest fire," he said.

"Because, my man, the guy used det cord. Which is why we didn't go inside when we first arrived. I saw the sucker on my phone screen laying it all out. I didn't know when it'd blow. Or if he knew what he was doing in the first place."

"You think he blew himself up?"

"Not unless he was an idiot."

Maria yelled out Mason's name. He immediately dropped into a crouch then shined his flashlight toward her, holding the light away from his body.

"It's me," she said as she hurried toward him.

"Were you in on our little Fourth of July display?" He stood and crossed to her in five long strides.

She grabbed his arm, his shoulder and wrapped herself into his chest. "Oh my God, I thought...."

"Pretty exciting," he said as he held her against him.

The mineshaft oozed mud and rifle parts. Wooden crates, reduced to kindling, spiked between twisted shafts of steel and endless dirt.

Local law enforcement appeared on various ATVs as a pristine crimson sunrise pushed rain clouds off the eastern horizon.

Maria stepped as close to the rim of the huge indented minescape as she dared, while Mason and several of the badged men watched the entire setup over again on Mason's cell phone screen. "That's why the contents were going up while the earth was going down after the explosion.... see there? He's wrapping the det cord all the way around the crates as well as over the top of them and around their base."

"I thought det cord was a fuse that sets off other explosives," one of the men said.

246

I betcha it was loud in here with all the ammo going off along with the dynamite," another one said. "Too bad the camera blew out."

"Apparently this guy didn't want a crater the size of a small planet," Mason said. "He just wanted to ruin what was in the mine. If he'd used dynamite this whole place would be on fire. Pentrite is containable and det cord is very specific."

She made her way back over to the little group of men, and said to Mason, "I'd like to watch that again when we get a chance."

"The ORCA guys will be really pissed off their little cache of armor is ruined," she said. "How did you land a helicopter in the woods?"

"Denny's a good pilot. He set us down in a pasture not far away. We walked from there and arrived right before the explosion."

"You're just as handy as a pocket on a shirt—all kinds of toys. You must work for the government."

"Uh huh."

CHAPTER 35

Rising sunshine outlined the tree trunks in gold, offering no warmth as Maria dialed Tom's cell phone. An overlay of dust hovered around the explosion site like fog on the still air.

Mason crunched through the ground mulch to find Denny. "Tom, I don't expect you to be up since it's barely seven a.m., but you should probably contact the sheriff's office in Dahlonega right away. The old mineshaft on my listing blew up this morning. Apparently nobody was inside. Talk soon."

Mason returned to say, "I've sent Denny on back. It's going to be a zoo around here for quite a while. You should probably go on home. I'll get a ride from somebody and pick up my car later." His obsidian eyes reflected their excitement in the early light.

Focus, Maria told herself. "Why would an ORCA member blow up their own weapons? It had to be a lot of work to haul all those cases through the woods."

"I've been thinking about that."

His nearness started a wave of radiation through her body, even though her nose had lost its feeling.

"Maybe the guy," he indicated the shaft with a wave of his arm, "wasn't part of ORCA."

"Maybe somebody who couldn't stand competition?" she offered. "It doesn't make sense that ORCA would destroy the weaponry just because they found out the Feds were onto them. They could have moved it instead."

His intensity and the little quotation mark between his eyes made her ache.

"I agree. It was either a subversive or a rival."

"In any case," he continued, "we'll be going from here right to headquarters. I'll walk you back to your rental."

Headquarters?

She found no reason to stay with him in the drizzling woods. Now her knees were so weak she wasn't sure she could walk on them. She needed to figure out how to follow up on her contract with Bonnie anyway, so she turned with Mason toward where she'd parked.

Grateful for daylight, she'd forgotten just how dark the countryside was without streetlights or stars. She resisted pressing herself against Mason in farewell, started the SUV and drove toward the paved road.

After she reached the freeway she called to pick up messages from the old answering machine at her home. She found three—her cousin Arthur's voice said her mother was doing fine, having Christmas Dinner with their family and he'd call again soon. He did not leave a phone number or name.

The second message was from Emily, wishing Maria Merry Christmas. She added that she'd seen an old friend of Maria's and wanted to relay a message.

Emily didn't know any of Maria's old friends, thank God. As much as she didn't want to talk to Emily, she did need to know what her stupid cousin meant, so she reluctantly dialed her number.

"Hello?"

"Emily. I just got your message. What's up?"

"Oh, Cuz, I'm so glad you called. Listen, Frankie has gone missing and I need your help."

Strange. Emily without her nonsense. "What do you mean 'gone missing'?"

"I was supposed to meet with him last night, but he didn't show up. That's so really not like him. He told me some things last Wednesday, at our normal meeting time. Things that worry him. About AJT Enterprises."

"The consortium? What things?"

"Well, he heard your partner and his partner fighting... and then he didn't show up last night. I think you should call his home and find out if he's there."

"Why don't you call him yourself?"

"Because his wife will answer and I don't have any reason to be calling him. But you do. You have a contract."

Of course I do. "You want me to call the man's wife?"

"You can see that I can't call him, can't you?"

"He's probably spending Christmas Day with his family."

"Here's his number. You call him. We'll talk."

Emily gave her a number and then hung up.

Maria couldn't believe it. What nerve of the woman, to order her around. She put her phone down on the passenger seat. Frank Denning heard Bonnie and probably Daniel Duke fighting. There were other partners, but Duke was the principal one. She wondered, not for the first time whether Daniel Duke and Bonnie were an item. She quickly put out of her mind any visualization of them together, shuddered at that ugly thought. Not exactly a match made in heaven. Besides, she remembered, Duke was married. She hadn't known Denning was married, which figured, knowing her cousin. But Bonnie? The woman was 72 years old. Come to think of it, Duke probably was about the same age.

She realized she'd been taken for a sucker, but got a pen and notepad from her purse then redialed Emily's phone number. "Okay, give me Frank's phone number again."

It was only after she turned her phone off she remembered she hadn't asked who the old friend was.

* * *

A woman answered when she called the number Emily gave her. "May I speak to Frank Denning, please?"

"I'm afraid Frank is out of town. May I help you?"

"Do you have a number where he can be reached? I'm the listing agent on one of his consortium's properties, and I need some additional information."

"Oh. I've been expecting him to call me any time now. I can take a message if you'd like. He's been out of phone range."

Yeah, I bet. "Okay, this is Maria Sebastian." She related the phone number. "Thank you." They said their good byes and Maria hung up.

She called Emily. "No Frank—he's out of phone range."

"Ohmigod. Maria, this isn't good. Frank's never out of phone range. We've got to find him.. Something has happened to Frank."

"Emily, call the police if you're worried. He could be taking care of a business issue."

"Christmas Eve? I don't think so. I can see me calling the cops: "Uh, excuse me, my sugar daddy didn't show up to bring me my Christmas diamonds, so you go find him? Can you spell laughter?"

"I take your point. I can't help you with that, I've got problems of my own. I can't find the realtor representing the buyer." She reiterated the story to Emily. "And the listed property was being used to stash a couple million rifles and guns. Somebody blew it up this morning. That's where I was when you called earlier."

"See? See? That's what your partner and Daniel were fighting about. The listing." Emily's voice had raised a couple of decibels.

"No, I think they were fighting about having it listed with me since I got blamed for not being able to find the agent who

252

sent the contract. Duke wanted to cancel it. But I can't imagine why Bonnie would defend me to him."

"Oh, this is starting to make sense... uh huh. Frank told me the contract was a hoax, and that's what they were fighting about. Duke said they'd never be able to explain it. Bonnie said it was the only way they could buy time."

"Time for what?"

"He didn't know, but if they'd known he heard them discussing rifles—they probably killed him."

Maria's blood turned cold. "Emily. Don't be so dramatic. The contract is not a hoax—it's signed, sealed and delivered—a legitimate document."

"Then why can't you find the agent?"

"I've been running all over the woods since four o'clock, for one thing. It's just a mix-up. I need some time to straighten it all out. And Frank will probably come waltzing in the door any minute." *I hope.* Too many people had been hurt over this land. Surely not Frank as well.

"I've got a bad feeling about this," said her cousin.

CHAPTER 36

Bradley Owen looked up from his keyboard. "I can probably handle this right now. Let's see what you've got."

Christmas Eve day, Maria was surprised to find his business open, even though her watch said ten thirty. The stenciled door read GEEKS PLUS ONE across its glass face. Bradley dabbed at his wet forehead with his right hand as his eyes passed over her.

"I found this flash drive in my grandma's desk when I cleaned out her things." She added, "She died, you know."
Yeah, sixteen years ago.

"Oh, I'm sorry." He stood and stepped toward another computer terminal blinking its myopic eye as designs peeled across its screen, his face sympathetic. "Isn't it hard trying to figure out a person's life after they've gone? My wife had to do that with her parents' things after they died. And the paperwork is incredible, isn't it?" He held out his hand. "I don't get many octogenarians who even know what a flash drive is." He beamed at her.

"I know. I didn't expect to find this in grandma's desk. I think her old computer was built before I was born." Maria just wanted that flash drive opened before somebody else got hurt.

Brad sat down at the chosen computer screen again and ran through a couple of menus and selected topics while Maria watched.

"Oops," he said. "We need a password. Any guesses what your grandma would have used?"

"I really can't see her making the drive herself. My guess is somebody sent it to her and she couldn't open it either. Maybe one of my cousins sent her Christmas pictures of their children. Can you bypass the password?"

"Let me see." His fingers flew across the keyboard.

Numbers and letters continuously flashed on the screen but in milliseconds were replaced by others.

Fifteen minutes later, Salali popped up on the screen in a little red box. "You recognize this word?" he asked, indicating the screen.

Donnie Salali Sebastian.

Maria's breath caught as she created another lie. "I think it's one of my cousin's middle names. But I don't know what it means.

"Just a sec," Brad said. He wheeled his chair around to yet another computer screen. Playing the keyboard like a musical instrument, he brought the computer to life.

He turned to look at Maria and said. "Salali means 'Little Squirrel' in the Cherokee language." Without pause, he rolled himself back to the first computer and danced his hands again across its keyboard.

All activity stopped and a list of names, addresses, and phone numbers appeared on the computer screen.

"Oh," Maria said as she stood beside him and scanned the list, thinking about what creative explanation she could come up with now. "It's an old list of my aunts, uncles and cousins. This is great! Can you print it?"

Two more keyboard taps, and a printer in the back of the jumbled room began to whine.

Maria excitedly grabbed the sheets Brad offered her, and paid him the only bill in her purse—a twenty, even though he told her it would only be six dollars. He reached into the computer slot and pulled out the flash drive, and handed it to her. "Don't forget this."

Her eyes scanned the list before she started her car. She read some of the names out loud. "Arnold Evans. David Longworth. James Ackworth. Thomas L. Wainright. Jonathan Dever. She didn't recognize any from the first column. Sure there would be somebody she knew on it, she made herself read more slowly. Daniel Duke. "Isn't that interesting?" She said out loud.

This is weird. Maybe the list is of all the people who own the property

She thought about fifteen people would make up Duke's consortium, not forty-six. Maybe this is another bunch entirely. But then why would Duke's name even be on a list from Norman's house?

The addresses were all over the place.

She noticed no women's names were on the list.

With Daniel Duke's name being there, she half expected to see Bonnie's as well.

When she drove into her driveway, she found a tiny package tucked into her mailbox. Old-fashioned brown paper covered a box on which her name was printed in a child-like hand.

She threw it back into her mailbox. Since it was so small and she'd noticed a return address printed in the upper left hand corner, she got a grip on herself. *Now I'm getting paranoid expecting bombs to be mailed to me. What an idiot.*

She reached into the mailbox again and retrieved the package. Navarro was printed in the return address corner. It was from Wanda. She could swear she felt the woman's ghostly vibrations on the paper covering that box.

It was taped almost entirely with wide, clear, packing tape.

Inside her house she fished a small envelope opener from her desk drawer and used it to pry, then cut through the tape and paper covering the box. She slipped the opener into her pocket and opened the lid of the box. Three little fetishes lay in the box.

A stab of remembered pain shot through her chest. Wanda had sent these right before she'd died.

Tears sprang up in her eyes again. She dropped the paper and tape into her office trashcan, set the box beside her lamp and vowed to think about the fetishes later.

She picked up her cell phone to call Mason, but thought better of it and slipped it back into her purse.

She hadn't told him about the list from the flash drive in the first place, hadn't really known its significance until she saw Duke's name. What were the chances a death in Arizona could be tied to a death in Georgia? If she could talk with others on the list of names, maybe she could figure out the connection. Maybe they were names of golfers, of antique car enthusiasts. It could be an innocent coincidence. Mason would want her to give the flash drive to the authorities.

If what her father said was true, she could be in trouble for removing the flash drive from the house where Wanda died. She had been only thinking of poor little Donnie. She didn't want to draw the attention of the legal system. She'd probably get put in jail for messing up a crime scene. She'd lose her real estate license and have no means of income. She leaned back in her chair and closed her eyes.

How could I be so foolish?

Deciding to try again to find the missing agent co-opting on her land sale after the holidays, Maria hurriedly put the final touches on a chicken and set it in the oven for her Christmas dinner with Emily. Maybe for Mason as well, she hoped.

Just as the kitchen began smelling spicy and wonderful, the phone rang.

Tom said, "Hey there. I've been talking with a buddy at the Dawson sheriff's office. He said the morning's explosion was set up by one guy."

"Exactly. Who would think one person could cause such a mess."

"You saw it on camera?"

"It's recorded on Mason's PDA. The camera played a delayed recording because Mason didn't answer the phone when the cameras deployed and called Mason's cell phone number. He didn't hear it for some reason, so it was stored as a saved message." She didn't add just why Mason hadn't answered the phone. Nobody had asked.

"My office will be conducting the investigation because the Bureau of Alcohol, Tobacco, Firearms and Explosives will handle it in the end. They want us to do the preliminary reports."

"I'm glad nobody got hurt," she said.

"Yes, me too, but I sure hope there is a clue or two to justify the paperwork."

Maria thought about the hat she saw on whoever set off the explosion.

She threw together a pumpkin pie from the recipe on the Libby's can and some roll-up refrigerated pastry dough she'd found in her freezer, and put it in the oven with the chicken. She hoped they would cook at the same time, but suddenly wasn't too concerned about it.

She was more interested in what the Internet would say about the people on the list from the flash drive. The first five she Googled showed nothing in Wikipedia, a few news articles about same-named individuals, and one showed a criminal record. None appeared to be the same persons as on the list.

Each name did have an address and phone number, but she couldn't figure how to use that information effectively. About to start over with the next five names, she typed in Daniel Duke's name to see what the 'Net had to say about him.

The first site she went to under his name read a list of accomplishments that seemed impossible in one lifetime.

From developing site feasibility reports to demographic analyses, implementing aerial photographs, bidding out massive development projects and actually ramrodding physical site development, it seemed nothing was beyond his knowledge.

Three other listings held essentially the same type of job assessments, none of which made any sense to Maria or tied Duke to subversive groups in general or ORCA specifically. She needed help with this, but where could she get help?

When her doorbell rang, she was about to start calling everybody she knew.

Maria reached for the doorknob, expecting to see Emily standing on the porch wearing something ridiculous: a turkey costume or Santa Claus boots. She knew at the split second she heard the blast outside the door that something was terribly wrong.

CHAPTER 37

As the heavy, steel-encased front door flew open against her entire right side, she was crammed into the adjacent wall like a woman sandwich.

Blackness took her. When she surfaced, she fought for air, heard scuffling feet, grunts of exertion. She wanted to fight but couldn't breathe. Rough hands grabbed her arms and legs, dragged her. Blackness won again.

Next time she woke, at least she could breathe, but her hands wouldn't work, her legs were bound from hip to feet. She couldn't see. God! Was she blind? Eyes open, she blinked, saw fabric. Dark fabric.

She was in a bag. No. Her fingers felt fuzzy carpet. Her head was in a bag. And it throbbed. She was on her back trussed up and claustrophobic. She began to hallucinate, to sympathize with roasting chickens, but then made herself concentrate.

A motor hummed, and she rumbled around on the fuzzy floor, bouncing and swaying. With great effort she moved her legs, tried to sit up. Lightning bolts pierced her head when it hit something hard. She fell back onto the fuzzy stuff, nauseated. Slept.

Next time she woke, she smelled oil, gas, and rubber. She must be in a car trunk. Okay, she'd have to move her legs, get ready to kick when the trunk opened.

If it opened. If it didn't then she'd die here. A lump formed at the back of her throat at that thought. Was she going do die? Now?

When the car stopped, she'd yell for all she was worth. What if they drove the car into the lake to get rid of her? Sweat ran down her face in the cold. Tears joined the sweat. She thought of Mason. He'd always wonder what had happened to her. Would someone find her bones some day, like the poor guy in the mineshaft? No name, no gravestone to say she'd ever been on the earth. Lost. Dead.

She figured she'd been in the car trunk about a half hour, but not knowing how long she was out, and couldn't be sure.

Her hands were tied with some kind of plastic rope and tape. She couldn't move them enough to feel her legs and didn't know why they felt glued together.

The car bounced, her head bounced with it and hit the floor. Her yelp was muffled and pitiful, even to her ears. She didn't want to think about drowning or being left, abandoned to die. It must have taken two people to maneuver her into the trunk, since she couldn't walk. Two loose people to one tied-up person made bad odds. Kicking was a bad idea. If her abductors thought she was still unconscious, she might be able to learn who they were, or something—anything to help her escape. Maria tried deep breathing to relax the pounding in her head, the feeling of suffocation like she got in elevators and closets.

A series of creaks and lurches threw her body into trunk detritus. She recognized the end of a tire iron under her cheek. A jack rattled against her shoulder, a couple of cans of something rolled into her side on turns. Nuts or bolts slid around her, bruising her as her body found them in new positions with each jolt. Apparently off road, the vehicle turned right then gnawed across a gravel or rock-based road, maybe a driveway. They moved very slowly now. Movement stopped and the motor quit. She listened to the tinny ping of the cooling engine. *Why weren't they getting out of the car?* Maria wondered.

Panic spurted through her brain. She yelled as loud as she could, screamed, "Help, get me out of the trunk!" She lifted her legs together and bashed the trunk lid, hoping to raise dents, attract somebody's attention.

The car swayed from her exertion, but when she stopped the noise, she heard nothing.

Regrouping courage, she did it all again.

Sweat ran into her eyes inside the head-covering shroud and the headache which had subsided, came roaring back.

She had to do something. She spun around so her head was at the outside edge of the trunk and kicked at the backseat with what remained of her strength. Just as she felt the seat begin to cave, the trunk lid popped open.

With her feet against the back seat springs, her plan to kick her abductors evaporated.

They dragged her out over the trunk edge, painfully scraping her from her neck to her waist. She yelled at the hands pulling on her, shrugging, struggling against them. "Coward," she yelled. "You can't stand and fight like a man, you have to tie me up because you're scared I can take you." She bucked and kicked to no avail. "Well, I can take you. Make the field level, and we'll see who's the better man."

She heard laughter as they carried her past an upright post, bashing her right arm. She was plunked down on a hard floor.

Feet moved away from her. The sound of a door or board scraping concrete echoed in what seemed to be a hollow room. A door slammed shut. Something banged on the outside of the door. Then there was nothing but a foul odor.

A blinding headache overpowered her senses and she lost track of smells and movement inside wherever she'd been dropped. Lying as prone as her bindings would allow she tried to meditate her headache away so she could think. They didn't want her dead, or she'd be dead. *Why not?* she wondered. She wasn't prime for a ransom. Nobody she knew had any money. Did they want to keep her out of their way? Why?

"Hello," a tentative voice said.

"Screw you," she gasped, and kicked out against nothing. She forgot her tender arm as she squirmed back from the sound, listening for movement, ready to aim her kicks better.

"Hey, they're gone. They threw me in here a couple days ago. Sorry about the odor."

There was another prisoner?

"Are you tied up too? Blindfolded?" she asked.

A sigh. "Yes."

A little flicker of hope fizzed out. "Sorry. What do they want?"

"They think I know something."

"Do you?"

"Ha! If I do, I'm not telling them. Anyway, they haven't asked."

"Who are you?"

"Frank Denning. Who are you?"

"Frankie! Emily told me you were gone, but I had no idea you were kidnapped. It's me, Maria Sebastian."

"I thought somebody would come looking for me by this time. But I don't know where I am."

"If we're blindfolded, it's because we'd recognize where we are."

"Do you think they're going to let us go?" Frank asked.

"I don't know, but if they're crazy enough to kidnap us, they're crazy enough to do anything." Maria shuddered. "We have to escape."

"I always thought Dan liked me."

"Dan? Do you mean Duke? He kidnapped you? Us?"

"Yes."

"Did you blow up the mine?" she asked.

"What do you mean?"

"Somebody blew up the mine this morning. It was full of explosives and rifles, which made for a big show. Oh, yeah,

Emily said you've been missing for two days. Have you been in here for two days?"

"Three days I think. Was anybody hurt? I didn't even know the explosives and rifles were in there till I overhead these guys talking. Shows you how dumb I am. I just wanted to sell the property."

"Nobody seemed to be hurt. Shows how dumb we all are. That's what I wanted, too. But I can't even find the selling agent now."

"That's what I mean. There is no selling agent. Duke got somebody to send a fake contract to you to buy time to take the rifles and ammunition out of the mineshaft. They didn't want other people showing the property and finding the explosives."

That's why she couldn't contact the agent. "Well, why did they list it? It never would have come up if they'd just held onto the property. They could have continued storing things in there indefinitely."

"I messed them up when I came to you to help me find a new investment so we could sell that land. It was so remote; I thought commercial property would be a better investment. Dan said he'd been working with Bonnie to do the same thing, but you actually found a new property for us that's far more attractive than bug heaven stuck in the outback. I always wondered why Dan and Bonnie wanted us to invest in that land in the first place. If I'd known what they were going to do with it, I never would have gone in with them."

"Were the rifles for some raid they planned?"

"Yes. Ever hear of ORCA? Organization for Radical Changes in America? These nutzos think they're going to overthrow the government like a military junta. They must have thousands of followers, from the way they talked. Hundreds of caches of weapons stockpiled all around the country. While I was listening they discussed at least twelve locations and mentioned cells of people responsible for them. The one here never would have been found out if you hadn't decided to poke around."

"Did Bonnie know about it?"

"I think so. She must have, otherwise the fake contract could not have been signed. She found the paperwork for us, paid somebody to call you and set you up."

"When did you find out about that?"

"I overheard Bonnie and Duke fighting about it. They're always fighting, but this time they were accusing each other of trying to take over. I was curious and listened in.

"I couldn't believe they were talking about our land. About cases of rifles and explosives hidden there. I told them to get the damn stuff off the property before somebody found it there."

"Do you know who might have blown it up?" Maria asked.

"No. It might be the Bureau of Alcohol, Tobacco, and Firearms, you know, getting rid of product. But that would be odd. They usually confiscate things like that."

"How often do the kidnappers come back to check on you?"

"So far about every twelve hours, near as I can guess. They bring me protein drinks with straws. I've been living on those since I've been here."

"How long?"

"Best I can figure, about three days. I've lost track of time. What day is this?"

"December 24. Merry Christmas."

"Then it's been two days." He shuffled around on the floor. "I can't get these ropes off my hands. Can't feel my hands any more either. I guess gangrene won't matter if they kill us."

"They better hurry if they're going to kill us. Are your hands tied behind your back?"

"Yes."

"Okay, I have an idea."

CHAPTER 38

"Recite the alphabet or something so I can find you, I'm coming over," Maria said.

Frank droned "A, B, C, D...," and Maria inched toward him, scooting on her butt toward her feet, then pushing them out and scooting again, until she felt his body radiating heat and stink. She hadn't noticed how cold she was until then. Her fingers seemed to belong to somebody else.

"Are you facing my voice?" she asked.

"Yes, I think so."

"I'm going to scoot around with my side to your hands and I want you to reach into my right hand jeans pocket."

"Look, I appreciate the thought, but we're in a bind here...."

"Pay attention!" She kicked him, not knowing what part of him she hit.

"Ow."

"I've got a letter opener in my right front jeans pocket. It's only plastic, but it's got a razor blade in it. And don't drop it."

She felt Frank's hands move against her side, wishing her jeans weren't so stylishly tight.

They were both on their knees, her side pressing into his back, trying not to fall over while he groped for her pocket. "At least they're not men's pants—men's pockets are so deep I'd never get the thing out of there."

She felt him claw at her side. "What are you doing?"

"I'm trying to scoot the thing upward to the top of the pocket so I can get it out. If you didn't have such a sexy butt, you wouldn't wear your pants so tight."

"Shut up and get the thing out."

He made little grunts. "I almost have it out. Okay, okay, I've got it. It's not very big. Why didn't Duke's guy take it from you?"

"It's small enough they didn't know it was in my pocket."

"Are you sure it'll work?"

"No, but we don't have a lot of choices here. Let me try it since I've used it before."

He felt for her hand then passed the letter opener to her. Maria pushed failure from her mind. She gripped it, not being able to feel its landscape with her numb fingers. When she assumed she held it in the right position, she remembered to be cautious enough to not break the stem as she slid it between the tape and his skin and worked it up and down in tiny strokes.

"Hey, I think it's working." He sounded incredulous.

"Try to keep the tape taut so it'll tear as I cut it." She hadn't realized she was holding her breath till she heard a little rip and it all ran out at once. Sweat stung her eyes even though they were tightly shut. She minced away at it through the beginning of a different strip till he could twist away from the remaining wrappings.

"I can just unwrap yours I think," he said as he found the end of the tape on her hands and wrists. They came away quickly with the ends released and her hands restored to their natural shape. She then reached to do the same with her ankles, but she'd pulled so hard on the bindings that she had to resort to the letter opener to get a start on a cut.

Maria snatched the sack off her head, stamped her feet to get the circulation flowing through them again, then looked around their prison. They were still locked inside of what seemed to be a block building with a wooden door and shuttered windows. Dim light barely peeked in from under the door and around the window edges.

Frank's watch lit up when he pressed a button. "It's five o'clock. Where are we, anyway?

Five o'clock and she was still stuck inside with a stinkpot. "It's a building on the property's grounds... I thought it stored shooting equipment, but I never got a chance to find out."

"It's a block room," he said, trying the barricaded window then moving toward the door. "Do you think somebody is outside, watching the building?"

"Probably not, since we were trussed up and locked in."

Frank walked to the back of the small room and peeked around the dark corners into an attached room. "Nothing in here but stacked boxes. I've never wanted another pair of pants so badly."

"We're going to worry about the pants thing later. What's in the boxes? We could use, um, a rifle, some food, maybe dynamite." She'd also like some car keys, a cell phone and a car parked outside. Maria took Frank by his arm, crossed the room and aimed his wrist to shine the watch's light against the top box. "Eprifam," she read.

"Huh, that's the brand name of some children's sheets." A cloud crossed the sun in her mind. After it passed, she remembered. "It's also the name on the label of the coat the dead man wore. I mean the bones we found in the mine."

"You think there are clothes in these boxes?"

She used what was left of the maimed letter opener to dig a fingerhold into the lid of the top box, and jerked it open. She reached inside and pulled out a heavy piece of wool. Another flash from the tiny watch light revealed bright red cloth. A red wool man's jacket with the Eprifam label. It was too hard to read the tiny writing on the box label, so she tore the damp gooey label off and stuck it in her jeans pocket. "We really need to get out of here."

269

"Maybe there's some pants too?" Frank felt through the jacket box, then sighed.

Maria stepped over to the door and shoved on it. Tiny shards of light showed through both the wood of the door and the doorframe. On the outside of the door, she saw the bar across the doorframe at the location of the doorknob. Days of practice on her grandmother's French doors when she was a child refreshed a memory from her past. "Frank, do you have any credit cards in your wallet?

Frank fumbled with his wallet. "I don't know which one this is… are you going to wreck it?"

She ignored him, felt around in the dark toward him and followed his arm to the card in his hand, and slipped it through the doorframe and door. She flicked the card upward. The door quietly swung open.

"I'm not even believing this," Frank said.

They stepped outside into the cold twilight.

Surrounded by deep woods, Maria took a few seconds to scan the area where the hut stood. To their left, steel plates sat six feet off the ground, lined up like ducks there for the shooting. They were at the range Maria had found when she and Eileen came to walk the property of the new listing—Frank Denning's consortium property.

"Don't you recognize this place?" she asked. "The mine you own is just over the hill behind us."

"No, I've never seen it. It was just an investment for me. I had no idea all this was out here. I thought it was plain old wooded land."

"Unfortunately for us, it's a million miles from nowhere. The good news is, I know the way back. But I wish I had my cell phone. It's going to be a long walk." She grabbed Frank's arm and led him toward the burned out mineshaft, hoping somebody was still there continuing the investigation.

As they topped the hill between the firing range and the blown up gold mine site, they heard footsteps crunching through leaves on the opposite side of the range hut they'd just left.

With strength she couldn't have, Maria grabbed Frank's arm and in a panicky whisper said, "Trouble. Hide!" and dived into the bushes with him.

CHAPTER 39

Maria landed with Frank under a dense mountain laurel bush. She heard a vehicle motor ahead of them, and when she peered through the everygreen branches, she saw a white SUV making its way through the path the sheriff's deputies had cut the night of the explosion. When she looked back toward the hut again, she saw that Daniel Duke had discovered their escape and stood looking through the trees at them. They turned and ran toward SUV, over the hilltop.

"Where'd you two come from?" the Lumpkin County Sheriff Deputy said as they ran up to his SUV. "Stop where you are and show me your hands."

"There's a guy with a gun after us," Maria gasped. "He was right behind us." She held out her hands and looked back at Frank, hoping he was doing the same. "Look at the marks on my arms where we were tied up."

"Get in the truck," the deputy said, and then clicked the lock of the vehicle open.

Frank and Maria jumped in. She realized they were caged in a prisoner transportation SUV as the door slammed and locked. She looked down toward where the door lever should have been. It was gone.

The deputy ran around the vehicle to the side opposite the way Frank and Maria had come. He stooped, rested the weapon that had materialized into his hand on the hood of the SUV and waited.

Maria pictured them stuck in the backseat of a sheriff's unit while Daniel Duke shot the deputy then did the same to her and Frank.

Duke never came over the hill. "He might circle around and come in behind you," she said through the glass while it fogged up from her breath.

The deputy's blue eyes darted around through the trees, then he turned back, stood stock still and listened.

He touched the mike on the radio on his shoulder. He ran a litany of code numbers through his teeth into the radio as he maintained his surveillance stance.

"Let us out of here and I'll go back up the hill and see where he is," she said.

The deputy ignored her. Sweat trickled down his face, even though the temperature had dropped. After fifteen minutes of listening to a crisp wind ruffling leftover leaves, the deputy got into the truck, started the motor, and backed it up. A bullet came through the window and clanged into the headliner. A spider-web blossomed across the center of the front windshield. Frank and Maria fell into a tangle on the backseat.

"This guy shoots at a firing range all the time—he's probably a pretty good shot," Maria shouted from the floor where she had scrambled with Frank.

The SUV bolted forward, gouged the side of a leafless red oak tree, but kept on going. Maria peeked up to see if the deputy was okay, but saw only the top of his head snapping back and forth, while he tried to watch all directions at once. He'd slid his body down behind the steering wheel but he was definitely still alive. The vehicle continued through the colonnade of trees.

Another shot thunked into the vehicle's body somewhere, spurring the deputy to step harder on the gas. Ditches and hillocks made invisible under the ground mulch tossed the SUV on a bleak crispy sea, throwing Maria and Frank into each other, banging her head into the cage between her and the driver, then slamming her ribs onto the hump in the floorboard, while Frank landed on top of her. "Frank, I can't breathe," she said.

"S-sorry," he managed to say as he rolled off her onto the bench seat.

"We gotta be out of range now," the deputy said. "Unless he has a rifle." He twisted the steering wheel to the left and they lurched around a corner, Frank's head banging against the left rear windshield. Maria recalled the way she'd felt the night of her icy car wreck, and winced.

They came upon a black sedan parked in the woods and the deputy slammed on his brakes, idling the motor. He seemed to make some decision, then continued forward.

A movement deep in the woods on their right caused the deputy to turn the unit toward it, slam on his brakes and jump out, using the door as a shield between whatever it was and himself.

Daniel Duke had his hands up in the air and walked toward them slowly. Behind him, Roland shoved his shoulder with a handgun and spouted a running litany of Spanish.

Relief flowed over Maria for a short second until she realized Roland could be shot by the deputy. "Wait," She hollered at the deputy, "that's the guy who was shooting at us— the one in the front. I know the other guy. He's my bodyguard. Don't shoot him."

"Stop right there!" the deputy yelled. "Drop your weapon, step forward and lay down on the ground." Daniel Duke knelt. Roland tossed his gun reluctantly onto the leaves while spurts of words came back over the radio.

Roland pushed Duke on his face into the leaves, then sank to his knees and lay down.

Maria wanted to kiss the deputy. Her bones had suddenly melted and she sagged against the backseat.

Two more white SUVs appeared on the dirt path leading in toward them.

"Don't hurt the Guatemalan, the Spanish guy," Maria said to the deputy. "I know you don't know him, but I do. The other guy is the one who shot at us," she babbled toward the still open unit's door.

The deputy ignored her and approached the two prone figures. He patted Duke's pockets and legs, put handcuffs on him, then did the same to Roland.

The deputies in the two SUVs stepped out of their vehicles. One continued talking in his radio while the other one walked around the SUV from which Maria and Frank watched helplessly. He continued toward the deputy now searching Roland. He put rubber gloves on his hands then walked over to where Roland had dropped his pistol and picked it up. "Tip and Bronson are at the turnoff," he said to the deputy doing the search.

"Good," the first deputy responded. "It's about time you guys showed up. I was only supposed to follow up at that explosion site, and I ran into these people."

Maria had the shakes so bad she couldn't control her hands enough to check her ribs.

CHAPTER 40

Maria was afraid to move. Every twitch caused shooting pains to run all around her torso. She found the electronic button on the side of the bed that calls the nurse and pressed it while she looked up at Mason and asked, "Why don't you explain to me what this has all been about?"

"You know I'm not supposed to."

"Oh, please. My house has been ransacked; I was knocked unconscious by a hit-and-run driver, and practically run over by a runaway car. I was knocked out again, kidnapped and shot at. Somehow, I'm not dead, but I'm thinking of getting a permanent reservation at this hospital hotel. I think you owe me an explanation. Right now, I'm not sure you're even on my side. If you mean to sit there and tell me I don't deserve to know what's been going on, then just go on out the door. It's been fun, but it's over." She shut her eyes and tried to breathe through the aches caused by her newfound cuts and bruises.

"I take your point. And you're right. You deserve to know. I may have to shoot you after I tell you, though."

Her eyes flew open and she winced.

"Kidding. I was kidding. I wanted to see if you were awake. It's okay, calm down. I can't stand to see you so miserable."

A nurse in a pink scrubs outfit hustled through the door. Maria looked at her with the most pleading eyes she could manufacture. The nurse handed two little paper cups to Maria, one with water splashing over the top and one with a blue pill nestled in the bottom. "I thought you'd be calling soon," and gave Maria a little pat on her shoulder. She turned and looked at Mason briefly, then cruised back out the door.

Mason looked deep in thought, took a big breath. "Somebody, who shall go nameless, brought our attention to the mineshaft by blowing up the weapons inside. It seems this somebody felt justified in destroying anything ORCA had. He thought he could put them out of business."

"What is their business?" Maria asked.

"Their business is—I mean, was—overthrowing our government."

"Like a South American junta" she prompted, remembering the letter and email she'd received about ORCA.

"Exactly, only on a bigger scale. They have a network trained in methods to eliminate people. We're talking about raiding Washington, DC, killing all the members of congress, and eliminating our president and his cabinet."

"Could they have succeeded?"

"Who knows? ORCA started with a bunch of ragtag maniacs in Puerto Rico fifty years ago, and the movement has been building ever since. But to underestimate them would be foolish. Our new job will be finding all of them, which my men are making top priority as we speak."

Maria considered if this was the time to tell him about the flash drive. She wished she felt more confident that Mason-the-chameleon was who she prayed he was. "This person who blew up the weapons, will he be prosecuted?"

She noticed sunshine peek through the western-facing window blinds of her hospital room. Maybe Spring would show up sooner or later after all. Her eyes wandered to the IV hanging next to her, an ever-present mute puppy. The IV insertion point's purple bruise on the back of her hand made the previous one from her last hospital stay look anemic.

It didn't drip blood, only glucose, but made her wonder just how Indian blood differed from Caucasian blood. Only the guys with the microscopes would know that.

"I can't see how. All he did was help us out. Besides, we haven't found him yet."

Though Maria knew better, she'd never seen another person look the same way her father did wearing that hat.

"How was Bonnie involved with the ORCA people. What about the land?" she asked.

"Mr. Duke is Bonnie's brother. He's been using her as a front to find goldmine property so they could stash weapons where nobody would be likely to find them. They'd buy the property and slowly build up a huge amount of weapons. As they overran where they were storing the weapons, they'd already have another piece of land where they could move it. It was stored in the mines for their terror war. If you hadn't found the remains in the mineshaft and exposed ORCA, they would have begun killing people, no doubt in my mind."

A refreshing burst of something passed across her brain. Probably the pills. She smacked herself gently on her forehead. Of course Bonnie is Duke's sister. She'd thought they were lovers, but never considered them to be blood relatives. "Who was the man who died in the mine?"

"Probably Jaime Navarro. If it isn't him, his mother wouldn't have been killed.

"We found three more goldmines loaded with as many weapons as you and Roland found. Our guys are searching underground for all of the goldmines on record."

"But the map I have says there were some five hundred of them."

"Yep. It's going to take a really long time." He reached for Maria's hand, being careful to not touch bandages or tubes.

She watched him gently maneuver his hand into hers, watched his eyes select the route through to her fingertips. Did he know how to set bombs? Was he able to kill people then go home and have a good night's sleep? Would she ever know

279

Mason? She was ninety nine percent sure that whoever he was, he wasn't a subversive. It was all she could do, not to give him the flash drive.

In the end, was he really much different than Norman? Maybe she should talk to a shrink about how she managed to hook up with men addicted to adrenaline. In retrospect, her father had always been her hero and now she knew he was not who she thought at all. The man she knew from childhood misrepresented himself, just as Norman had done. Just as Mason also had. "At what point did Norman's name show up while you were investigating ORCA?" she asked.

He'd stopped working into a comfortable chair at the side of her bed, softly resting his hand under hers, and looked thoughtful. His appealing little grin was gone when he ran his eyes over her face. "We had cells of these guys all over the place—Oklahoma, Texas, Arizona, Louisiana, Georgia and Florida and other states. Some of them have been festering for fifty years, overall getting stronger and stronger, more weapons disappearing from the street after shipments went missing. When the link between Wanda Navarro in Oklahoma and Sebastian in Arizona was made—this was about two years ago, the two groups were put on a watch list."

"They were just being watched?"

"Yes, until you came along and found the body in the mine. When the FBI was notified with the possibility of it being associated with ORCA, our attention shifted. We never considered they were using old mines to hide weapons."

"I never thought Norman would want to overthrow the government, Maria said. "Say what else you will about him, as crazy as he was, he was loyal to America and hated what the politicians were doing to it. That's what drove him nuts. He does love America in his own cracked way. He lost all his tools for survival when he realized he fought for an ideal that was sold out. I suppose he took matters into his own hands."

"The reality is he never got into our crosshairs. It was his association with the Navarros that drew our attention his way."

"Poor, sick Norman. I've hated him for so long." She felt drained. "Do you know where he is? I came here because it was the last place he'd think to look."

"We've got him on ice."

CHAPTER 41

Maria's heart skipped a beat and she felt her eyes get too big for their sockets. "Holy shit. I've got to get out of here." She sat up suddenly, wondering if her clothes were in the closet next to the TV. Where was her coat?

"Wait a minute. I didn't say he was here," Mason said. "And I can't tell you where he is, but he doesn't know anything about you."

"He'll find out. He's not stupid and he can read newspapers."

"Wait a minute. You've got to remember his age. He's not going to do anything to anybody. We're bargaining with him, using his son as our big chip. He doesn't want the boy to be caught up in his wife's family's lifestyle, in his lifestyle, so he's cooperating all the way."

"Cooperating how? Promising to be good if he can keep Donnie?" Maria's blood scampered through her veins, pounded against her brain.

"Look, he's in Virginia at a veteran's hospital. He was in an accident, may end up in a wheel chair. When we run down the key ORCA members he'll be safe. Somebody waltzed into Child Protective Services and took Donnie out of the foster home. Sebastian went after him but ended up in the hospital."

"You mean that little boy is in the hands of crazies like Daniel Duke?"

"No, I mean he WAS in the hands of crazies. He's been brought back."

Maria clutched the front of her hospital gown, breathing hard, reaching for the floor with her toes, looking around the floor for her shoes. "Where is he then?"

"He's in Phoenix. He's safe." Mason patted her fingers.

"Why did your guys take him right back there for somebody else to kidnap him?" She stood on the cold floor in her bare feet, air drifting up her loose hospital gown. She realized she was still attached to the drip machine and pulled the tape carefully off the back of her hand. She took out the IV and stuck it into the plastic solution bag over her left shoulder.

"Maria. Calm down. Don't do that." He stood in front of her and placed his hands on her shoulders.

She turned away from him. "He's a little boy! Where is he exactly?"

"Okay, I didn't want to tell you this. Robert John Charles Walton, also known as Bobby Wahkinny, got him back and won't tell us where he is."

Maria fell back against the side of the bed as she groped for the rail edge. "My dad?" Her eyes had trouble focusing.

"He said Sebastian called him to take the boy. Sebastian went to the hospital, but needed specialty services only available in Virginia, so they shipped him there. He's got a 24-hour guard. I understand he won't be going home. He won't be able to take care of himself so he'll be in a veterans' home in Virginia till he recovers. If he's not in jail."

"Where's my dad?"

"That's another issue. We don't know. Sebastian told him to go to his house and get the list of ORCA members. The problem is, we've been all through that house and there is no list. Sebastian told him the list was supposed to keep his family safe. Instead it put them in harm's way. He's pretty defeated sounding, between bouts of screaming at everybody close."

"If, as you say, Norman wasn't involved with the ORCA members, where did he get such a list?" Maria stood on the floor again, Mason hovering around her, ready to catch her if she fell.

"He said Jaime had given it to Jaime's sister, Awinita as an insurance policy, he'd called it. Sebastian thought it was a bunch of crap, and told Nita to get rid of it."

Maria edged her way down the side of the bed to the closet next to the television and opened the doors. "Ouch," she said, grabbing her forehead with her left hand. "Mason, get my purse down there." She pointed to the bottom of the closet.

He handed it to her and she reached inside for her wallet, opened the money section and took out a fat, folded packet of papers. "Here's the list. It was on a flash drive and I had it printed."

Mason stared first at the papers she held out to him, then at her face. "But, how…."

She felt hot tears in her eyes. "It was in the toy I picked up from Norman's house when we found Awinita. Did you know that Donnie's middle name, Salali, means 'Little Squirrel'?"

Mason opened the packet of papers and looked through the list of names. "You didn't tell me about this."

"I didn't know about it until the toy fell off my bedroom bureau and a flash drive popped out."

He pulled his eyes away from the paper and looked up at her. "But when did that happen?"

"About a week ago. I didn't know what it was, and couldn't open it, so I took it to my computer guy."

"I could have opened it with my computer," he said, looking down again, eyes scanning the rows of print.

"I didn't know what it was. I tried to call some of the people but really haven't had enough time to find any of them. When I found Daniel Duke's name on the list, I started to worry about what it meant. I noticed Bonnie's name isn't there. You just explained the connection between her and Duke, though."

"You had to know how incriminating this is."

"But until you told me about Norman, about Donnie, I wasn't sure who you were, much less what the list was. I couldn't take that chance. I still don't know exactly what you do, but at least I'm comfortable that the overlap of what I stumbled into and what you have been pursuing isn't contrived." She looked down at her black and blue IV hole.

"You're a hard nut. But I can understand how you felt. It isn't easy working in the dark. You won't mind if I take this opportunity to send a couple of calls out to start rounding up these guys?" It wasn't really a question.

"Please. The sooner the better."

"We already have the ones you found for us." He smiled at her while he furiously texted on his phone.

Still trying to digest Donnie being with her father, Maria thought about all she'd been through in the last month. It seemed so coincidental, so unthinkable to accept there was a sea of activity going on behind her every day life... that her past life in Arizona could fast forward twenty years and dovetail into her current life bordered on the fantastic.

She watched Mason's fingers fly again, and wondered if she'd ever be able to work with such sophisticated electronics. She knew she'd have to sell something before she'd be able to afford a new BlackBerry. Now that the land deal was bogus through and through, it was a dry hole that would have to be made up as soon as possible. She had to get out of this hospital. She stood up again and inched her way to the closet.

The hospital room door opened slowly as a huge bunch of lilies, crocuses, and irises floated in. Behind the flowers, Emily Louise Tandy's big smile beamed. "See what I have brought for you *ma cherie*!" she said.

"Emily!" Maria spouted in surprise.

Her cousin walked to the rolling table at the foot of the bed and placed the huge bouquet's vase on it. She turned to Maria.

"Honey, your butt is showing. Eww, don't you have something better to wear? A little silk nightie or something? Are you feeling all right?"

Maria said, again, "Emily!"

"Oh, I suppose you're not feeling well." She looked at Mason, seeing him for the first time. "And, who do we have here? Oh yes, I remember youuu."

Mason had worked his way over to the bathroom door and turned on the light. He quickly terminated what he was doing after poking a few more buttons and slipped the unit back into its holster on his belt. He quietly walked over to Maria's bed and sat on the end of it.

When Emily turned back to Maria, she winked. "Do you want me to come stay at your house when they let you out of here? I have a *tres* sweet recipe for *poultre a jus*. Why are you not answering *moi*?"

"I'm waiting for your first act to end," Maria said as she pulled the tails of her gown together and backed toward the bed again.

"Okay." Em draped her leather-clad body across the window seat.

"The flowers are gorgeous, Em. And they're so fragrant! I love them." She suddenly felt close to Emily, which surprised her. Love is the only reason she could think for Emily coming to see her.

"You feel guilty for yelling at me about the fashion show, don't you?" Was this her way of asking for forgiveness?

Maria smiled at her. Mason smiled at her too. How could Mason not be right for her if he'd put up with her family?

About the Author...

Melody Scott was born in San Diego, California but raised in Riverside, California, a town near Los Angeles. She graduated from California Polytechnic College in Pomona, California, and was employed by The Press Enterprise newspapers for six years.

After marrying and moving to Cumming, Georgia, she became enamored of the land and obtained her Georgia Real Estate license in 1978. Buying and selling, moving and investing became a way of life until she was drawn to write novels about the land, the history of which still holds a mystique for her.

Melody has had several short stories published in various magazines such as Confection, The Lyric, Promises to Keep, Woman, Horizon Magazine, and The North Georgia Star. Her acrylic paintings, wall murals and watercolors are becoming known among the art community.

Today she is a licensed Realtor and belongs to her local Board of Realtors, the Chamber of Commerce, two writing groups, a book club, Sisters In Crime, and Southeastern Mystery Writers of America.

She's managed to remain married to the same saint of a husband and now has two adult children and three grandchildren traipsing the same land about which she writes.

CPSIA information can be obtained at www.ICGtesting.com
Printed in the USA
238257LV00002B/52/P